DEAD FIT

Praise for In The Past

'An excellent summer read. I'm a fan of Agatha Christie and Dick Francis. Once I started I found it really difficult to put down. The story kept me guessing right up to the very end. I would definitely recommend it as an excellent summer garden read. I enjoyed it so much I've ordered the next one.'

'Engaging and gripping. Would love to read more from E M Elliot.'

'A really enjoyable and page turning read from start to finish. Looking forward to the next one please!'

Praise for Opportunity for Death

'A must for mystery addicts! Read it!'- Dorothy Simpson

'Superb read. A classic whodunit brought up to date.'

'Start to finish in an evening, not able to put down.

'Intriguing and totally absorbing. A wonderful and fascinating tale of the intrigues of English village life... beautifully written and well told, a brilliant book to disappear into.'

DEAD FIT

BY

E M ELLIOT

Copyright © E M Elliot 2023

The right of E.M.Elliot to be identified as the author of this work has been asserted by her in accordance with the Copyright, Designs and Patents Act 1988

All rights reserved. This book is sold subject to the condition that it shall not, by way of trade or otherwise, be lent, resold, hired out or otherwise circulated in any form of binding or cover other than that in which it is published and without a similar
condition including this condition being imposed on the subsequent purchaser.

This is a work of fiction. Names, characters, places and incidents are either the product of the author's imagination or are used fictitiously, and any resemblance to actual persons, living or dead, or to actual events or locales is entirely coincidental.

Cover Illustration by Alexandra Blake
Cover copyright © E M Elliot

To

Frances

and

Pippa

CHAPTER ONE

As the biting January wind whipped around the gathered party, Kitty Muier glanced across over the bleak funereal hole at Bastien's stooped figure and whispered to her close friend and ally, Bella Sparkle.

'Look at him. My heart breaks at what he's been through. First his parents five months ago and now Dolly. She's been like a second mother to him since they died. Now who has he got?'

'Mmm,' replied Bella distractedly, flicking the collar of her long navy wool coat up in an attempt to prevent the icy blast from further seeping down her already frozen neck, annoyed that she'd forgotten to put a scarf on when she had left the house. Her diminutive 5'5" frame shivered in the mid-afternoon bleakness.

Kitty looked sharply at Bella and raised her eyebrows questioningly, then narrowed her gold-flecked brown eyes as Bella studiously avoided her gaze. Kitty knew what Bella's "Mmm's" tended to signify; not "Mmm, I'm agreeing with you," but, "Mmm, there's more to this than meets the eye and I'm suspicious."

The final words of committal from the Rev. Jeremy Haslock, vicar at both All Saints Wynenden - where they were currently standing outside in amongst the ancient headstones in the churchyard - and St Nicholas Church

Monhurst, drew Kitty away from her musings as Dolly Broom, aged 88 at the time of her death, was laid to rest.

The gathered party of approximately 100 local residents - for Dolly had been an active member of the church and community for the past twenty years - started to move off in the direction of the village hall, which was adjacent to the church, for the wake which the local Women's Institute had organised in memory of their friend and devoted member.

Ted Armstrong, Kitty's partner, walked around the open grave to Bastien and put a comforting hand on his shoulder. Bastien, whilst only 36 years of age, looked older and smaller as he hunched his already rounded shoulders still further. The stress and grief of the past few months were etched across his forgettable face, the tips of his large protruding ears red from the bitter cold, his short brown hair ruffling in a gust of icy wind.

'Come on Mate,' said Ted, though they were more acquaintances than friends. 'Let's go over to the village hall and warm up, it's freezing out here.'

Bastien frowned but allowed Ted to gently steer him in the direction away from the grave. Ted's kind, normally sparkling, blue eyes were clouded with concern for Bastien.

'So?' repeated Kitty, nudging Bella in order to get her attention.

'So? What?' replied Bella, feigning innocence.

'You know what!' laughed Kitty.

'Not here. Not now. Later. Ok?'

'Oh all right,' agreed Kitty reluctantly, impatient to discover what she believed were Bella's implied suspicions surrounding Dolly's demise.

Kitty herself was a relative newcomer to the - what she had originally thought would be - sleepy Kent village of Wynenden, having arrived 18 months ago. She'd bought a wreck of a house called Wynenden Farm and subsequently spent months renovating and extending her dream project - a dream she had held for many years, even more so after her husband had left her for a younger woman and the subsequent divorce. Eight months ago she'd moved into the property and quickly settled into her adored Grade II Listed farmhouse, despite her occasional struggle with memories of the devastating discoveries of two skeletons during the renovations; a mother and her child murdered ten years previously - 16 year old local girl Cecilia Stillingfleet and her baby son. Kitty knew that she would never forget, but always endeavoured to look to the future with positivity.

Kitty had first met Bella, who lived in the neighbouring village of Monhurst, when she volunteered to help out at the annual Monhurst Village Fete - a widely renowned traditional fete to which many flocked every summer. Instantly they had clicked and over the past seven months a firm friendship had developed between them, feeling as though they had known one another for decades rather than mere months. Their curiosity and interest in life and people was inherent within them. Combining this with the fact that they had both previously been unwittingly caught up in criminal investigations, provided them with a great deal in common - Bella five years earlier having been involved in dramatic events which had taken place in Monhurst shortly after she had moved into a rented cottage located on the edge of the village green.

The village was where her best friend from school lived and it was she who had persuaded Bella to move there for a change of scenery from the small Norfolk town where she had been resident for years with her husband Hugh, a police officer, who had died tragically in a car accident seven years previously.

Bella had originally planned to stay for just six months, however the warmth and support she had received from the village community during that period had made her feel as though she had, after seven years of feeling displaced and bereft, come home, that it was the place where she should settle.

Kitty and Bella, trailed by Ted and Bastien, slowly followed the melange of mourners, impatient to get out of the freezing weather, frost still sparkling in the weak mid-afternoon sunshine. The elderly friends of Dolly, who were walking ahead of them, cautiously picked their way along the intermittently slippy path all too aware of what a fall could mean, desperate to avoid physical breakages or worse.

'I can't believe how bitter it is,' muttered Kitty, blowing into her cashmere gloved hands in an attempt to thaw them out.

'Me either,' replied Bella. 'It's years since we had this kind of cold weather and snow has been forecast for imminent arrival.

'I hope not,' groaned Kitty, 'I imagine it'll be a nightmare getting to work from my house if it does.'

Kitty actually loved snow, had it not been for the fact that the new term was about to start at the preparatory - Prep - school where she worked part-time as an administrator, she would have been eagerly awaiting the arrival of the first snow fall since she'd moved into her house. Wynenden Farm was nestled in five acres of land up a narrow country lane on the edge of the village. Inevitably, given the remoteness of the house, it was more than likely that a deluge of snow would cut the lane off from the main road. This, combined with the fact that the school was 15 miles away and also located in the middle of the countryside, created a potential maelstrom to ensure that she would be unable to get to work.

Whilst her role at the school wasn't in anyway critical to the running of it, Kitty loathed not keeping up-to-date with her work. She had even contemplated going to the school, prior to the snow arriving, in order to collect a pile of work to get on with at home. Not for the first time since the weather had turned wintry had she had second thoughts and regretted her initial decision to not proceed with the installation of a generator as a source of backup power should there be a power failure, which was not unheard of in the countryside during inclement weather. However, the cost had been far higher than she had budgeted for, but had she been too short-sighted about it, she now mused?

'You could always stay at Ted's,' suggested Bella. 'I'm sure he wouldn't mind ferrying you around in one of his four wheel drive vehicles.'

'Seriously?!' Kitty rolled her eyes. 'I'm sure he wouldn't, but he's got far better things to do with his time - like work for example!'

'Just a suggestion,' laughed Bella. 'Finally!' she added as they entered the modern village hall which had been built six years previously to replace the crumbling old rotten one. Constructed of glass and cedar wood in a nod to sustainability and energy efficiency, with solar panels on the zinc roof, it had initially caused controversy in the village.

The traditionalists were keen for an identical structure to that which had been there for decades to be constructed. This view was diametrically opposed by the more forward thinking members of the community who took the long view for the future of the village and the environment. The persuasive arguments made by those more forward thinking had won the approval of the majority of Wynenden Parish Council and the planning application had been met with enthusiasm by the planning department of the local council. The cedar had mellowed and the building had now begun to blend into its surroundings. Grudgingly, those who had originally opposed the design had come to agree that the right choice for the village had been made - particularly once they saw how minimal the running costs were proving to be.

The delicious warmth inside the hall engulfed them as they shuffled their way through the foyer and into the large, light, airy main hall. The volume from conversation was steadily rising in parallel to the thawing out of the chilled mourners. Kitty and Bella peeled off their outer garments and hung them over the backs of a couple of chairs. They waved at a few of their friends who were on the far side of the hall and chatted to one another as they queued to get a cup of tea. There would be no alcohol at the wake. Dolly had been a life-long tea-totaler. She had never had any objection to other people imbibing the odd tipple, but her friends at the W.I. were keen to serve Dolly's favourite beverages and food. Therefore, what was on offer was tea or coffee and a selection of traditional sandwiches and cakes - definitely no fancy canapés or champagne - on such a chilly day the thought of a hot drink was an appealing concept to those who had stood minutes earlier around Dolly's grave.

'Hello you two,' came a voice from behind Bella and Kitty.

'Kim!' exclaimed Bella, smiling. She kissed her friend on both cheeks in greeting.

Kim smiled back and reciprocated. Her cropped blond hair looked a little wild, post removal of her hat, and her arctic blue eyes shone in delight at seeing her friends. Her clear skin glowed red from having been outside and the fine lines around her eyes crinkled up when she smiled.

'You should have sat with us during the service,' commented Bella.

'We would have done,' said Kim referring to herself and her husband Seb, 'but someone,' she glanced pointedly over towards her husband who was busy conversing with other people, 'was late getting back from work so we had to slide in just after the service had started.'

Renowned for always going that bit further and being incredibly kind, subsequently resulted in Seb having a reputation for being late. It infuriated Kim who was obsessive about her time keeping, but she loved him all the more for his generous and compassionate nature.

Kitty and Bella chuckled. They adored Seb, how could anyone not with such a kind person? Bella in particular had a soft spot for them both. Her friendship with Kim had developed into one of mutual respect and compassion after the death of Kim's first husband, Rupert. She loved the fact that two such perfectly matched, made-for-each-other, people were now so happily married. Their adoration and love for one another was clear to anyone who met them and their four year old daughter, Matilda, completed their happy family.

'So, how's it going?' asked Bella referring to the business Kim had opened three months previously, an upmarket gym and studios - Oast Gym - which was located in a triple kiln Kentish Oast House originally built in the late 19th Century for the purpose of drying hops for brewing. The oast was situated down a country lane between the villages of Monhurst and Wynenden and had previously housed Oast Wines; a business set up by Kim's late husband, which had since relocated to a warehouse on the outskirts of a nearby town. Customers could still visit Oast Wines in person, where they were warmly welcomed, but the business model and customer demand had shifted from shop-based to internet-based, thereby making a large retail space of several thousand square feet redundant; expensive to run and with declining footfall.

Kim smiled broadly in response to Bella's enquiry. She adored her new "baby" and found the thrill of running her own business incredibly exciting having developed it from a seed of an idea now through to fruition. She aimed to offer cutting edge classes within a contemporary setting along with a state-of-the-art gym and had carried out extensive research in order to do so and still kept a keen eye on what was trending and being developed across the globe. Kim wanted to be ahead of her competitors, introducing new concepts before they started appearing en masse, whilst also keeping some more traditional, but still popular, classes too. She paid close attention to members feedback and acted on it where necessary. Kim wanted to attract a varied range of clientele; from those who were as passionate and enthusiastic about fitness as she was, to those who required a more nurturing approach to exercise such as those who felt they "ought" to join a gym and do some exercise, but who never actually utilised the facilities or reaped the benefits.

In addition, Kim wanted to encourage those who desired to get fit or become fitter; be it for health reasons or other, but who were too terrified or intimidated to join a gym in the fear that they would be judged for their lack of ability, knowledge or size and who envisaged that gyms were only utilised by those who were slim, toned, super-fit and who always knew what they were doing, which was not necessarily the case. Kim wanted to encourage those reticent about exercise to gain confidence in themselves and feel comfortable in the environment. With that in mind she was trying to develop times where the facilities would purely be available for such potential customers whilst being mindful of the needs of current members. Additionally, Kim was looking into the possibility of being able to offer rehabilitation exercise courses in conjunction with local healthcare providers.

'It's brilliant,' replied Kim in answer to Bella's question. 'I absolutely love it. Exhausting but exhilarating, though not without its challenges.'

'I can imagine. It is…' Kitty was interrupted by a male voice shouting, "No!" and turned to see Bastien shoving Andrew Battle away from him, then storming out.

'What was that about?' exclaimed Bella.

'Andrew, being Andrew I imagine,' replied Kitty grimly. Personal experience had taught her exactly what he was like and just what he was capable of, and it wasn't good.

'Should… Oh, there goes Seb.' Bella had been about to say "should someone go after Bastien?" but Seb was clearly ahead of her.

Meanwhile Ted, Kitty's partner and Estate Manager of the private Wynenden Park country estate owned by Sir Geoffrey and Lady Susan Percevall-Sharparrow, strode over to Andrew. From his body language, though his back was to her, she could tell that he was "suggesting" Andrew leave. With a contemptuous shrug, Andrew sauntered insolently out. Bastien meanwhile returned, having been persuaded to do so by Seb and the remainder of the wake passed without incident.

As Kitty and Bella put their coats on to depart, Kitty said. 'Don't think I have forgotten.'

Bella looked quizzically at her.

'About your "Mmm" earlier.'

'Ah,' replied Bella, having hoped that Kitty had indeed forgotten.

'Well?' persisted Kitty.

'How about coffee tomorrow?' suggested Bella.

'Okay, as long as you promise to tell me then.'

'I promise. My place? About 11 a.m.?'

'Great.' Kitty kissed Bella on the cheek and left.

CHAPTER TWO

Bella lived in a moderately sized detached, four bedroomed, Edwardian red-bricked house up a drive off the village green in Monhurst. She had bought it a year ago having rented other properties over the previous four years.

When she had first moved to Monhurst she had managed to secure the lease of a picturesque, semi-detached cottage on the green from the owners who were in Hong Kong for a year. Bella had fallen in love with the village, the green and the surrounding area. She knew that if she were to put down permanent roots and buy a property in the area, then location was top priority, in which case, for her, it had to be a property located on the green. However, such properties rarely came onto the market. She had had to rent outside of the village whilst she waited, sometimes despairingly, in the hope that one would come onto the market and be in the price range she could afford. The problem was that properties in that specific location tended to stay in families for generations precisely because of the desirability of the location.

So when an Edwardian house became empty after the demise, at the age of 97, of the sweet old gentleman who had owned it, Bella had contacted the solicitors who were acting on behalf of the deceased's Estate and stated her point of interest in the property. She had felt that it was rather ghoulish of her to do so, with the gentleman barely cold in his grave, but she knew that there was no time for sentimentality if she were to be in with a chance of successfully purchasing the house and could not be complacent. The fear that if she were the property might be snapped up in a bidding war or - even worse - bought by Andrew Battle who, in his own inevitable way, would over-develop the 1.5 acre plot by cramming in as many new properties as he could and consequently in doing so it would risk ruining the ambience and rhythm of the village green.

As luck would have it, the beneficiaries of the Will were after a quick sale. Once probate had been granted the purchase of the house, if rather on the high side price wise, swiftly moved to exchange and completion of contracts. Needless to say Andrew Battle - who never knowingly wanted to miss out on the opportunity to make money, irrespective of how it would affect people living in the vicinity - was outraged and subsequently held an unwarranted grudge against Bella.

Upon completion of the purchase of the house, Bella oversaw a six month renovation project of the property using Kitty's builder Dougie. Now, six months on from having moved in, she was starting to feel settled and loved the fact that she could once again walk to village amenities; the post-office-cum shop, the deli/coffee shop, the pub and the church - which could be seen from her house and of which the churchyard backed on to Bella's extensive, partly walled, garden.

Unusually for Kent it had been minus ten degrees celsius the previous night, so when Bella opened the door to welcome Kitty inside, the day after Dolly's funeral, a blast of bitterly cold air greeted her and she noticed that the front garden and drive were covered with a heavy white frost.

'Morning,' she said cheerily to Kitty.

'Brrr,' responded Kitty hurrying inside. 'Morning. It's absolutely freezing out there!'

'It certainly is.' replied Bella, swiftly closing the sage-green coloured front door behind her.

Kitty followed Bella through the uncluttered hall to the back of the house where the spacious kitchen, despite the heavy greyness outside, was warm and welcoming. Large casement windows lined three walls providing a triple aspect of westerly light along the length of the kitchen, southerly and northerly light on the other two.

'Coffee?' she said

'Yes please,' replied Kitty, shivering and leaning back against Bella's new deep-purple coloured Aga "Aubergine" the Aga catalogue had said. Would it be sold as an "Eggplant" colour in the USA, she randomly wondered as the warmth started to seep into her from it? The kettle began to boil on the hotplate behind her and she shifted to the side so that Bella could take it off and finish making the coffee.

'I lit the fire in the morning room, it's such a gloomy day I felt it warranted it.' Bella picked up the tray with a cafetière of coffee, she'd tried various new coffee machines and had disliked them all so stuck to her trusty - if a little dated - cafetière, milk in a jug, fine bone china cups and saucers and walked across the hallway into the morning room.

The fire burned merrily in the hearth warming the room deliciously and they each sank into an arm chair on either side of the fireplace and settled back with their coffee.

'Go on then. Explain,' demanded Kitty, referring to Bella's comment from the previous day.

'It's nothing,' replied Bella.

Kitty snorted. 'I don't believe that for one minute. Come on. Out with it.'

'Well,' Bella paused, 'it's just a gut feeling really.'

'About?'

'Oh, I don't know.' Bella searched for the right words. 'I suppose the circumstances surrounding Dolly's death don't sit right with me.'

'In what way?'

'I know she was elderly, 88 is a good age to reach, but she was so active and strong and still cycled every day. And, even though she lived in your village, I saw her most days out on her bicycle around here - albeit a little slower than a few years ago - but incredibly impressive all the same.'

'Oh I agree. She was an example to us all of how to keep fit and age well. She must have been fitter than many people a quarter of her age. I'm sure keeping so active helped her stay so physically strong when many of her peer group seem to hobble about, sleep a lot of the day and in general are inactive.'

'Exactly! That's my point!' exclaimed Bella.

'What is?' Kitty's brow furrowed in puzzlement.

'How could she just slip over, seemingly on nothing, outside her back door and not be able to get up again or at least crawl inside to phone for help?'

'I don't know. Maybe she felt dizzy and blacked out. Nothing suspicious was raised regarding her death. It's lucky that Seb found her when he did and managed to get her inside before calling for an ambulance, just a shame she died before they were able to get there to help her, but at least Seb was able to sit there and hold her hand so she wasn't alone.'

'Absolutely.'

'So I still don't see what you are getting at Bella?'

Bella pursed her lips then blew out a long sigh. 'It's something I overheard Seb saying to Kim.'

Kitty raised an eyebrow in scepticism.

Bella continued. 'I'm sure I heard Seb mention that he was convinced he had glimpsed Bastien hurrying away round the back of Dolly's garden and into his garden, when he turned up to deliver Dolly's organic veg box.'

'Hmm. You think you heard Seb say that, but can't be sure, and that he thinks he may, or may not have, seen Bastien hurrying away when he arrived?'

Bella nodded an affirmation.

'So who are you accusing of what then?'

Bella shrugged. 'I don't know really. If Bastien had seen her lying there, why didn't he help her? Why would he leave her all on her own?'

'I don't know. Maybe he was going to call an ambulance. Maybe he wasn't there at all.'

'But why wouldn't he use Dolly's telephone?' persisted Bella. 'He's known her for twenty years, ever since she bought the section of the house Bastien's parents had separated off into another dwelling in order to raise some capital.'

'No idea, but I think you are barking up the wrong tree. Have you asked Seb? Because if he didn't say it, or hadn't seen Bastien, there's nothing to it.'

'No, I've not seen Kim or Seb to really talk to since Dolly died. What with Christmas and New Year in-between everyone's been rather busy and it would hardly have been appropriate to ask him at the funeral yesterday.'

'Have you mentioned this to Dave?' asked Kitty referring to Bella's on/off partner who was a Detective Inspector in the local constabulary.

Bella snorted and laughed. 'No! He'd think I was delusional!'

Kitty giggled. 'I think he probably would. All a little fantastical don't you think? Are you bored and looking for something to do?'

'No! Seriously though, something just doesn't feel right.'

'The simplest thing Bella, is for you to just ask Seb outright, then you'll know if he thinks he saw Bastien or not. You're like me, I know that you won't rest until you've got a satisfactory answer. But what are you going to do if Seb says he believes he *did* see Bastien hurrying away? You can't really go sniffing around for evidence, much as you love to, you'll just be accused of stirring things up and being disrespectful to both Dolly and Bastien. She's dead and he's lost the three people who were closest to him in a short space of time. And let's face it, the reality is she was old, she could have hurt her head when she fell or slipped and as a consequence died; it's not unusual at that age.'

Bella pursed her lips again then took a contemplative sip of the aromatic, slightly nutty-with-a-hint-of-spice, coffee and thought. On the one hand she was inclined to agree with Kitty, but on the other something just wasn't sitting right with her about Dolly's death. In the past, when instinct had alerted her to something, nine times out of ten she was proved right. However, her best friend from school, Mia, had on more than one occasion pointed out that perhaps her behaviour was erring on the side of meddlesome, prying and intrusive into the lives of other people, which sat uncomfortably with Bella. She didn't want to be that sort of person, but equally couldn't help her inquiring mind and gut instinct.

'Perhaps you're right,' she conceded, changing the subject. 'How was your Christmas and New Year? I've not seen you to really ask.'

'Oh, lovely thanks. To wake up in my new home on Christmas Day was such a joy. To enjoy the peace, serenity and beauty of the house and its location was really special. I don't know why it felt so much more so than any other morning since I moved in last June, but it did. Hearing the church bells ringing, the sound drifting across the fields whilst I ate breakfast, the sun streaming in through the windows and the frost outside so crisp, white and beautiful. It's a moment snapshotted into my memory.' Kitty smiled dreamily as she remembered. 'The rest of the day itself was perfect too, despite Ted being with his family in Oxfordshire. He did invite me but I wanted to be here, to experience my first Christmas in my lovely home, after all I, and it, have been through it felt right. I went to church, then had Libby, James, Henry and Alice over for lunch. At ten and eight, Henry and Alice are still so excited about Christmas, it was enchanting to see. Ted came home a few days later and we had a quiet New Year's Eve at my house, it was perfect. Then of course it's back to reality and what can sometimes feel like the mundanity of life. And you? How was yours?'

'Pretty similar really. I went over to Mia and Fred's on Christmas Day and had a lovely time with them and Tess, I can't believe she's 22 and in her final year at uni! I then spent New Years Eve here, Dave came over but mid-way through our meal he got called out and that was that.' Bella shrugged resignedly.

'Oh, what a nuisance! Such a shame.' offered Kitty sympathetically.

'Goes with the territory really. You'd think I'd be used to it having been married to a policeman for 20 years and then dating another one on and off for five.'

They continued to chat for a while. It never ceased to amaze Kitty how similar their lives were. They had both moved to new villages. They had both, albeit on different scales, refurbished their dream house. They had both moved into them during the past year. They had both been married for a long time and now weren't; Bella widowed, Kitty divorced. They were both in relationships and ambivalent about committing. They were both inquisitive and social whilst still relishing time on their own. They both had best friends from school who lived in their same respective villages and, above all, they liked one another.

CHAPTER THREE

Kim drew up and parked in the pristine car park at Oast Gym. It was the start of the second week of January and she had just dropped her daughter Matilda off for her first morning at the local Montessori Kindergarten. She sniffed and dabbed the tears from her eyes. Whilst her four year old daughter had skipped happily off, excited to see a couple of her friends with whom she had grown up with after their parents had met at pre-natal NCT (National Childbirth Trust) classes, Kim had felt bereft. The loss, the end of an era she felt. She adored her daughter and had cherished every moment with her. Between Seb, herself, her parents and an occasional few hours from an excellent nanny, Matilda had had a stable home life surrounded by those who loved and worshiped the ground she walked on.

But Kim knew that, in order for her daughter to grow up into a well balanced individual and continue to learn to treat everyone equally and with respect, irrespective of their backgrounds, she needed to spend time with children from as broad a range of backgrounds as was possible in rural Kent. Neither Kim nor Seb wanted their daughter to grow up into a spoilt individual with an attitude and sense of superiority over others because of her privileged up-bringing. So from today Matilda would spend the term split between two mornings at Montessori and one morning at the local play school in the village hall. After Easter it would then increase to two mornings at the local play school. Kim knew that it would not only benefit Matilda in a multitude of ways, but it would also help Kim herself who had struggled to find the right balance between work and looking after her daughter.

Knowing this didn't stop her from still feeling torn, on the one hand she wanted to be with Matilda 24/7, but on the other hand she had to, and wanted to, oversee the running of the businesses her late husband Rupert had left her, even though she was now taking less of an active role in the daily running of them whilst she concentrated on her second 'baby' - Oast Gym - a dream come true. It was, however, a business and it needed to at least cover its costs and, hopefully, one day turn a profit. The fact that Kim was so passionate about the project it made it feel less like a job and more like the best kind of hobby. However, the guilt she felt from working and not spending all her time with her daughter never left her, even knowing that Matilda was having fun and being well looked after by Seb, her parents and now at kindergarten, didn't ease it.

Dabbing her eyes again, she flicked down the visor in her car and inspected her face in the mirror. It didn't look as bad as she had feared it would. In fact, unless you knew her well, you wouldn't even notice that she'd been crying. Her normally sparkly blue eyes were a little red, along with her nose, but nothing too obvious. She was pleased she'd decided to have her eyelashes tinted the previous week which negated her requiring to wear mascara and in turn saved her from potentially looking like a panda from running mascara. She rummaged in her bag for her pale pink lipgloss and slicked some across her lips, took a deep breath in, then out, and forced a smile onto her face.

The car park was beginning to fill up with cars as parents, who had dropped their children off at school, arrived either for a workout in the gym or to attend a fitness class. Kim smiled as brightly as she could muster, waved cheerily at them and got out of the car, ready for the morning ahead.

Oast Gym was situated in, not surprisingly given the name, a traditional Kentish Oast House. Constructed of mellow red brick walls under a Kent peg tile roof and with the requisite kilns - triple in this case; each kiln being circular in structure within which, years ago, hops had been processed, dried out and stored for brewing. Atop of each of the conical tile roofs was a white cowl, made of wood, which would swing around in the wind and indicated from which direction it was blowing.

Extending from the kilns was a double, almost triple, storey rectangular building. Further away, on the far side of the car park, was a double height brick and white weatherboarded, Kent peg tile roofed barn which had been converted into offices - from which the behind-the-scenes running of the business took place - and in part of the first floor a small one bedroomed flat, currently occupied by Zeno, the most popular member of the Personal Training Team.

What you saw on arrival was very Kentish, very historical, very traditional and in no way hinted at the modern transformation which had taken place within. The fields surrounding the property consisted of traditional apple orchards, their branches bare and naked in the bleak winter morning except for a random leaf here and there which clung resolutely on for dear life, frosted and preserved. In Spring the trees burst into a riot of white blossom, edges tinged with pink, and looked stunning.

The simple oak door - one of the stipulations of planning permission being granted for the change of use of the building from offices, wine shop and storage, to a gym - led into the reception area on the ground floor of the main building. The area was spotless. White walls, the use of concealed, carefully positioned, subtle lighting and white porcelain flooring created a calm and serene ambiance. The semi-circular reception desk, hand crafted in a rich dark-coloured cherry wood, was topped with a pristine, milky-white, glass surface. Behind this, interspersed along the length of the wall, were wide vertical sections of clear glass, providing glimpses into the vast gym area and one of the two studios - the second studio being located on the first floor. Inside the gym and both studios were full height exterior glass walls proffering spectacular views out over the orchards with a south-easterly aspect. It had taken a great deal of persuasion on the parts of both Kim and her Planning Consultant to persuade the local council to allow the walls of glass to be installed at the rear of the building, but eventually the planning authority capitulated.

The ground floor of the spacious three kilns were divided equally between a juice bar/cafe, male changing rooms and female changing rooms. The male changing rooms combined dark cherry wood, mood lighting, teak floors and leather banquettes to exude a sense of luxury and led through to the powerful rainforest showers, steam room and sauna.

In contrast, the female changing rooms were light, airy, indulgent, clean and crisp. Teak floors mellowed the ambiance, vast mirrors were carefully lit and several windows with opaque glass brought daylight into the area which also contained several individual, spacious, changing cubicles. An array of accoutrements was provided for the drying and styling of hair along with a selection of body and face care products. The showers were vast but, unlike those in the male changing rooms, the shower heads had several different settings to choose from. There were the requisite steam and sauna rooms and large fluffy-white towels were stacked up in the bespoke shelving unit ready for members to envelope themselves in.

Equally as luxurious were the two separate changing rooms, each with all the facilities, located at the opposite end of the main building, specifically designed for those with additional needs. Additionally, they were available for those who felt uncomfortable using either the male or female changing rooms.

Kim, dressed in tight-fitting dark blue jeans, a cream silk blouse, pale pink super-soft cashmere round-necked jumper, matching scarf and pristine white sneakers with a single pink stripe slicked across each outer side, held open the door for several members, all dressed in the latest sportswear designs, then followed them inside. Every time she walked through that door into the reception area she felt a frisson of excitement combined with disbelief. Excitement because she burst with joy and pleasure at seeing what had been created and disbelief that her long dreamt of business had actually come to fruition.

She was delighted with the team of staff she had so carefully chosen, proud of how they worked so well together and by the positive and energising way in which they interacted with club members. She had wanted the best and had been prepared to pay for it. Hence her staff were paid generously, something which was relatively unheard of in the notoriously underpaid and often under appreciated leisure industry. Her accountant had done his utmost to dissuade her from doing so, urging her to pay fair salaries but not well over and above the market place average. He argued that the gym was a business and financially it had to at least break even. But Kim had refused to be persuaded and stood her ground. It felt right to her and, even though the club had only opened three months previously, she was convinced that she had made the right decision and that it would pay off in the long run. In her mind, staff who felt appreciated and were actively listened too, would feel more inclined to create a positive and happy environment, one which members would pick up on and be the sort of environment that they would enjoy spending time in. Kim herself had been a member of numerous gyms over the years, all too often the atmosphere was oppressive and where staff would moan to members about their pay, conditions or employer and which subsequently created a toxic and negative atmosphere.

She waited for Zeno to finish greeting the members who had preceded her before speaking to him. He was temporarily covering reception for Tara; the blond, bubbly, fizzing-with-enthusiasm young woman of 23 who was on Reception duty that morning and who was currently carrying out the first of the regular checks of the building. Detail was everything to Kim and she wanted perfection, additionally she felt it was important that every single member of staff - from cleaners to managers - have an understanding and appreciation as to what was involved in their colleagues roles. In order to do so staff regularly rotated and shadowed one another for a few hours.

'Morning Zeno. How are you? Nice weekend?' enquired Kim pleasantly.

'Hi Kim. Great thanks and you?' His emerald-green eyes twinkled back at her.

From the moment Kim had met Zeno at his interview she had known that he was precisely what she was looking for in a Personal Trainer (PT) for Oast Gym. Exceptionally well qualified, passionate about fitness and health, incredibly knowledgeable on the topic all combined with a bright and happy disposition which was infectious. In the four months that she had known him, Kim had never once seen Zeno exude anything other than happiness and a zest for life. To top it all, his six foot frame was toned to perfection; muscles beautifully shaped and firm, but not bulging in an over-developed, over worked sort of way, abs which many aspired to and a smile which radiated and lit up a room the moment he walked into it.

Zeno's flirty manner had a private reserve about it, attentive enough to make female members feel special, but not overtly so in a way which might make them feel uncomfortable. With dedication and hard work on their part, Zeno encouraged his clients to achieve goals which were realistic for them as an individual. As far as Kim could see, members loved Zeno.

Zeno provided Kim with a run down of events over the weekend, attendance figures, new membership enquiries and so on. He then briefed her on the day ahead, all interspersed with pleasantly greeting members who passed through reception either on the way into, or out of, the gym or a class. Just as they were joined by Tara, the entrance door burst open and Jennifer bounced in.

'Ugh! It's *freezing* out there,' she exclaimed rather over-dramatically, flicking her long curly rich-chestnut-coloured, glossy hair in a flirtatious manner towards Zeno. Her deep chocolate coloured eyes smouldered at him from beneath her long, luxurious - completely natural - eyelashes.

'My gorgeous Jennifer. Ready for our session this morning?' he twinkled at her.

'With you Zeno, always,' she replied in a coquettish manner.

Kim smiled, amused by one of her closest friends and gave her a kiss on the cheek.

'Morning Lovely. On fine form as ever I see. Hmm,' she stepped back and stared intently at Jennifer's face, there seemed to be an extra glow about her this morning. 'Nice weekend?' She asked, gazing meaningfully into Jennifer's eyes.

'Perfect thanks Kim.' replied Jennifer non-committally. 'And you?'

Zeno interrupted them. 'I'm all set up. Ready when you are Jennifer. I'll wait for you in the gym.'

Jennifer gave a lingering look at his retreating rear.

'Don't think I'm letting you off that easily,' whispered Kim, tittering.

'No idea what you mean Kim,' smirked Jennifer in response. 'Better go and dump my stuff in the changing room,' she said in reference to her coat and gym bag, 'don't want to keep Zeno waiting.'

'Clearly not.' smiled Kim. 'Coffee after?'

'Yup. But you're not going to succeed in getting anything out of me,' she laughed as she strolled off to the changing rooms.

Kim turned to chat to Tara before doing her own walk-through of the building then headed over to the offices for an hour or so. She liked to work between the two buildings, whilst the club was managed from the offices, she felt it so important that she, and her staff, were visible, present and accessible to members. She wanted members to feel that this was a real club, where they were valued, not faceless individuals or a number in an impersonal club.

Jennifer bounced into the gym itself looking forward to her PT session with Zeno. When she had met him three months ago - Kim had generously given a handful of her closest friends a years complimentary membership - she had still been feeling very down and disconsolate after the break up, three months prior, of a two year relationship, one which she had hoped would lead to marriage and babies. At the age of 36 Jennifer felt that she was starting to run out of time, her biological clock ticking ever louder as a reminder and knew that she had to take stock of her life and what she wanted from it. Zeno had helped to bring a little spark of joy back into her life. He was an excellent listener and made her feel good about herself whilst simultaneously helping her to become the fittest and strongest she had ever been.

To the uninitiated, Jennifer seemed to have it all, but inside she was insecure and often lonely. As she sashayed through the gym to the far side of the room where Zeno had set up for her session that morning, female members who were already working out, eyed her 5'8", curvy, busty figure, with long, slim, very shapely legs, high pert buttocks and innate sense of sensuality, with a mixture of envy and jealousy, but little did they know.

'Ready for your Monday morning blitz?' smiled Zeno good-naturedly.

'As ever.' Jennifer grinned back.

Despite the intensity of the session, the hour flew by and before Jennifer knew it she was flat on her back on a mat with Zeno carrying out additional assisted stretches to her legs. It felt intimate but not sexual, yet she was aware that some of the women were surreptitiously eyeing her enviously, wishing that they were in her place instead. He gently manipulated her legs and though she could feel her muscles protest a little it wasn't painful and she knew that she would feel all the better for it later on.

'You look like you're enjoying yourself way too much there,' quipped a soft, gentle voice.

'You're just jealous, admit it!' laughed Jennifer as she turned her head to look at the young, tall - at over 6' - very slim and very beautiful, 35 year old woman. Jennifer had only recently met her but had instantly liked her and felt an immediate connection, subsequently, a firm friendship was developing between them.

Ditzi van Vizier was relatively new to the village of Wynenden. She'd moved into Wynenden Hall, a stunning Queen Anne style house, with her much older husband Dezo, two years ago, but Jennifer had not met either of them until they had joined the gym. She'd heard about them, plenty in fact, but took the gossip with a pinch of salt knowing all too well from personal experience what utter rubbish could be made up about someone based on nothing remotely factual.

'Don't worry, there's plenty of me to go around,' grinned Zeno broadly.

Jennifer got to her feet and kissed Ditzi lightly on both cheeks. 'He's all yours,' she laughed, 'but I have to warn you, he's being particularly brutal this morning.' She winked at Zeno who tried to feign innocence. 'See you on Thursday for our next session Zeno. Thanks very much.' She blew him a kiss, smiled cheerily at Ditzi and sashayed back through the gym stopping to chat as she went.

Showered and changed, Jennifer walked through into the juice-bar-cum-cafe, ordered a super green juice; packed full of as many green vegetables as possible along with herbs, ginger, lemon but no other fruit, no sweetness of any kind, which tasted as though it had to be doing you a lot of good but which was palatable to only hardcore juice aficionados. To accompany this she ordered a decaf, oat milk latte and a vegan oat and seed flapjack. She settled into one of the comfy cream armchairs adjacent to one of the full length windows overlooking the surrounding orchards and waited for Kim.

'Good session?' enquired Kim, placing her coffee down onto the table then dropping herself with a sigh into the chair opposite Jennifer.

Jennifer looked up from her phone, tucked it into her bag and smiled. 'Yup. He's an excellent trainer, really pushes you but never beyond what you're capable of. He's a real asset to this place.'

'Thanks. Yes, I think I struck gold when I found him. He's such a kind person and he really cares about his work. Anyway,' said Kim, smiling mischievously at Jennifer, glancing around to ensure that they wouldn't be overheard. 'You were going to tell me about your weekend.'

'Was I?' smirked Jennifer.

'Oh yes. You came in with the distinct air of someone who had had a very good weekend...' Kim raised an eyebrow expectantly at Jennifer.

Jennifer's cheeks tinged pink and she paused to consider how to respond. 'Well. Yes. It was a good weekend. Best one I've had for months in fact.'

'Do tell! Who is he? Where does he live? Have you known him long? Where did you meet him? Anyone I know?' Kim fired off.

Laughing, Jennifer replied. 'You can stop with the interrogation. And who says that a man is responsible? Anyway,' she conceded, 'my lips are sealed as it is very early days. Probably nothing serious. I'm trying to be relaxed and enjoy dating, a bit of flirting, you know. After...' her face clouded briefly, then cleared. 'Well, you know.' She shrugged, referring to her previous relationship and its subsequent breakdown. 'I don't think I'm ready for anything serious yet.'

'Fair enough. I'm just delighted to see you looking happy, you've had a horrible time of it. He-who-shall-not-be-named was a complete git to you. You deserve so much better. Are you not even going to give me a hint?' Kim pleaded hopefully.

Jennifer giggled. 'Let's just say that I am broadening my horizons and leave it at that.'

Recognising defeat when she saw it, Kim changed the subject. 'Have you seen Ariadne since new year?'

'No, I was going to ask you the same. Do you think she's gone back to L.A.?'

'Possibly, but I'm sure Sophie said that Ariadne was going to stay in the flat above their garage for a while, something about her writing a tell-all autobiography. Now that could be a very interesting read, I expect she knows an awful lot of secrets. Whether she'd dish the dirt or not is another matter.' Kim was referring to global mega-star actress, Ariadne Veasey, who, at the age of 41, had had a stellar career as an actress over the past two decades. British born, she had started her career with bit parts in television before the lure of Hollywood beckoned and she had decided to take the risk and move out to Los Angeles. Unlike the multitude of other hopeful's who arrived in L.A. with dreams and aspirations of a glittering career, but ended up either never being successfully cast or being offered roles so minuscule and so sporadically that they had to look for alternative employment to support themselves financially, Ariadne had been in the right place at the right time. She had met the profile of what was being looked for at that time and was also very talented. Since then she'd been in ten blockbuster movies, but the last one had proven to be a flop. A one off or the descent of her star? No one knew and, out of nowhere, not having visited her school friend Sophie for over a year, turned up in the village just after Christmas.

'Do you think she's hiding out? Hiding from the press? Or from someone or something else? asked Jennifer.

'Maybe. She didn't seem her usual effervescent self at Sophie and Harry's New Years Eve dinner. Perhaps getting panned by the press over her last movie has affected her more than we thought, particularly after the phenomenal success she has had and having been fortunate enough to consistently remain one of the darling's of the media until now. It can't be very nice when the tide turns.'

'I imagine not. Though, I would think you'd need a pretty thick skin to work in that industry.'

'True. But I think it felt more personal because it was her first foray into producing/directing as well as starring in it. It must have hurt. Some of the things which were, and still are, being said are horrible, simply vile.'

Jennifer nodded in agreement, convinced that she herself would be unable to deal with such a barrage of abuse.

'I'll drop by Sophie's on the way home and see how they are and find out if Ariadne is still around.'

'Let me know, won't you?'

Jennifer nodded, then exclaimed. 'I forgot to ask! I'm so sorry. I'm a terrible friend! How are you feeling? It must have been hard dropping Matilda off for her first morning of kindergarten?'

Kim's eyes welled up at the mention of her daughter and she gulped, then re-composed herself. 'Heartbreaking. I adore that little person so much. She's my baby and always will be, but I know that it's beneficial for her on so many different levels to be at kindergarten - goodness knows what I will be like when she starts school in September! This was bad enough, it felt like it was the beginning of the end. I know that's me being completely melodramatic, but I can't help it.'

Jennifer got up and gave Kim a big hug. 'Oh you poor thing. I can only imagine how emotional it must be for you.'

Kim sniffed again and dabbed her eyes with a crumpled up tissue. 'I'll be fine. Thanks Jennifer. It's not like I'm the only parent in the world who has experienced this.' She laughed half-heartedly.

'No. But it's the first time you have, so don't beat yourself up about it.'

Kim glanced at her watch. 'Only another two hours and I can pick her up. I guess I ought to get on, lots more to do before then and I have taken the afternoon off to be with her.' She rose from her seat and kissed and hugged Jennifer. 'Thanks so much Jennifer. Let me know how you get on at Sophie's.
'

CHAPTER FOUR

Ariadne's eyes fluttered open and she yawned sleepily, stretching her slim, willowy body under the rumpled duvet and smiled to herself as she remembered the previous evening. Unexpected, but utterly delicious, her body tingled with pleasure at the memory of it.

However, as her eyes focused, her mood plummeted when she remembered where she was, or rather why, making her feel as though she had been dropped from the top of a lift shaft. The oppressive mood which had engulfed her in the previous few weeks wrapped itself tightly around her again. She sank back down into the warm, soft bed and sighed miserably. The same old reel of mental self-abuse playing out in her head, tormenting her; "You're a failure. You're no good. You've had your time. You're too old. You've no talent. You can't act. You can't produce" repeated itself on a loop, all fuelled by her recent, near constant, feeling of futility about her life.

What had she really achieved? Ariadne was actually aware of how extraordinarily lucky she was to own two lovely homes and have sufficient funds saved and invested so that she need never work again. But she had no partner, no children, no family and most of her so called industry "friends" seemed to have melted away since the disastrous flop of her last film. She felt guilty and selfish for even thinking this way with so many people suffering across the globe. There were few who knew what she did under the radar to help others. The support she gave physically, practically and financially to charities and individuals. She didn't want, or need, any recognition for what she did and that was how she wanted it to stay, despite her agent, publicist and manager urging her to allow it to be "leaked" to the press. They argued that it would raise her profile in a positive way and deflect from "the flop". But Ariadne was resolute and they were bound by strict NDA's. Even reminding herself of the financial help and support she freely gave didn't make her feel any better in that moment.

Since "the flop", she felt that the projects being submitted to her agent had proved to be either uninteresting or rather dubious, consequently she had filmed nothing since. In hindsight it may have been a mistake to reject the projects outright. However, prior to the release of "the flop", as she continued to label it, she had already decided to take some time off to properly relax, recover and recuperate after years of relentlessly working back to back on projects, with the aim being to come back more energised than ever. What had actually transpired was over a year of stress, pressure, despair and rejection. The whole process of her foray into acting/producing/directing had been mired with problems from start to finish and continued with one thing after another on set and location; sickness, tantrums, delays, accidents and so on, consequently, long before the film had even been released, there had been negative whispers and rumours circulating in the press and on social media which stoked the flames of negativity towards the film. The ensuing slating of it subsequently ensured that preconceptions of the paying public kept them away in droves.

As a result, Ariadne had become even more exhausted, drained, emotionally wrung out and on the edge of a breakdown, exacerbated by the fact that exciting projects which had been in the pipeline suddenly disappeared.

Despite Kit's (Ariadne's Manager, long term friend and one time lover) best efforts, little of interest was forthcoming. Watching his friend spiral down, he feared that she would be tempted back into her old ways; partying too hard fuelled by drink and drugs - despite having been clean for 14 years - to obliterate the pain he could see she was feeling. It was his suggestion that she go and stay with her oldest school friend, Sophie Easingwold, her husband Harry and their six year old daughter Jemima, in the rural Kent countryside. A place far removed from the often toxic world which Ariadne frequented.

Sophie and Harry had welcomed Ariadne with open arms. Sophie knew her friend better than anyone, the real Ariadne; insecure, kind and thoughtful.

They would have been delighted to have Ariadne stay with them in the house, however, when Ariadne saw the the newly converted, light and airy flat above Sophie and Harry's garage (a small converted barn and hay store), which they had been intending to rent out to supplement their income, Ariadne decided to ensconce herself in it rather than with them in the main house. She insisted on paying them rent at the going rate, despite Sophie and Harry doing their utmost in trying to persuade Ariadne otherwise and to stay as their guest free of charge. Ariadne did not want to deprive them of the income, income she knew that they intended to save towards Jemima's future school fees, adding to what they had prudently been saving since the day Jemima was born. With school fees seemingly spiralling out of control, they needed every penny they could get.

The flat was comfortably furnished, spotlessly clean, bright and fresh and had one bedroom, one bathroom and a large open-plan sitting-cum-kitchen room. It was far removed from Ariadne's spacious flat in London and capacious house in L.A. and reminded her that particular morning of where she felt her life was at; one big floundering mess with no idea as to how to extricate herself from it. Yet, despite the smallness and relative simplicity of the flat, it felt womblike and at times comforting.

Ariadne glanced at her chunky, diamond-encrusted watch and sighed. It was 6 a.m. and still dark outside, yet, in an attempt to convince herself and others that she was "fine", she had committed to personal training sessions at 7 a.m. three mornings a week with Zeno at Oast Gym. Generally that time of the morning was a little quieter, falling between the early morning members who arrived spot on 6 a.m. finishing, yet prior to the post school drop off rush and afforded Ariadne a little more privacy during her session.

She reluctantly rolled out of bed, plodded into the bathroom and gazed at herself in the mirror. Ordinarily she liked how she looked and took great care of herself, she had to, for the industry she was in was ruthless, there were always bright young things snapping at her heals ready to trample on her to further their own careers. Ariadne had become obsessed with exercising, feeling that she had to have the "perfect" body for work. She regularly had botox to keep her face line free, though she still wanted some movement and expression in her face in order to be able to visually purvey emotions on screen. Her lips were plumped with collagen and she'd had a small face-lift in her mid thirties. Yet now, as she looked at her reflection in the mirror, all she could see was a façade behind which despair and depression lay, a mask which hid her true self.

She felt ashamed of the selfish and self-centred traits she had begun to develop over the previous few years, how hurtful and tactless she had been at times. Being surrounded by people who only ever told you how wonderful you were, what an amazing person you were, how beautiful you were, how successful you were and who never said no to you, had stoked her ego and she had eventually succumbed and begun to develop a false sense of self-importance and relevance within her. For where were those people now? Gone. Deserted her like rats from a sinking ship. She tormented herself in her head as she recalled over and over again all the horrible things she had said and done, her body flushing in embarrassment from the memories of it all, forgetting all the good that she had done and the kindness she had shown towards others. Big fat tears fell rapidly down her cheeks in shame as she clung tightly onto the white porcelain sink. After a few minutes she forced herself to pull herself together, washed then dressed.

At five minutes to seven Ariadne drew up in the Oast Gym car park, the sleek drive lights threw a warm glow across it in the dark frosty morning. Her eyes were still red, nose swollen and cheeks flushed from crying, but she felt a little brighter, as though a small weight had been lifted from the burden she had been feeling, releasing some of her inner turmoil had proven to be cathartic.

Taking in a deep breath of cold air she put on her "happy" persona and strode with purpose into the building, gave Tara a cheery greeting as she passed through reception on the way to the changing rooms.

Alone in the main body of the room Ariadne examined herself closely again in the mirror, took more deep breaths and pushed the forced smile back onto her face, attempting to make it look as genuine as possible. She had to admit that what reflected back at her was a fairly feeble attempt but it would have to do. She fiddled with her over-sized diamond solitaire stud earrings, tweaked her navy - she found black looked too harsh on her - very expensive, form-fitting gym gear and mentally prepared herself for her session with Zeno.

At precisely 7 a.m. - because she was making herself become a stickler for punctuality - she walked into the gym and waved at Zeno who was on the far side. The three members who were working out on various pieces of equipment, glanced up or looked at Ariadne's reflection in the wall of mirrors. She smiled at them in a cheerful manner as she walked elegantly across the room, her long, golden-blonde ponytail swishing gently from side to side as she went.

'Morning darling, how are you?' she asked Zeno, giving him perfunctory kisses on each cheek.

'All the better for seeing you, my sweet,' he responded.

Zeno loved his job. In fact, he adored it. He was a natural people person, being with others was like oxygen to him; he needed it to survive and thrive. It didn't matter to him who his clients were in terms of status, money or fame, it was irrelevant to him. The inner person was what he looked for, the true person behind the "face" his clients often presented with for the benefit of others. Being a P.T. to him was an intensely personal and intimate job, one which he took seriously and with a great sense of responsibility. Over time, as his clients trust grew in him, they tended to open up, often confiding their deepest, darkest secrets and most innermost thoughts. To be the recipient of such information felt a privilege to Zeno, his clients knew that they could trust him and he never betrayed that trust. Ariadne was more of a challenge because, despite her very best efforts, Zeno could see the emotional and mental pain she feeling but she was so used to not trusting anyone on a deeper level, to not exposing her vulnerability - or too afraid to do so - that she had encased herself in a hard protective shell which seemed impenetrable.

'Ok. Let's get you warmed up and then I will show you no mercy,' he grinned at her. When Kim had asked him a couple of weeks earlier to meet a new client at her house he was surprised, but Kim had explained that there were exceptional circumstances, that it was a potential client who was an exceedingly private person and that this person, on Kim's recommendation, wanted to meet Zeno to see if they would be the right "fit" i.e. that this person would feel comfortable and confident enough in his ability to help achieve the physical and fitness goals she wished to and, above all, could be trusted.

All very mysterious Zeno had felt, but the moment he had met Ariadne he had understood the cloak and dagger approach. She told him what she wanted, what her goals were and that she would commit to training hard and with dedication. He in turn had told her that he would help her to obtain the results she was after, that she could achieve the level of fitness, tone and strength she desired, but that it would be on his terms, in his way and she would need to trust him, that he wasn't prepared to burn her out or have her injure herself from excessive or inappropriate training.

Ariadne had admired him for standing his ground with her. Her trainers in L.A. had been good but she had felt that they were easily dictated to and she hadn't felt that she'd achieved the results she had been after - to say nothing of the expense. When Kim had informed her as to how much a single session with Zeno would cost, she thought she'd misheard, that Kim had left a zero off the figure? But no, she hadn't. This added fuel to her growing sense of dissatisfaction about her life in L.A. In only the five sessions she had had so far with Zeno, she had noticed that her body was already beginning to feel stronger, leaner, fitter and more flexible. Admittedly over the past few months she had, by her standards, let herself go and not worked out obsessively six days a week, but perhaps that had been a good thing? Allowing her body some time to rest and recuperate after years of relentlessly pushing herself to extremes. Every session with Zeno was different which gave her muscles no opportunity to become familiar or complacent with a repetitive routine.

Ariadne grinned at Zeno, her spirits lifted just a little by being with him. 'No mercy is it? Better get this over with then!'

As she warmed up in preparation she chatted to him. 'So, who's heart have you broken this week then?' she smiled.

'Me?' he responded, feigning innocence.

'Yes. You! You are such a flirt. I've only been here when the gym is quiet but have still seen the way women swoon over you, so I can only imagine what it's like when this place is packed!'

He laughed good naturedly. 'A gentleman never tells. You won't get anything out of me!'

'Spoil sport,' Ariadne teased. 'I bet your flat could tell a few stories if it could speak.'

Hi grinned. 'I couldn't possibly say... Instead of grilling me, how about I grill you? Anything you want to tell me?'

She snorted with laughter in an attempt to cover up the flush which rushed through her as snatches from the previous evening flashed through her mind. 'Most definitely not!'

Ariadne loved the fact that Zeno treated her like an ordinary human being rather than a celebrity. He spoke to her as he would anyone else, not afraid, fearful or full of revere for her status and not treating her with kid gloves or being nervous around her as so many were. Every hour she spent with him took her mind away from her own problems and though she was reluctant to get up and go to the gym so early, once she was there with Zeno it boosted her morale.

At that moment Venka walked in. Colleague of Zeno's and also Kim's trainer for the past six years. Late thirties, 5'2", small but powerfully built, short blonde choppy haircut streaked with bright pink - a colour which she changed regularly depending upon her mood or the season. She was super toned, strong and flexible.

'Zeno. Ariadne,' she said, giving a brief nod in greeting before turning back to focus on her client who had followed her in.

Perspiring heavily, her body zinging from the intensity of her workout, endorphins rushing through her providing a brief boost and sense of wellbeing, Ariadne felt energised as she walked out of the gym back into the reception area with Zeno. Walking towards them was a tall, blonde, very slim, naturally beautiful woman. Ariadne frowned, sure she recognised her and flipped through her roller-dec memory for the information.

The woman started in surprise. This was not someone she had seen for years.

'Ariadne!' she smiled.

'Ditzi!' remembered Ariadne just in time to avoid the awkwardness which came from not being able to put a name to a face.

They hugged one another, genuinely pleased to see each other.

'It's been too long. But what are you doing here?' Ditzi was more than a little taken aback to see Ariadne in a gym on the edge of a small Kent village located in the middle of nowhere.

'I could say the same to you!' Ariadne said. 'Last I heard you'd married Dezo and were living in London.'

'We were but we needed a change of pace. We live in the next village along, at Wynenden Hall, moved in two years ago. You must come over, it would be really lovely to have a good catch up with you and I know Dezo would be delighted to see you. You've got my number? It's not changed. Call or message me please.'

'Ok. Thanks. I will.'

'Presumably, as you are here at this gym, you are staying close by? Are you here for long?' enquired Ditzi, curious.

'I'm staying with friends nearby. Not sure how long for but I will definitely give you a call to arrange a catch up. Anyway, apologies, but I've got to go.' Ariadne was anxious to vacate the premises before the morning rush.

'Great. I won't hold you up. I've got P.T. with Zeno anyway. See you soon.' Ditzi smiled broadly at Ariadne, then pushed the door to the gym open.

Ariadne hurried off to collect her bag and coat.

'So how do you know Ariadne?' enquired Zeno, intrigued.

'Oh, we go way back,' replied Ditzi. 'Our paths crossed a few times when I was modelling. That was in the early days of her career. She was always very sweet to me when we saw one another. Really supportive.'

Bella, who had somehow managed to miss seeing Ariadne, listened with interest to what Ditzi was saying, noticing that she wasn't the only one doing so.

CHAPTER FIVE

On her way back from the gym Bella stopped at the village shop in Monhurst and went in to buy her morning paper. She chatted with Sharon, who had run the shop-cum-post office with her hen-pecked husband Ron for many years, fount of all alleged knowledge, Sharon was well meaning but a terrible gossip. It was, however, hard to dislike her as underneath it all Sharon was a genuinely caring and kind person, it was just that her mouth had a tendency to run away with her.

The shop bell tinkled as the door was pushed open, signalling the arrival of another customer and they both glanced round to see who it was.

'Bastien!' exclaimed Sharon. 'How are you my chicken?' she said, using the term of endearment she saved for those whom she felt needed mothering.

Bastien didn't say anything but looked rather like a startled rabbit dazzled by the glare of car headlights. He had deep dark splurges underneath his eyes from lack of sleep, his shoulders were rounded even more than usual and his hair looked like it had not seen a hairbrush for a month. He shrank further into himself at Sharon's question and Bella could see pain and grief written over his face as he tried to hold it together.

Suddenly, the door banged open violently and the towering figure of Andrew Battle stormed in.

'You bloody moron!' he shouted. 'What the fuck do you think you were doing? Are you trying to kill me or something?' he yelled at Bastien.

'Andrew!' remonstrated Sharon. 'I will *not* tolerate having such foul language used in this shop. Now wash your mouth out and refrain from using such despicable language again. I've warned you before, if you keep using those sort of words in here you will be barred from the shop.' Sharon crossed her arms firmly across her ample bosom with an air of both indignation and determination to show that she meant business.

Bella found that she was trapped, her exit blocked by Andrew, though she was intrigued by what was unravelling before her.

Bastien ignored Andrew and walked off to choose a couple of packets of biscuits, tea bags, milk and several yoghurts.

'Oy! You pathetic little oik!' Andrew lunged towards Bastien and grabbed him. Bastien's provisions tumbled from his arms onto the floor, yoghurt exploding over it from the impact. 'Look at me when I am talking to you,' Andrew spat the words out ferociously.

In a split second Bastien metamorphosized from an introverted, weak-looking specimen into a ball of fury, punched Andrew in the face and stormed out.

Bella and Sharon stood there open mouthed in astonishment, though not as stunned as Andrew was. Seconds later he let out a roar, turned and hurried in pursuit of his quarry, slamming the door behind him as he went.

Silence pervaded the shop. Sharon shocked into silence. 'What just happened?' blurted out Bella.

Regaining her composure Sharon stuttered. 'Oh my. Oh my goodness. I've never seen anything like that in my shop. And that poor Bastien. What has Andrew done to rile him up so much? Bastien's always so quiet and pleasant. Betty says so too,' she said, in reference to her counterpart gossip who ran the village shop in Wynenden, where Bastien lived.

'I really can't imagine. But then we know what Andrew can be like,' muttered Bella darkly. His reputation preceded him, the way he had treated Kitty over her house had been despicable and was still fresh in Bella's memory.

Once Bella was sure that Sharon had recovered from witnessing the outburst she left, her mobile ringing as she did so. It was Kitty.

'Hiya. How are you doing Kitty?' she enquired.

'Morning Bella. Good thanks. And you?' Kitty continued without waiting for a reply. 'Do you fancy meeting up for a drink tonight? We could go to The Orchard Pub in your village, now that it's re-opened, and have a look at what they've done? Or have you been already?'

'Sounds like an excellent idea. Nope, not been in yet, it only opened on Wednesday. I do feel sorry for them, they've ploughed so much time, effort and money into it, for the works to overrun so badly meaning they missed out on the profitable Christmas and New Year trade must be so frustrating, not to say financially detrimental. I don't understand why they changed the name of the pub though. I liked The King's Head, not so sure about The Orchard, sounds a bit wishy-washy to me. What time?' She paused for breath.

Kitty laughed. 'I'm with you on that. How about 8 o'clock?'

'Perfect. See you then.' Bella replied, but before she had the opportunity to recount what she had just witnessed in the shop, Kitty rang off.

Minutes later, just as Bella was opening her front door, her mobile rang again. This time it was Jennifer.

'Hi Bella. How are you?'

'Good thanks Jennifer, and you?' Bella shoved the door closed with a backward push of her foot and attempted to shrug out of her coat, swapping her phone to her other hand as she did so. 'Sorry, I missed that, trying to get out of my coat.'

'No worries. I was just asking if you wanted to go for a drink at the pub tonight?'

'Funny you should ask, Kitty has just phoned and suggested that too. Come and join us, we're meeting at about 8 o'clock.'

'Lovely. I'll see you then.'

A little after 7.30 p.m. Bella pulled on and laced up her sheepskin-lined winter walking boots. They were black, sturdy, practical but surprisingly stylish, many a time she had been asked where she'd purchased them from. She was trying to drum up the enthusiasm to venture out into the bitterly cold night having been curled up on the sofa in the sitting room all cosy and warm by the fire. The temperature outside was still falling, having been below freezing since mid-afternoon and snow was forecast for later that night.

She wound a bright pink cashmere scarf around her neck, put on her black padded coat, a thick navy cashmere beanie with matching gloves and braced herself for the blast of cold air. She shivered as she stepped out into the dark, the drive lights flicking on automatically at the movement, lighting the area with a gentle luminosity.

'Brrr.' She said to the empty night, a plume of white, icy, exhaled breath wafting in front of her. As she walked, attempting to be brisk but wary of the ice on the ground beneath her, her cheeks began to glow from the cold in contrast to her warming body. Reaching the end of her drive by the edge of the green, she flicked on her small L.E.D. torch to light the way towards the pub as there were no street lights in the village - previous attempts to have them installed had always been met with a barrage of objections from residents - consequently the only splashes of light were from outside the front doors of properties edging the green, along with those located on the main road through the village and now, across the green, Bella could see the pub brightly lit inside and a posse of people within it.

Her torch picked up snatches of frost as she walked, sparkling and twinkling under its beam and she felt as though she could almost smell the approaching snow in the air.

The pub was packed, not rammed to the rafters, but full enough for Bella to have to weave her way around people as she searched for Kitty and Jennifer. She glimpsed the back of Jennifer's long, curly, glossy, rich-dark-chestnut coloured hair and slipped around the end of the bar to get to her.

The atmosphere of the heavily beamed, low ceilinged, 16th Century building was one of jolliness and relief. Relief that it was Friday night, meaning for many no work for the following two days and the prospect of having the opportunity to relax.

The old pub, pre-refurbishment, had felt very much like a traditional village pub, one which locals had frequented for years, indeed decades and generations. Run down and rustic, with tables which wobbled, chairs which were uncomfortable and had seen better days, a dark red swirl-patterned carpet worn and torn from at least a couple of decades of use and from which the stale smell of old beer and cigarette smoke had pervaded. A posse of old men, bent and crinkled from the years and who had grown up in the village, had been resident at the bar pretty much from opening time to closing time on most days, more so in the winter when there was less work for them to carry out in their allotments and for whom the chilly air seeped into their rheumatic bodies making it too painful to work outside for prolonged periods of time. There had been an unspoken rule locally that the three stools to the left of the bar were theirs and locals would never have dreamt of moving, sitting on or using them. The old men had muttered, grumbled, hacking-coughed and cackled their way through hours and had been as much a part of the fabric of the pub as the fixtures and fittings, they gave character and a sense of place to the pub. Stoic, resilient and with tales to tell which went back through the generations of their family, having all been born, brought up and lived in the village their entire lives and who now found the modern world a mystery.

But now where were they? Bella had heard the rumours over the past few months whilst the pub was closed, older members of the community had voiced their concerns and resistance to the alleged changes being made. Bella could imagine how they felt. Why would they want things to change when feelings of security and reliability stemmed from the familiar and didn't confront them to dwell upon the fact that times were changing, that they were getting older and with each day their lives were drawing closer to an end?

Arguments and division had broken out in the Post Office, the deli and at the farmers' market as debate raged on within the older members of the community. Not prepared, or wanting, to remember the changes they themselves had implemented in the village in their younger years. That they themselves had informed their elders that they had to move forward or be left behind. That village life, all life in general, was going to change whether they liked it or not. That what they had done back then, was happening to them now as history repeated itself.

Change could be good, could be for the better, but equally had the potential to be detrimental. Pubs were closing in their droves. How people drank, spent their money and their leisure time was rapidly changing, evolving at such a fast pace and the once packed old village pub had become quiet as customers trickled away. It was a vicious cycle, fewer customers meant that there was less money coming in - barely enough to break even and cover costs - which subsequently meant no surplus funds with which to maintain and keep on top of the decaying decor and structure and which in its self inevitably discouraged customers from returning.

With these thoughts in mind, Bella's first impression was that the refurbishment had been as radical as had been rumoured. It was like stepping into a different time and place, one which was in no way connected to what had been there for centuries. Gone was the stale, stained, worn, red-swirled carpet and in its place exposed, sanded and polished oak floorboards. The walls and ceiling were clean and crisp; painted in a soft, gentle, white. The beams had been sandblasted and were now a golden-honey colour giving glory to the ancient oak timber which had held the building together for hundreds of years; the grime, dirt and tar from cigarette smoke and wood smoke from the open fires, all blasted away. The battered old bar, which could have told so many stories and secrets, was gone and in its place was a modern, elegant but practical, oak base atop of which was a white, grey-veined, marble slab, an unusual choice for a pub felt Bella.

There were blue-flecked tweed fabric sofas on either side of each of the two large fireplaces which no longer had open fires but had more efficient, some would say safe but less atmospheric, wood-burning stoves. Gentle flames waved softly back and forth behind the glass and a powerful heat was emitting from them. The magic of the open, often spitting and crackling, fires had gone. Low coffee tables piled with newspapers and magazines were placed centrally between each pair of sofas. Carefully positioned at intervals across the rest of the bar area was a mixture of small, modern-style, light-oak tables and chairs along with several pairs of comfy looking arm chairs.

It must have cost a fortune, thought Bella, and that was without being able to see through to what would apparently be - in the not too distant future - a restaurant serving pub food, traditional-with-a-contemporary twist, and which opened out onto the garden.

This was not a place, felt Bella, where the posse of old men would feel comfortable or even welcomed she wondered, though she had no foundation upon which to come to this conclusion. From what she had seen so far the couple in their mid-thirties were congenial, had listened to the complaints and concerns raised at residents meetings and had appeared to be sympathetic. But they had a vision, they were focused, and they had the energy and enthusiasm to see the project through to fruition. They had argued that they wanted to breath new life into the village (which hadn't gone down too well with long-term residents who tended to be initially suspicious and wary of "incomers" as they referred to them), that they wanted to help keep the village alive and for the pub to become a hub for the community.

It would be interesting to see how it played out now that the pub was open. Would those who had been resistant to its changes weaken and give in? Curiosity getting the better of them? Or would they remain stubborn and unmovable in their opinions and attempt to be disruptive?

'I got you a red wine,' said Jennifer proffering a large glass of a deep plum-red coloured liquid, interrupting Bella's musings. 'Hope that's ok?'

'Perfect. Thanks. You know me too well,' laughed Bella.

'I managed to get a table over here.' Jennifer nodded towards a corner of the room. 'So how are you?' she asked as she sank into a comfy armchair.

'Good thanks. And you?' reciprocated Bella as she shrugged herself out of her coat then removed her hat and gloves, leaving her scarf snuggled around her neck.

'Fine thanks. Oh, here's Kitty.' She waved across at her.

'Gosh it's getting busy in here,' Kitty exclaimed. 'Good for business, let's hope it lasts. Was that Hetty I saw behind the bar?' she asked referring to the cheerful young woman who was normally seen behind the bar at The Speckled Goose in Wynenden where she also lived, renting a room from the landlord.

'Yes. I was just having a chat with her. Oh, I got you this elderflower cordial.' Kitty's drink of preference when driving. 'Is that ok?'

'Lovely Thanks Jennifer. You were saying about Hetty? She hasn't quit her job at The Speckled Goose has she?'

'No. Apparently she was looking for a change and was going to quit, she loves it there but had itchy feet. You can understand why, she's only in her mid-twenties and she's been there a few years. But the landlord didn't want to loose her, she's so good at her job.'

They glanced over at the smiling and laughing Hetty whose natural ability to engage easily with customers in a happy, welcoming and friendly manner, highlighted her innate effervescence.

'Anyway,' continued Jennifer, 'she applied for a part-time job here and the landlord at The Speckled Goose agreed to let her work part-time there with Hetty alternating weekends between the two pubs. She said it meant she got a change of scenery and working environment and also managed to negotiate a pay rise too. A win win result and quite right too, she is excellent at her job.'

'I agree' replied Kitty.

The three were chatting amiably when the front door was suddenly flung open with force, letting in a sharp blast of cold air followed by the 6'2" dominant presence of Andrew Battle. In fact, they had smelt him before they saw him, his tendency to be overzealous with overpowering cologne was renowned.

Deemed to be the least popular person in the area, particularly in the villages of Wynenden and Monhurst where he persistently tried to buy up and turn any piece of available land into a building opportunity to make money. Many felt that he was eroding away at the heart and uniqueness of both villages, turning them into sprawling masses of over-developed, insipid looking, concrete jungles.

Kitty in particular was not a fan of his. He had done everything in his power to try to buy Wynenden Farm before it was eventually sold to her by Sir Geoffrey Percevall-Sharparrow who owned the Wynenden Park Estate with its 2000 rolling acres of parkland, farmland and many associated buildings and properties. Sir Geoffrey's bitter dislike and instinct not to trust Andrew had been validated when the motivation behind Andrew's persistence, and seemingly increasing level of desperation, to get his hands on Wynenden Farm had come to light. It was the final piece of land he needed to acquire in order to provide enough access to the 50 acres he already owned - purchased and hidden through one of his companies - in order to have planning permission granted to develop a massive housing estate of approximately 1000 houses due to an unofficial verbal agreement made with his "useful" contact within the planning committee. When his underhandedness had been exposed, the village had been in an uproar, outraged and even five years later it was far from forgotten. But Andrew was as resilient as they come and no amount of negativity or hostility towards him seemed to break through into his being or conscience.

'I might have known he'd turn up,' muttered Kitty darkly.

Sensing her presence, he swaggered over. Bella tapped Kitty's foot to warn her as she had her back towards him, who in response rolled her eyes at Bella.

'Ladies. Always a pleasure to see you,' he oozed with a sense of sarcasm.

'Andrew.' Jennifer nodded politely.

'Kitty. How are you? Keeping well I trust?'

His fakeness made her skin crawl. He continued. 'It's going to snow. You know you'll get cut off at the house. Lose power for days. No heating. Burst pipes and so on. Why don't you let me take it off your hands. Find you somewhere central in the village, less remote?' He grinned at her.

His opportunistic and persistent attempts to persuade or provoke Kitty into selling him her house had been, and continued to be, both impressive and tedious. She had grown used to it, though it didn't stop her from feeling annoyed at his every attempt. She raised one eyebrow at him and said nothing.

'You know you'll give in one day. So why not make it sooner rather than later? You have my number.' He gave her a wink and a smile and sauntered off to the bar.

'Yuck! He doesn't get any better, does he?' Jennifer asked rhetorically. 'I don't know how Hetty does it. Look at her being all smiley and nice and flirty with him, he's lapping it up.'

'She's made of strong stuff, but he can't be the only odious character she comes across in her line of work. Hard though it is to believe,' added Kitty, glancing around at them. 'Anyway, what's with that bruise on his face?'

'I know!' answered Bella gleefully. 'Have either of you seen Bastien recently?'

Jennifer and Kitty shook their heads.

'Well. I was in the shop earlier to get my paper, when Bastien came in. A few moments later Andrew burst in and started shouting and swearing at him, accusing him of trying to kill him!'

'No!' exclaimed Jennifer and Kitty in unison a little too loudly, making some customers turn and stare.

'Why did he say that?' asked Kitty, lowering her voice.

'No idea, he didn't say. Anyway. Bastien, who was looking terrible by the way, ignored Andrew and went to get some biscuits and stuff. This incensed Andrew who lunged at Bastien, Bastien dropped his shopping and - I don't know what came over him - he punched Andrew in the face and stormed out! Andrew was so stunned that it took him a moment to recover, then he too stormed out in pursuit of Bastien, yelling at him. Sharon and I were so shocked we just stood there with our mouths open in surprise. I did wonder if I should have gone after them, just to make sure that Bastien was alright, but thought better of it. Do you think somebody should go and see how he is?' finished Bella.

'Wow!' said Jennifer.

'Gosh.' Added Kitty, astonished at the turn of events.

Bella looked expectantly from one to the other.

'I'll pop over sometime and check he's ok,' said Kitty eventually. 'I know it's not nice but...' she hesitated, 'I can't help thinking that it was about time someone punched Andrew in the face.'

'Yup, me too. I'm only surprised that it hasn't happened before, or more frequently for that matter, given the number of backs he's managed to put up,' agreed Jennifer.

'That reminds me,' said Bella, lowering her voice to a whisper and gesticulating for Kitty and Jennifer to lean in towards her. 'I don't know if you know but, and this is strictly "entre nous", apparently Andrew is buying Florence's old house.' Bella made reference to the dilapidated cottage located on the outskirts of the village, in the middle of nowhere, down a long track and surrounded by woodland.

'What? No!' spluttered Jennifer, horrified. 'He can't. You know what he'll do, he'll try to obtain - probably successfully knowing our luck - planning permission for a load of houses. It'll ruin the area and decimate that beautiful woodland.' she added, looking grim.

'What can we do though? We can't stop the sale to him, can we? Besides who is actually selling the house anyway?' asked Bella.

'Perhaps Kim will know?' murmured Jennifer thoughtfully.

'Worth a try asking her. If there's any way he can be stopped that would be good. Look what he's planning on doing to the land adjacent to the road through my village,' said Kitty. 'It is so sad that Bastien's parents sold those 15 acres to Andrew rather than to someone more sympathetic to the environment. But perhaps there was no-one else? No alternative?' she added thoughtfully. 'His obtaining permission for 300 houses on the site is disgusting, it's going to completely ruin the ambiance of the village. I guarantee that there won't be enough parking provided for each house - people seem to own a disproportionate number of cars these days - and they'll end up parking on the road causing disruption, chaos and inevitably the people who buy the houses won't get involved in village life. I've seen it happen before,' she ranted.

'Say what you really feel Kitty,' laughed Bella, used to her friend being presumptuous and getting on her soap box about over-development in the countryside. 'You know I agree with you, as does Jennifer,' she added.

Jennifer nodded. 'At least the parish council have managed to delay the start of the works a little by applying for a judicial review. You never know, they may yet be successful and manage to have the permission overturned.' she said hopefully.

'Come on. It's Friday night and we're here to have a good time together,' said Bella changing the subject. 'Same again or something different?' She nodded towards their empty glasses.

'Same again please,' they replied.

Bella weaved her way through the throng of people towards the bar, doing her best to ensure that she was as far away from Andrew as possible. He was busy lounging against it leering at Hetty.

'Same again is it?' asked Hetty, smiling at Bella.

'Yes please Hetty, thanks,' replied Bella who, as always, was impressed by Hetty's ability to remember her customers original orders. 'You enjoying the change of scene then Hetty, even though it has only been a couple of days?'

'Loving it thanks Bella. Great atmosphere and a complete contrast to The Speckled Goose. I think I have managed to achieve the best of both worlds. There we are,' she placed two glasses of red wine down onto the marble top bar along with a sparkling elderflower. 'That'll be…'

She was interrupted by Andrew's booming voice.

'Het's. I'll get those, add them to my tab,' he ordered.

'Thanks. But it's fine. I'll buy them,' replied Bella tightly, unwilling to be indebted to Andrew in any way. She attempted a polite smile but only managed to succeed in making it look more of a grimace.

'Nah. You're fine. Het's, ignore her, stick it on mine. And don't panic,' he looked directly at Bella, 'you don't owe me anything. I'm not expecting any favours. Just being a good citizen.' He winked at her.

Hetty looked apologetically at Bella, knowing full well that Andrew would get his way. For all his faults - and there were many - he was always generous.

'Well. Thank you,' replied Bella grudgingly.

He raised his half empty beer glass in her direction. 'Cheers,' he said as she hastened away as swiftly as possible without spilling the drinks.

'Why the thunderous look?' asked Kitty as Bella carefully put the glasses down onto the table.

'Drinks. Courtesy of Andrew. Couldn't get out of it. Sorry.'

The others glanced in Andrew's direction and over the top of the mélange of people he grinned and winked again at them.

'Oh,' was all Kitty could muster in response.

'So Kitty,' said Jennifer deliberately changing the subject. 'How's Ted?' She watched as a gentle glow came over Kitty.

'He's very well thank you.'

'You've been together now for what? Over a year?'

The evening passed quickly as they continued to chat and enjoy one another's company.

CHAPTER SIX

The snow had fallen lightly overnight, dusting the fields which looked as though they had been sprinkled with icing sugar, a hint at what was forecast to come; heavy snow for that night and the following day.

At the weekly Saturday morning Farmers' Market held in Wynenden Village Hall both stallholders and customers were out in force taking the opportunity to stock up on provisions before the expected deluge of snow. The village hall was modern, having been built six years previously to replace the rotting old building which had sufficed as one prior to that. It was light, airy, functional and warm, but it didn't blend into the landscape in the same way in which the village hall in Monhurst did. The replacement hall in Monhurst had opened in 1998 and had been built to look like a traditional Kentish weather-boarded barn conversion, which had subsequently mellowed over time.

Kitty decided to walk to the market, the winter sun was glowing and the clear blue sky lifted her spirits. She adored this kind of weather; clear, crisp, bitterly cold but with a hint of warmth, albeit a weak one, from the sun. She took a long route to the village hall, her lungs filling with the fresh air as she strode across the fields, arriving at her destination with glowing cheeks and feeling energised. She had been due to meet Ted at the market but he'd had to cancel, much to her disappointment. He was diligent in his role as Estate Manager to Wynenden Park and with the heavy snow forecast he had wanted to double check that everything was in place to ensure that the estate would still run smoothly no matter what the weather threw at them. In addition, he wanted to brief the team who would drive the tractors to assist with snow ploughing in the area in order to keep the local roads and lanes as operational as possible. So instead of Ted, Kitty was going to meet Bella. And Bella, who was eager to meet Kitty's new kitten, would drive her home.

Stomping the snow off her boots onto the large mat at the entrance to the hall, Kitty was then met by an invisible wall of warmth and chatter as she walked into the main hall, estimating that there were approximately 25 stalls present; not a bad turn out for a mid-January, snowy Saturday.

She chatted convivially to stallholders and other customers as she wandered round making her purchases. Even though not a month had passed since the rush, bustle and excitement of Christmas, Kitty pondered upon the fact that, to her, it felt like it had been a lifetime ago. Clearly, from the enthusiastic buying taking place, cupboards were deemed to be bare and the impending snow was appearing to motivate people to stock up on provisions. This, naturally, delighted the stallholders, whose previous experiences of January and February markets were ones of sparse transactions As a consequence, many of them often decided to take some time off during the early months of each new year.

Kitty purchased some local strawberry jam and honey - produced barely a mile from the village - a couple of individually sized butternut squash and leek tartlets, along with two individual blackberry and apple pies to pop into the freezer. She then hurried over to join the requisite queue for the bread. Bread Man, as he was nicknamed, would be arriving shortly - late as always - and the empty table would temporarily be laden with an array of enticing baked goods, before swiftly selling out.

'You beat me to it,' laughed a voice from behind her. It was Bella.

'You snooze, you loose,' joked Kitty back. 'How are you this morning?' teased Kitty.

Bella scowled. 'I blame you entirely for encouraging me to drink more than I usually do, you know how pathetically intolerant I am of alcohol these days. One large glass is more than enough for me now, but three! It feels like I had the equivalent of me having downed a few bottles in one night during my youth. Blame my age, or perimenopause, or whatever, my body just can't take it any more. So, in answer to your question, my head is banging and it feels like I am thinking through a fog. And before you start clucking like a mother hen, yes I have drunk lots of water and I took a couple of paracetamol before I came out. I only hope that they start working soon.'

'Oh, poor you!' said Kitty sympathetically. 'But you seemed to be having a good time, you even blew Andrew a kiss as we left. He looked rather startled!' Kitty chortled.

Bella groaned. 'Oh please tell me you're joking?' she looked hopefully at Kitty, who giggled and shook her head. 'What am I going to do when I next see him? Ugh! I feel all hot and prickly at the thought,' she grimaced.

'Probably a hot flush Bella,' Kitty laughed.

Bella gave Kitty a withering look. They'd had discussions about the menopause before and, despite the myriad of perimenopausal symptoms she seemed to be experiencing; tiredness, brain fog, occasional bouts of anxiety, aching joints and intermittent periods of low mood, hot flushes were fortunately not currently one with which she suffered. Occasionally she felt a little warm, rather as though the thermostat of her body had got stuck and wouldn't regulate itself, but nothing compared to some of her female friends in their forties and fifties. Bella had been holding out and resisting taking HRT in an attempt to let nature take its course, but she was weakening, the more debilitating her symptoms became and the more she read up on HRT - scientific fact not fiction - the more she was swaying in the direction of succumbing to it. Kitty, who was all for women being able to make an informed choice and decision for themselves, had pointed her in the direction of a couple of excellent websites, of which the factual information had been provided by medical doctors. As a result, Bella was coming to understand the potential long-term, not just short term, benefits there could be to her health, particularly with regards to heart disease and osteoporosis. As far as she could currently see, the benefits outweighed the negatives, but realised how important it was to be able to have a discussion regarding her options with a doctor who was well informed on the subject, something which was not always a given.

Bread Man arrived, interrupting Bella's musings and, once the offerings were on the table, the queue inched forward. When Kitty had purchased what she had wanted to, she went off to buy them both coffee, leaving Bella waiting her turn in the queue.

Kitty returned with two white, chunky, china mugs and placed them down onto the small wobbly wooden table where Bella had managed to secure two available chairs.

'Oh. There's Venka,' commented Bella as she sipped the strong black liquid, hopeful that some caffeine would swiftly help to perk her up a bit.

'Ahhh. She's got Valentina with her. She is *so* adorable,' said Kitty wistfully.

They were referring to the diminutive, but physically very powerful, strong and flexible woman in her late thirties who was a personal trainer at Oast Gym and who had been Kim's trainer for the past five years. Her demeanour could come across as rather ferocious, but she was incredibly kind and had a wealth of experience and qualifications. Her clients loved her style of training and the results which they were able to achieve. Valentina was Venka's cute-as-a-button two year old daughter. The little girls hair was blonde and her eyes were a deep sapphire blue, when she smiled her whole face lit up. Valentina was shy and hesitant with strangers, but those with whom she was familiar, she became a chatterbox with.

Valentina knew both Bella and Kitty from having met them in the villages when she was out with her mother and on the occasions when she was allowed a special visit to say "hello" whilst Venka dropped something off at work. On the whole members too were cast under her spell, for Venka was a stickler for good manners and was bringing Valentina up to be polite and respectful of others.

Wrapped up in her navy blue duffel coat, along with a bright pink knitted bobble hat, gloves and scarf; the colours of which matched the streaks of pink in her mothers blond hair, Valentina ran across and flung herself at Kitty. She immediately started to chatter away to them, both in turn captivated by the adorable two year old. Confident that her daughter was in safe hands Venka completed her shopping in solitude.

Usually buzzing with endless energy, Bella noticed that Venka appeared to have lost her fizz, fatigue was evident by the dark bluish/purple smudges below her eyes and worry was etched across her face. Bella assumed that it was caused by the pressures of being solely responsible for Valentina's upbringing, along with the relentlessness of being a working single parent and trying to be a full-time parent in part-time hours.

'Hello Venka, how are you?' asked Kitty over Valentina's continuing stream of chatter.

'Fine. Thanks. Come along Valentina, leave Bella and Kitty alone. Let's go to the playground.' Never one for small talk, Venka - despite her fatigue - glowed with joy when she spoke to, or about, her daughter, the warmth and love she had for her plain for all to see.

The prospect of a visit to the playground in the snow was clearly too much for Valentina and she squealed with the sort of excitement which was infectious and made Bella and Kitty laugh. In a cute manner, Valentina said goodbye to them, accompanied by a nod and a wan smile from Venka.

'She is such a sweetheart,' sighed Kitty at the retreating sight of Valentina, wistful for children of her own, ones she had not been able to have.

'Indeed she is,' replied Bella, mindful too of her own absence of motherhood. 'It must be such hard work though, being a single parent. Venka never mentions the father so I'm assuming that he's not on the scene, but I'd never dream of asking.'

'Me either,' agreed Kitty. 'If he's not around then I guess the burden of responsibility lies solely on her shoulders. It must be so stressful - and scary - I imagine, being completely and utterly responsible for the wellbeing of another human being.'

Their melancholic moment was interrupted by the ever glamorous and terribly sweet Ditzi, who was accompanied by her much older husband - at the age of 62 he was 27 years Ditzi's elder - Dezo. On first impression they seemed like an unusual match. To start with she was young enough to be his daughter, but also physically they were polar opposites too; she was 6'1", he was 5'8". She was slim, toned and fit. He was overweight and unfit, though he had recently begun personal training sessions with Zeno. She was rather shy and reserved upon first meeting. What he lacked in height he made up for in personality. But their devotion and love for one another was obvious by the bucket load. Clichés such as "made for each other" and "two peas in a pod" tended to pop into peoples minds, the age difference dissolving into irrelevance.

Jovial as ever, Dezo greeted them as he did everyone; full of energy, good humour and friendliness. 'Morning, lovely ladies. You are looking as wonderful as ever. How are you both?' He asked with sincerity, not simply out of politeness. Dezo had had, and still had, a long and successful career in the music industry. He had been in a band in his youth, they'd had a one-hit-wonder, but the band had split up shortly afterwards and his performing career had dwindled away. What hadn't dwindled though were the songs he had written, and continued to write, achieving a phenomenal level of success. His songs were performed by many artists; those who were well established and very successful, along with lesser known and up and coming artists, making him a stalwart of the industry and very wealthy in the process. Not only that, he was a music producer and had converted the stables at Wynenden Hall into a recording studio with ancillary accommodation so that artists could come down and stay whilst they laid down their tracks.

'All the better for seeing you two,' responded Kitty, smiling broadly. She was enjoying getting to know Ditzi, having first met her at Oast Gym, but had only recently met Dezo and liked them both immensely. 'Are you finding your P.T. with Zeno rewarding?' she asked Dezo. 'It looked like he was really putting you through your paces the other day.'

Dezo grimaced. 'He certainly wasn't going to let me take it easy. Ditzi's assuring me that it will do me good, though personally I'm rather attached to my baby,' he winked and patted his protruding belly.

Ditzi rolled her eyes indulgently. 'You know that I love you just as you are, but you need to look after yourself. I want us to be together, healthy and happy, for decades to come. She tucked her arm through his black leather clad one.

'I know darling, but I can't say I've discovered a passion for exercise yet and the same can be said for the healthy diet you've put me on.'

Ditzi laughed. 'There, there, never mind.' She stroked the back of his head and cuddled into him then addressed

Kitty and Bella. 'Kim is coming over next week for coffee. If you're free would you both like to come too?'

'I'd love to thanks Ditzi. When were you thinking of?' asked Bella.

'Kim was aiming for Wednesday, if that works for you?'

'That should be fine, unless we get snowed in,' replied Bella.

'Perfect for me. I don't work on a Wednesday now that I've reduced my hours and even if it snows I can still walk over,' added Kitty.

'Wonderful. Say. 10.30?' Ditzi suggested.

'Well. Well. Well,' said a soft voice from behind Dezo and Ditzi. 'I don't believe it. You really are living here now.'

Ditzi spun round, recognising the voice. 'Ariadne! It's so lovely see you again so soon.' She embraced Ariadne warmly with Dezo and Bella following suit.

There was a wave of excitement rippling through the hall as people recognised Ariadne, some of them not able to believe their eyes; a real live movie star was in their midst.

Kitty meanwhile remained seated at the table feeling awkward, not sure whether to stand up and introduce herself, but also a little star struck too. What was one supposed to say to a mega-star?

'Ariadne. Let me introduce my friend Kitty,' said Bella.

Kitty stood up, her mouth going dry.

'Nice to meet you Kitty,' said Ariadne pleasantly, offering her hand.

'You too,' stuttered Kitty, her mind going blank but taking the proffered hand and shaking it.

'So, what brings you to the rural idyl of the Kent countryside then Ariadne?' asked Ditzi.

'Oh, I needed a break, a change of scenery.' Ariadne shrugged non-committaly.

'Well, we are going to have to have a good catch up, apart from bumping into you at the gym it's been, what? How many years? Four? Five? Since I last saw you?' said Ditzi. From time to time they had come across one another when Ditzi had been modelling and she had always been touched by how sweet and kind - almost sisterly - Ariadne had been towards her. The advice Ariadne had offered her had proven to be invaluable, giving her the confidence, knowledge and ability to say "no" when unpleasant or potentially dangerous situations arose. Ariadne, to Ditzi, had felt like her guardian angel and she would forever be grateful to her.

'Watch out,' muttered Kitty, raising her eyebrows and tilting her head in the direction of the rapidly approaching figures of Sharon, who ran the shop in Monhurst, and her partner-in-gossip, Betty, who ran the shop in Wynenden.

Ariadne sighed. She was used to the curiosity, inquisitiveness and adoration of fans and general public, but part of the reason why she had chosen to stay in this rural area had been in an attempt to bring a semblance of balance and normality into her life. She really didn't feel like putting her "Hollywood" face on, but she knew that she had no choice. Any hint of unpleasantness from her in public and it would swiftly be all over social media and blown into something a million times bigger than it actually was.

'Morning everyone,' burst out Sharon, her eyes shining. She opened her mouth to continue but was beaten to it by her comrade, Betty, the grey-haired, heavily permed-into-tight-curls woman in her sixties who always meant well, but was a terrible gossip - though she couldn't see it herself.

'Have you heard?' she blurted out.

'Heard?' enquired Kitty politely.

'About what happened at the gym?' She searched their faces for any sign of comprehension as to what she was making reference to.

'Oast Gym?' asked Bella.

'Yes!'

'No idea what you are referring to Betty?' Kitty paused and braced herself, she knew she was playing right into Betty's hands and was annoyed with herself for taking the bait, but it was too late now to backtrack. 'What about the gym?'

Both Betty and Sharon were fizzing with excitement, but it was Betty who spoke.

'Murder!' she said triumphantly.

'Nope. I really have no clue as to what you are referring to.' The others looked just as puzzled as Kitty.

Visibly puffed up with self-importance, Betty continued. 'There's been a murder at the gym!'

'What are you talking about? That can't be right. Where did you pick that up from?' snapped Bella, irritated by what could only be unfounded gossip being spread by Betty.

'I drove past the gym on the way here and there are police cars and police officers swarming all over the place!' added Sharon.

'But that doesn't mean that someone has been murdered,' interjected Kitty.

'I have my sources and have it on good authority that someone has been,' replied Sharon sulkily. How dare they be so high and mighty, she thought, tempted not to tell them who the victim was.

Dezo stepped in, smiling pleasantly at the pair of gossips, keen to escape but knowing full well that they wouldn't be able to until the pair had had their say.

'Ladies,' he dazzled them with a broader smile. 'Would you care to enlighten us as to whom you believe to have been murdered?'

Sharon visibly wilted with delight from the attention of the wealthy, well-connected, influential man in front of her and fluttered her eye lashes at him.

'Of course, Dezo, of course I will. For you,' she added coquettishly. 'It was one of the personal trainers. Zeno.'

There was a collective gasp. Dezo paled. Ditzi wobbled and clutched onto him. All of them stunned into silence.

Satisfied that their job was done, Betty and Sharon prepared to retreat.

'We just though you'd like to know,' added Betty, 'given that you are friends with the owner.' She directed her gaze at Bella and Kitty.

'Yes. Yes. Thank you,' uttered Kitty.

CHAPTER SEVEN

Seb opened the door to the generously proportioned Tudor farmhouse where he and Kim lived. Despite his warm smile, Kitty and Bella could see worry and stress etched on his face - hardly surprising given the circumstances.

'How is she?' asked Bella as he led them down the hallway to the back of the house and into the recently updated, light-flooded kitchen. The expansive room was light and airy as a result of the numerous windows and pair of French doors which opened out onto the terrace providing views of the garden and tennis court. The newly installed kitchen units were in a crisp-white with chrome bar handles along with a vast centre island made from maple wood atop of which was a deep green, iridescent-flecked, marble work top which shimmered in the light like the flash of a kingfishers wings At the opposite end of the room was a glass and chrome rectangular table with eight white leather chairs.

Kim was sitting at the table drawing with Matilda. Traditionally on a Sunday morning the family went to the 9 a.m. service at St Nicholas Church, Monhurst, where children were particularly well catered for. The children stayed with their parents for the first part of the service and then went off to do activities related to the days theme in the newly created space; glazing fitted between the arches and architecture of the Norman building, off to one side towards the rear of the building, a good use of space within the church. The children returned towards the end of the service to show the congregation what they had made and had been learning about, then re-joined their parents.

But this particular Sunday Kim had not felt up to facing the inevitable questions which would be asked, too concerned and distressed about what had happened to Zeno. She gave them a wan smile as they walked in, dark smudges and bags visible underneath her eyes which were also red-rimmed and hence enhanced the look of utter exhaustion on her face.

'Kit Kit! BB!' squealed an excited Matilda, who slid off her chair, ran over and flung herself at them. Delighted by such an enthusiastic welcome, Bella and Kitty squatted down and in turn gave the adorable four year old a cuddle.

'Coffee?' asked Seb.

They nodded as Matilda dragged them by their hands over to the table in order to show them what she had been drawing. They listened earnestly to her explanation; apparently it was her, mummy, daddy and a kitten.

'Kitten?' murmured Bella to Kim questioningly. Apart from the long haired rabbit called Boris, she wasn't aware that they had any other pets.

'Don't ask.' Kim rolled her eyes. Matilda was proving to be particularly persistent in her campaign for a kitten, which had intensified since she had started at nursery school, where one of her new little friends had been given a kitten for Christmas.

'Why don't you get mummy or daddy to bring you over to my house and you can have a play with my kitten?' suggested Kitty.

Matilda squealed and clapped her hands in excitement. 'Please can we Mummy?' her eyes shone. 'Can we go now? Please. Please. Please!' she begged.

'Not now darling,' interjected Seb. 'But I'm sure Mummy or I can take you over some time soon. How about that?'

Disappointment flashed across Matilda's face and her bottom lip trembled.

'That will give us time to go and choose a little present for her. Wouldn't it?' added Kim hastily as tears started to well up in Matilda's eyes.

The tactic worked and Matilda started clapping her hands again and doing little bounces of delight.

'Come on Matilda. Let's go and make the coffee.' You can help carry the cups and saucers over,' said Seb, gently taking his daughters hand.

Easily distracted, particularly if it meant being grown up and helpful, Matilda trotted off to the other end of the kitchen.

The five of them chatted whilst Seb made the coffee, then he discretely took his daughter off to play with some toys in another room. The three women looked at one another, waiting until the door had clicked closed behind the pair of them before speaking. Tears welled up in Kim's eyes, Bella reached out and took her hand, feeling the coolness of Kim's skin despite the warmth of the kitchen. Outside the snow had begun to softly fall.

'How are you, really?' she asked.

Big fat tears splashed down her face. Kim withdrew her hands from Bella to brush them from her face and blow her nose which had started to run.

'Not brilliant. It's awful. Terrible. I can't believe it. How could it happen? And to Zeno?' Kim looked bleakly from Bella to Kitty. 'I just don't understand. I really don't.'

'Oh Kim. I'm so sorry. And for Zeno too. And for his family. Do they know?'

Kim sniffed and shook her head. 'His mother died a couple of years ago and he never knew who his father was. He had no siblings and I believe his grandparents are both dead, from what he told me he has no other living relatives.'

'Oh, that is so sad,' said Kitty, who had so far remained silent.

Kim nodded. 'I know. It felt as though the gym community was becoming his family.'

'So, do you know what happened?' asked Kitty.

Kim shook her head. 'No. I don't know. They haven't told me. The police are investigating, which I suppose they have to do in such cases. I just hope…' she paused, 'I just don't know what will happen if…' she trailed off.

'If what?' asked Bella gently.

'If he doesn't make it,' she blurted out.

Kitty and Bella glanced at one another, confused.

'What do you mean, "if he doesn't make it"? He's dead. Isn't he?' questioned Bella.

Kim looked surprised. 'No. No he isn't. At least, not yet. He was still alive when I spoke to the hospital an hour ago.'

Kitty and Bella looked dumbfounded.

'Why did you think he was dead?' asked Kim, puzzled.

Bella rolled her eyes. 'Betty told us. We should have known that she'd got her facts wrong. How stupid of us. So what injuries did he sustain?'

'He's got a head injury. Apparently he hit the back and side of his head. I'm assuming that he tripped.' answered Kim.

'Where did it happen? In his flat?' asked Bella.

Kim shook her head. 'No. He was in the gym. As he lives on site he had asked if he could use it after hours - there's no space in the flat for his gym equipment, other than a few hand weights. I agreed. I got him to sign a waiver so that, should he injure himself or something, the gym would not be liable. Never in a million years did I think anything would *actually* happen to him. He's so sensible, responsible and experienced. I know he would *never* take any risks or put himself in danger, so I really do not understand what could have happened. And even though he agreed to sign the waiver, and indeed had done so, I still feel responsible. If I hadn't agreed to allow him use of the gym out of hours, this would never have happened.' More tears welled up and trickled down her face as she said this.

'You can't think like that.' said Kitty, in an attempt to reassure Kim. 'It's not your fault. He could just as easily have tripped or fallen at home, or anywhere else for that matter.' Kitty reached over and squeezed Kim's hand to offer some comfort.

'What about CCTV footage?' interjected Bella. 'You've got security cameras up everywhere, surely they will offer an explanation as to what happened and at what time?'

Kim shook her head. 'No. He tended to switch them off when he was in there on his own. I did speak to him about it because I felt that he should leave them on. But he was very persuasive and I trusted him. I even asked my solicitor only last week to look into the legality of it and had told Zeno that I'd done so. '

'But what about the ones in the car park? Weren't they on? Surely they would show what time he went in?'

Again Kim shook her head. 'No. I don't know why they were off because, as far as I was aware, they were left on 24/7.'

'Strange,' murmured Bella thoughtfully.

'What have the hospital said then? Presumably they've carried out a barrage of tests? Are there any results? What's the prognosis for him?' asked Kitty inquisitively.

Kim sniffed then blew into her tissue. 'Well, I think they've done lots of tests and scans and I have a feeling they may have operated on him,' she paused, 'I'm not completely sure. My mind has gone totally blank. I can't remember. Other than that the next 24 to 48 hours are critical. I'm so pathetic. I really can't remember and yet I only spoke to the hospital an hour ago.' She looked bleakly at Kitty and Bella.

'You're still in shock. It's hardly surprising.' Bella patted Kim's hand reassuringly.

'Bella's right. We just have to hope and pray that he will be alright. He's young. He's fit. He's - I am assuming - healthy, that will surely work in his favour and give him a better chance of recovery.'

'Really?' Kim looked hopefully at them.

'Definitely. Kitty's right. If anyone can pull through this, it'll be Zeno.' Bella spoke with more confidence than she felt.

They were interrupted by a persistent banging on the front door. Kim's brow wrinkled.

'Who on earth is that?' She arose to go and answer it, but on hearing Seb walk down the hallway, sat down again.

They could hear raised voices and then Seb saying, 'Stop!'

Intrigued, they all strained to listen to the subsequently lowered voices in the hope of discovering the cause of the commotion. Moments later Seb came in.

'Sorry Kim. But I think you need to come out here.'

Hearing footsteps behind him, Seb turned.

'Look. I asked you to wait in the hall whilst I fetched Kim. You can't just barge in here,' he said crossly, feeling protective of his wife.

'I know. I know. But I can't wait,' barked a man's voice. 'I have to know now. The hospital wouldn't tell me anything. What's happening? How is he?' Dezo burst in, red faced, looking as though he was about to erupt like a volcano.

'Dezo.' said Seb sternly. Kim shook her head at Seb.

A little face peeped around the door and a quizzical Matilda looked between the adults, confused by what was going on.

'Seb darling. Why don't you go and continue your game with Matilda. Or maybe take her outside to play in the snow?' suggested Kim.

The squeals from Matilda in response offered no doubt as to her preference. Unwittingly, the sweet interruption had helped to diffuse the potentially explosive situation, dampening Dezo's apparent simmering anger.

Kim waited until Seb and Matilda had left the room and the door firmly closed behind them. Calmly she turned to Dezo. 'What can I help you with?' she asked.

'I thought I had made that clear,' he blustered. 'Zeno. How is he? What happened?'

'Why do you want to know? ' said Kim

'Because…' he spluttered, 'I do.'

Kitty and Bella raised their eyebrows at one another, sceptical.

Limiting the amount of information she offered, Kim omitted to say that the accident had taken place in the gym, after hours or that the police were investigating.

Dezo opened his mouth to speak then closed it.

'The gym is closed again today and also tomorrow but open as usual from Tuesday. I'm sorry for any disruption this may cause to you and Ditzi. Venka will step in and cover as many of Zeno's clients as possible and will do her very best to keep to his time slots, but there may need to be some flexibility over this. If you have any issues, with regard to the gym, please don't hesitate to get in touch with myself or one of my team - at the office,' she said firmly.

'Well,' harrumphed Dezo. 'I suppose that will have to do. I'm a very busy man and have a tightly packed schedule, I cannot have it disrupted by this. Venka had better be good, though I doubt she will come close to Zeno. And you can tell her that I expect her to fit in with my schedule, not hers.'

'I am sure she will do her utmost to accommodate you Dezo,' said Kim with impressive restraint. 'I will update my staff the moment I hear anything significant. Even though the gym is physically closed until Tuesday, it will still be staffed in order to answer any telephone queries.

They are, and have been, phoning members to inform them of the temporary closure and to re-schedule Zeno's clients for the foreseeable future. You should receive a phone call from them today. Now, if there is nothing else, I do have rather a lot to be getting on with.'

Dezo, who was used to getting what he wanted, felt disgruntled, but realised the futility of pushing for any more information, so politely said. 'Kim. Thank you. I will be in touch. Ladies.' He glanced at Kitty and Bella, who had not uttered a sound throughout the exchange.

'Bye Dezo,' they said, as Kim ushered him to the front door.

'Poor Kim. She could have done without that,' muttered Bella.

'Agreed,' replied Kitty. 'It's astonishing that he could be so self-absorbed and insensitive. Traits I am not enamoured with to say the least.'

Kim came back in and shut the kitchen door behind her. 'Phew! I need another coffee after that. Same again?' she offered.

'We ought to be going. You've got a lot on,' said Bella, rising from her chair.

'No. Please stay. It would be good to talk, I worked all day yesterday and into the evening and I am back there again this afternoon. It was Seb who insisted I take a break this morning. I didn't want to, but he was right, it'll help me re-focus for this afternoon and has meant that I could spend some time with Matilda. So please, stay a little longer, I don't think Matilda's going to want to come in from playing in the snow for the foreseeable.' She glanced out of the window and smiled as she watched her little daughter running around, leaping and throwing snow as she did so, carefree and exhibiting unbridled joy.

Barely had Kim sat down again with a fresh cup of coffee in her hands when there was further knocking on the front door, this time less frenetic.

'Now what?' groaned Kim. 'If he's come back to harangue me again, I'm not sure I will be able to remain so calm,' she said, referring to Dezo.

Kim returned, grim faced, followed by a serious looking tall, thin, wiry man with short greying hair and kind blue eyes. A man known to them all.

'Dave!' cried Bella, jumping up and going over to give him a kiss. 'I wasn't expecting to see you today. I thought you were…' her voice trailed off as realisation dawned, 'working.'

'Yes. I am afraid that I am here on official business.'

Dave Ormonday was a Detective Inspector within the local police force. He also happened to be Bella's on/off - currently on - partner, and as a consequence was well acquainted with Bella's friends.

'Oh. Is everything alright?' she asked.

'I need to have a chat with Kim. In private please.'

'We can do, but I don't mind if Bella and Kitty are present' replied Kim.

'Perhaps we should go into another room, leave Bella and Kitty to chat?' he suggested diplomatically.

'Well. Ok. Would you like a coffee to take through?'

'No. Thank you anyway.'

The door closed behind the pair as they headed to the sitting room. Bella and Kitty looked at one another nonplussed.

'Hmm,' said Bella.

'Indeed,' added Kitty thoughtfully.

'I can only assume it's about Zeno. Don't you think?' suggested Bella.

'I can't imagine it would be regarding anything else. But if it was really nothing more than an accident, why would Dave be involved?'

'He wouldn't,' replied Bella grimly.

'So, either it has nothing to do with Zeno or the gym, or there are suspicions that it wasn't an accident.' said Kitty, echoing Bella's thoughts.

'Precisely.'

They sat in silence, burning with curiosity. From outside joyous squeals could be heard emitting from Matilda. Seb blissfully unaware of who was paying his wife a visit.

Approximately half an hour later Kim and Dave returned to the kitchen. He gave Bella a kiss and bade them farewell, insisting on letting himself out, but not before he had given Bella one of his beady "don't interfere" looks, for he knew her too well. If there was even the tiniest hint of intrigue, he knew that she would not be able to resist sniffing around in an attempt to uncover information.

Bella smiled beatifically at him with an air of innocence and chose to ignore his unspoken communication.

'Would you like me to take over from Seb?' offered Kitty, having noticed Kim gazing worriedly out of the window at her husband and daughter.

Kim hesitated, uncertain as to what to do next. Seb should really be the first to know, she thought. However, he and Matilda looked so carefree she didn't want to break the spell, so shook her head.

'No. Thanks Kitty. They're having so much fun out there, I don't want to spoil it.'

'Are you ok?' asked Bella. 'Why don't you come and sit down and I'll make you a nice cup of camomile tea.'

Kim lowered herself heavily onto a chair.

They both were eager to know the content of the conversation but managed to restrain themselves from asking questions for the time being, more concerned about Kim who was looking very pale.

Bella added a couple of spoons of honey to the tea; a little sweetness to help with shock, and handed it to Kim who took it gratefully, clutching it in her hands, watching the steam rise from the clear yellow liquid.

'I imagine you're wondering what that was all about?' she said, looking from one to the other.

'Well. Yes. But you don't have to tell us,' replied Bella.

'He wanted to have a chat and ask a few questions about Zeno. I thought it was a bit strange that he was here,' she said, half to herself. 'So, anyway, they think that what happened to Zeno may not have been an accident, that someone else may have been involved.'

Kitty and Bella gasped, though neither completely surprised.

'Really? But why do they think that?' asked Bella.

Kim shook her head. 'I can't remember. He did tell me something, but I was too stunned. I mean. Why would anyone want to hurt Zeno? He's so sweet and kind.' She looked at them, bewildered.

'I've no idea.' said Kitty.

'Mmm,' murmured Bella thoughtfully to herself.

CHAPTER EIGHT

The predicted snow storm had still not materialized by Wednesday morning, but what had gently flurried down over the weekend still lightly dusted frostier pockets in the lay of the land and on north facing roofs. Consequently, when Oast Gym had re-opened the day before, members had been able to access its isolated location without issue and it had therefore been busier than normal for a Tuesday due to a combination of those who had felt deprived of their previous days workouts turning up, along with those whose regular day was a Tuesday. Naturally, the main topic of many a conversation was related to the event of the previous Friday evening. Unsurprisingly, the local rumour mill had gone into overdrive and all kinds of outlandish scenarios were being banded about. However, the staff remained bright, chirpy and helpful even though the stress and worry hidden behind their smiles had not gone unnoticed by the more observant members of the club. Kim too ensured that she was a highly visible presence around the club, politely answering questions whilst studiously ignoring outlandish gossip.

Curiosity from members still persisted on Wednesday, so it was with reluctance that Kim took the decision to pull out of the pre-arranged coffee with Ditzi that morning, feeling that her priority needed to be the business. She had been looking forward to seeing her friends, particularly as she was feeling in need of support; her stress levels had been building up like the pressure in a pressure cooker. Seb, as always, continued to be an amazing support and listener but she did not want every moment they spent together to be dominated by her off-loading onto him, despite him reassuring her that it wasn't a burden and he wanted to be there for her.

So it was, without Kim, that Kitty drew up outside the vast wrought iron electric gates to Wynenden Hall at 10.30 a.m. excited to see not just Ditzi and Bella but to also set eyes on what was, apparently, one of the most delightful and impressive houses in the area. Having buzzed the intercom she waited for the gates to swing open, observing a couple of discreet security cameras whilst she did so. Slowly the gates began to open, as Kitty glanced in her rear view mirror she saw Bella grinning and waving at her from the car behind her.

They drove in convoy along the immaculate, tree-lined, gravel drive until, once the drive had curved to the right, the magnificent Queen Anne style Georgian house, built in the early 18th Century, came into view. In front of the house was an expansive gravel area where a couple of expensive four wheel drive vehicles neatly parked beside one another. The setting looked exquisitely picturesque with snow still dusting the lawns and roof.

Bella got out of her car, walked over to Kitty and kissed her cheeks. 'Wow!' she breathed, gazing up at the house. 'It is sooo beautiful, even more stunning than I had imagined it would be. Everything is so… so…' she struggled to find a suitable word to express what she felt.

'Perfect?' offered Kitty, equally overawed.

'Yes. Perfect. Absolutely perfect. Can you imagine living somewhere like this? It's the sort of dreamy house one sees featured in Country Life.'

'Oh absolutely.'

They stood in the freezing cold breathing in the icy air, their out breaths whisping an icy mist which curled around them. Their musings were interrupted by the front door opening. Looking equally as darling and perfect as the house, dressed in soft oatmeal-coloured cashmere leggings and an oversized chunky cashmere jumper in an arctic-blue hue, was Ditzi who waved and smiled broadly at them. If the pair hadn't already known that she was a model they would now have been left in no doubt that she was, or should be, for she looked photoshoot ready and had the location to match.

'What an incredible home you have,' said Kitty, as she walked up the steps to the front door.

'Absolutely stunning,' added Bella.

Ditzi blushed, murmured her thanks and ushered them inside into the capacious hall. She adored the home she shared with Dezo, but occasionally felt embarrassed to be living in such a large and opulent home and lead the privileged life that she did. She often felt undeserving of it all, painfully aware of the struggles so many had to deal with on a daily basis. She and Dezo had worked, and still worked, hard. None of what they had achieved had been gained easily or handed to them on a plate. But Ditzi knew that millions of people worked just as hard, if not harder, and never came close to attaining the level of financial security that she and Dezo now benefited from. The unjustness of it, as she perceived it, had a tendency to gnaw away at her despite the financial support that they gave, generously but very privately, to a broad spectrum of charities locally, nationally and internationally.

'Wow!' uttered Bella again, as she looked up at the high ceiling, the ornate staircase and galleried landing. Central within the hall was a large, exceedingly expensive looking, glass circular table, atop of which was an enormous display of fresh, pale pink roses.

Ditzi led them past the floral arrangement, staircase to the left of them and through a door into a generously proportioned sitting room which ran the full depth of the house. The large double-aspect sash windows ensured that the room was filled with light on the crisp, blue-skied January morning.

Despite the opulence of the room it had a comfortable, welcoming feel about it. Put together by a well reputed and respected interior designer, it was beautifully curated with comfortable sofas, side and coffee tables, splashes of colour which included greens, berry purples, reds and yellows. There were incredible pieces of artwork hanging on the walls by a mixture of contemporary and impressionist artists, all synthesising wonderfully together.

'Gosh!' exclaimed Kitty. 'Is that an *actual* Monet?!'

Ditzi nodded. She had a passion for Art, including Decorative Arts, and had read avidly on the subjects over the years, the result being a substantial book collection covering a broad spectrum of subjects including, but not limited to, specific artists, collectors, museums - anything which fed her thirst for knowledge.

I have *never* seen a real one in someones home,' uttered Bella, almost speechless.

'It is beautiful,' breathed Kitty as memories drew her to Giverny where Monet had lived and worked for many years. 'And that's a Lichtenstein isn't it?' she added, pointing to another work. Ditzi nodded. 'How amazing. You must get so much pleasure from these. I know I would if they were in my sitting room.'

Ditzi blushed again, a mixture of pride and embarrassment. 'Thank you,' she replied simply. 'You're interested in art then?'

Kitty nodded. 'Yes, but I am not at all well versed on the subject. I've read a few books on various art related subjects, but the more I read the less I feel I know, which can be rather overwhelming and makes me feel a complete ignoramus. I tend to go with my gut instinct, which probably isn't the right thing to do, if I like it, I like it, irrespective of who the artist is or the value of it. If I don't like it, I ask myself why? What is it about this piece of art that I don't like?'

'You probably know more than you think you do,' encouraged Ditzi who became more animated the more they discussed their shared passion.

Throughout this exchange Bella had remained silent, art was not really her thing. She liked it on a superficial level and enjoyed the occasional trip to an art gallery or museum, but did not share the ardour for the subject in the same way that Kitty and Ditzi did.

'I'll get us some coffee, or would you prefer tea?' asked Ditzi, having noticed that Bella had glazed over during the conversation.

'Coffee would be lovely please.' replied Kitty.

'And for me too. Thank you.' added Bella.

'With milk? Without milk? Milk preference? Cappuccino? Latte?'

Bella laughed. 'You must have one of those fancy coffee machines?'

Ditzi rolled her eyes. 'Dezo is obsessed! It's such high maintenance though! It always seems to need something doing to it; de-greasing, milk pipework cleaning and so on. You can guarantee that it won't make any demands when Dezo gets himself a coffee, but as soon as I want one a message will pop up on the display telling me what needs to be done and won't allow me to make a coffee until I've done it!' she laughed. 'However, I did ask Dezo this morning to sort the machine out so, in theory, I won't have to do anything other than press the relevant choice of coffee style on the display…'

'Gosh. It sounds very sophisticated. A cappuccino with cow's milk would be lovely thanks?' said Bella.

'And a latte for me please,' added Kitty

'Perfect. Won't be long. Make yourselves at home.' Ditzi closed the door behind her as she hurried off to the kitchen.

Kitty and Bella looked at one another.

'It's incredible isn't it.' said Bella rhetorically.

'Completely and utterly. Far exceeding anything I had imagined. So, so beautiful. The house, the interiors, it is all stunning. Absolutely stunning. And yet Ditzi and Dezo are so down to earth. I suppose I imagined that anyone who lived in a place like this would have airs and graces, be aloof to the hoipoli like us. Naivety, ignorance or stupidity on my part I suppose,' shrugged Kitty. 'Though now I think about it, Geoffrey and Susan are completely down to earth in their own way, even though they are members of the aristocracy.' she added.

'I get what you mean,' agreed Bella, who had moved towards one of the windows which overlooked the rear of the property. 'Come and look at this. These gardens are beautiful. Just imagine how they must look in summer when they're in bloom!'

Kitty hurried over to join Bella. The view did not disappoint. Spread out before the pair of them were immaculate paths, pristine boarders, clipped-to-perfection hedging, a dormant water feature and much more. It was obvious that a professional garden designer had been engaged in its creation and Kitty suspected that several gardeners were required to maintain it.

They were still admiring the garden when Ditzi returned with the coffee. She set the tray down onto a deep purple, velvet, studded ottoman which was carefully positioned, central to one of the seating areas; the open fireplace on one side, with an ornate eighteen century clock ticking on the mantelpiece, and three sofas completing the other three sides of a square. Kitty and Bella settled themselves on a comfy sofa each, Ditzi seating herself on the third.

She proffered them delicate white porcelain side plates, of which the rims were scattered with tiny hand-painted insects, and invited them to help themselves to the indulgent, but dainty, chocolate biscuits laid out on a larger plate of the same design.

Kitty and Bella felt deliciously decadent sipping their coffee from the matching cups and saucers. Their previous experiences of drinking from such refined vessels were from the very rare occasion when either of them had taken afternoon tea at a luxury hotel.

Kitty sank back into the deep, squishy, exceedingly comfortable sofa, nibbled on a dark, richly-chocolatey biscuit and, in that moment, felt that life couldn't be better; a cold winters day, settled in an extraordinarily beautiful, snuggly-warm room with two delightful people, and sighed.

'Everything alright Kitty?' asked Ditzi.

'Perfect. Thanks. Sorry, did I sigh out loud? I didn't mean to.'

Bella looked quizzically at her.

'A sigh of contentment and savouring the moment,' added Kitty hastily.

Ditzi smiled with relief. They chatted for a while before the subject turned to Zeno.

'Any news?' asked Ditzi.

'Nothing more since Sunday, other than that he is stable, which has to be a good thing, but I imagine Dezo is already aware of this anyway?' replied Bella.

'Dezo?' said Ditzi, looking quizzically at Bella. 'Why should he be?' she added, rather defensively.

Bella and Kitty glanced at one another, both realising that Bella had, metaphorically, just put her foot in it.

Bella hesitated whilst she deliberated upon what to say. 'He seemed most concerned when he popped in to see Kim on Sunday, so I naturally assumed that he had spoken to someone for an update.'

'He went to Kim's house on Sunday?' Ditzi looked confused, puzzled as to why Dezo had not mentioned it to her.

'He came over to ask about Zeno - we were there having coffee with Kim. We were just as confused as he was, what with Sharon telling us the previous day that Zeno was dead. When Kim told us that he wasn't, it was a shock - in a very good way obviously - and she had only just done so when Dezo arrived.'

'I had no idea.' Ditzi paused for a moment. 'He does have a tendency to be a little obsessive sometimes. He doesn't like things to not go according to his plan. If he has something set in his mind then any kind of disruption stresses him out. Possibly the fact that he is finally on a mission to improve his fitness level - or rather complete lack of any fitness level - and had settled into a routine of having P.T. with Zeno, upset his mindset.'

'That must be it then,' interjected Kitty quickly, seeing the scepticism on Bella's face and eager to steer the conversation onto safer ground before Bella began to interrogate Ditzi. To Kitty it seemed logical. Her path had crossed many a high achieving parent at the school where she worked to understand that a proportion of them disliked any sort of unexpected change or disruption to their routine, so Dezo's behaviour was therefore not exceptional nor exclusive to him.

'How *is* Kim by the way?' asked Ditzi, who had been disappointed that she'd been unable to come that morning. 'I saw her at the gym yesterday, not to speak to as she was busy fielding questions from other members. She seemed very calm and was holding it together. If it were me, I think I would fall to bits.'

'Well, obviously she is very worried about Zeno and praying the he makes a full recovery,' replied Bella, 'but she's focussing on the members and staff, endeavouring to ensure that the staff are fully supported and also that the gym continues to run as smoothly as possible, given the circumstances.'

They were interrupted by the door opening and Dezo popping his head around it. 'Ladies.' He smiled broadly at them as he came over to properly greet them. 'How are you? Can I get you another coffee?' As quickly as he had appeared, he disappeared off to do just that.

'Has anyone seen Bastien?' asked Kitty, completely changing the subject.

'Yes. I popped over to see him,' replied Bella. 'It does sound as though rather a lot of people have also done so which is nice, though I rather got the impression that he was feeling a little jaded by all the visits, however he seemed none the worse for wear after his altercation with Andrew.'

'Andrew?' Ditzi looked quizzically at Bella.

'Yup. Bella was in the shop in Monhurst when he came in...' replied Kitty before Bella could, who then in turn interrupted Kitty in order to recount the event to Ditzi herself.

'I've met him a few times,' replied Ditzi, in reference to Andrew. 'He tends to accost Dezo whenever he sees him in an attempt to persuade Dezo to be involved, financially, in one or other of his deals. However Andrew's reputation precedes him...'

'Whose reputation precede's him?' asked Dezo as he returned with the coffee.

'Andrew Battle,' replied Ditzi.

Dezo rolled his eyes. 'Oh. *Him*. Too smooth for his own good and far too full of himself. Does like to think he's a big wheeler dealer, but he's small fry. Why are you talking about him?'

Kitty reiterated what she had just said about Andrew.

Dezo snorted with laughter. 'Serves him right. I'm sure it's not the first time someone's punched him in the face. Anyway, I'll leave you ladies alone, just thought I'd pop in to say hello.' He kissed his wife, squeezed her hand tenderly and left them to it.

CHAPTER NINE

Bastien fondled the soft golden ear of George the ancient family Labrador as he sat in the kitchen feeling empty, gazing unseeingly into the now cold mug of instant coffee in front of him on the cluttered table. All around him were piles of neglected paperwork, months worth of unopened bills tossed carelessly aside, dirty dishes and pans caked with hardened remnants of food were littered across the remaining surfaces and the sink was rammed full with similar detritus. The air was rank from the putrid smell emitting from the bin.

His bereavement leave from work had run out a long time ago but as he worked in I.T. he had been able to work from home thus avoiding what had been the daily grind of a two hour return commute into London. He'd split up with his city-based long-term girlfriend four months previously and the appeal of being in London had subsequently lost its allure. Whilst his volatile moods could be put down to the grieving process, it had brought to a head the dwindling fires of their relationship and he moved permanently back into the family home where he had spent the majority of his life and of which he had inherited upon the untimely death of his parents.

A sense of overwhelming despair washed over him, these days he felt like he was drowning, the tide of futility ebbing and flowing, giving him moments of hope that all would be okay, but these were few and far between. Punching Andrew had been a momentary cathartic release from a little of the explosive pressure of emotions festering within him, but it had not made him feel any better in the long run nor come close to helping to him to start to feel like his old self again. He did not know how to handle the loneliness and the emptiness inside him. He was alone in the world - an adult orphan - no family left, no one to care whether he was dead or alive. His parents were dead. Dolly was dead. Yes, he had the house and the opportunity, thanks to Dolly leaving her portion of the house to him in her Will, to reinstate it into one complete house again, back to what had been his childhood home and of which he had brooded over since his parents had had to sell, out of financial necessity, a third of the house in the late 1990's to help them through a difficult period. But he had wanted the whole house to be for all of them, for his parents and for himself. The dream of being able to come home for weekends with a wife and children. To be one big happy family. To watch his parents relish in the joy of being grandparents. And now? Nothing. Pointless. No parents. No wife. No children. Nothing.

George whined and nuzzled his wet nose into Bastien's hand. Bastien blinked and looked down into the dogs worried eyes. George whined again.

'Yes. That's right old boy. I have you. You need me don't you fella?'

George thumped his tail, wagging it hopefully, then stood up and gave his "is it time for a walk yet?" look. He may be 12 years old and not as agile or as nimble as he used to be, but he still liked the fresh air and the opportunity to sniff and smell whatever was around outside, even if he wasn't now fast enough to catch a rabbit or chase some other animal.

'What's that? A walk? Is that what you want?' said Bastien patting George's side. George wagged and swished his tale even faster, then hurried as fast as his slightly arthritic legs could carry him over to where his lead was kept.

Bastien yanked his black anorak off the back of his chair. George, realising that his strategy had worked, started running - albeit slowly - around in circles, then stood by the back door wagging excitedly.

'Come on then,' said Bastien, leaving the back door unlocked, not caring either way if someone entered the house and stole everything.

His lungs filled with the fresh, crisp winter air and for a moment Bastien felt a flash of something within him, a glimmer, a brief ebb in the tidal wave of depression. George trotted ahead down the unkempt gravel drive, pockets of frost sparkling where the sun hit it and others white, pure, untouched in the shadows of the trees.

George reached the end of the drive and sat down to wait patiently for his master to catch up. He watched from behind the gate as cars whizzed by too fast on the road.

Bastien crossed the road cautiously with George close at heel then stepped onto the recently constructed pavement and turned left in the direction of the centre of the village. He did his best to avert his eyes from the high metal fencing which had been erected on the opposite side of the road, adjacent to his house and garden, and which was draped with an enormous banner running the full length of it announcing the new housing development which was supposedly "coming soon". He felt bile rise in his throat at the sight of a grinning Andrew Battle plastered all over it. As far as he was concerned, Andrew had swindled his parents out of the 15 acres of land. Andrew had persistently cajoled and eventually succeeded in persuading Bastien's parents to sell the land to him, preying on their weak spot - lack of funds and a big repair bill for the roof looming - and paid them a paltry £10,000 for the 15 acres of prime development land. If Bastien had known what was happening he would have stepped in and halted proceedings, or at least negotiated a price closer to what he believed the land to be worth, which he felt would have been the equivalent current rate of 600-850k per acre. Bastien blamed Andrew for his parents death. Andrew was the root cause, as far as he was concerned, and he wasn't going to let him get away with it. The fire of resentment burned brightly within him competing with, and compounding, the malaise he had sunk into.

'Morning Bastien,' said a female voice, interrupting his contemplation. 'How are you?' The cropped blond hair, green sparkling eyes, brow wrinkled in concern, belonged to Audrey Stillingfleet who was looking intently at him. Audrey lived in a relatively modern house, built 22 years previously, set within an acre of land and which faced the driveway to Bastien's house, opposite but slightly to the left.

He shrugged. 'Oh. You know…'

And yes, out of anyone within the village, she knew what it was like to go through trauma and bereavement and feel dragged down into the darkest depths imaginable, to a place where there seemed to be no way out and where the so called "light at the end of the tunnel" simply did not exist. But she felt lucky, for she had received a huge amount of support from friends and acquaintances, along with the important medical intervention, but crucially she had felt able to ask for help. So many didn't feel up to, or able to. The stigma of suffering from a mental illness was still shockingly prevalent in society, with sufferers too ashamed or embarrassed to ask for help, feeling that it was a sign of weakness and seeing how others, who were brave enough to speak out, being told to "snap out of it" or "count your blessings, what do you have to be depressed about?" which compounded the fear, sense of failure and isolation within those who didn't receive - for whatever reason - help and support, often with dire and tragic consequences. In Bastien she could see this pain and feel the suffering he was experiencing even though he tried, as many did, to hide it.

'I'm here for you Bastien. Anything you need. If you want to talk, or even if you don't want to. I am here.' She reached out and squeezed his arm. 'You're not alone. Okay?'

He looked at her kind face and forced back the tears which were threatening to burst forth in a torrent, fearful that if he started crying he wouldn't be able to stop. Fearful of what other emotions it might release.

'Thanks Audrey,' he mumbled. 'I'd better go.' He indicated towards George who had been sitting patiently beside Bastien watching the traffic go by.

'Just remember what I said. Anytime, day or night. I'm here for you.' Audrey walked towards her house whilst Bastien turned right down the lane where Wynenden Hall was situated. He'd not gone far when a black Range Rover pulled up beside him and the drivers window slid down.

'Bastien. What a pleasure,' sneered Andrew. 'You'd best be careful on this road. No pavement. Lots of ice. Better keep your dog on a lead. Wouldn't want him chasing after something and being hit by a car would you?' he goaded.

Bastien could feel his blood begin to boil again but determinedly carried on walking, ignoring Andrew as best he could.

However Andrew chose to drive slowly alongside Bastien, music blasting out from inside his vehicle, shattering what had a been tranquil silence. He cruised along in an attempt to intimidate and provoke Bastien, toying with him like a cat malevolently playing with a mouse.

It took every filament within Bastien to prevent himself from reaching in through the open car window and grabbing Andrew by the throat until the smirk was wiped off his face. But he didn't. He would get his revenge on Andrew soon enough. Apathetic though his malaise made him feel, the desire for revenge continued to burn fiercely within him. Instead, he focused on the road and shortly came to a footpath on his right hand side which led across the fields, where he would then emerge back onto the main Wynenden to Monhurst Road, just a little distance further beyond his house, but the route would make it impossible for Andrew to follow in his car and continue with his current harassment of him.

CHAPTER TEN

Kitty sank back into her azure-blue velvet sofa and snuggled the tiny ginger ball of fluff to her chest, her much adored new kitten Daisy. From the moment that they had met at the cat rescue centre it had been love at first sight for the pair of them. Daisy had climbed onto Kitty's shoulder and nuzzled and purred into Kitty's neck, emitting an occasional high pitched mew of delight.

Now, curled up in the crook of Kitty's arm, Daisy purred like a little engine, her eyes closed as she settled down for a nap, her tiny paws padding into the air, fine little claws as prickly as cocktail sticks rhythmically moving in and out. Kitty gazed at her with complete and utter adoration and an overwhelming sense of love for her; to Kitty, Daisy was her baby, a substitute for the one she had never been able to have and which created a fierce sense of protection within her towards the kitten.

On the sofa next to her was Ted who in turn was gazing just as adoringly at Kitty, a scene which could have been - albeit obviously from a different era - snapshotted from a renaissance painting. 'You know,' he said, shifting himself around, his blue corduroy trousers blending into the sofa, 'if I were a jealous man, that kitten would be in trouble.' He smiled at them and reached over to tickle Daisy under the chin. Eyes still closed, the quietening purring increased in volume again to demonstrate her pleasure.

Kitty grinned. 'And jealous you should be! She has stolen my heart. I'm not sure that Ella is too impressed though,' she said, referring to Ted's seven year old black Labrador who was currently sprawled out on the rug in front of the fire which was blazing merrily in the wood-burning stove set within the large inglenook fireplace. Ella swished her tail in a sleepy wag upon hearing her name.

'She'll be fine. She seems to be getting used to - or rather tolerant of - Daisy clambering all over her. They were so sweet earlier, it was rather as though Ella was taking Daisy for a horseback ride as she plodded around the kitchen with Daisy hanging onto her back.' Ted was as devoted to Ella, as Ella was to Ted. 'And I can't not bring Ella over when I come, particularly when I'm staying over. Anyway, how's your week been?'

They chatted contentedly for a while then Kitty said. 'What I don't understand is how Zeno managed to hit his head like that? Kim was so relieved when she received the news that he was out of danger and was making good progress though it's going to be a while before he fully recovers and is back at work, but at least he's going to be okay.'

'Absolutely,' agreed Ted. 'I thought he'd tripped or something?'

'That's what most people think, but Bella was telling me today that the police are still investigating and I don't think they'd do that if they believed it was an accident.'

Ted narrowed his eyes in suspicion. 'Kitty. What are you up to?' He knew her propensity to dig around where she shouldn't if she scented a mystery.

Kitty opened her gold-flecked, brown eyes wide, feigning innocence. 'Nothing! I just think it's a bit odd and so does Bella.'

Ted rolled his eyes. 'Honestly, you two are as bad as each other. I suppose she somehow managed to extract this nugget of information from Dave?' he said, referring to Bella's on/off partner D.I. Dave Ormondy.

'Actually, no. Kim told her. They've been asking more questions. The police that is.'

'Hmm. Please don't get involved Kitty. It will probably turn out to have been an accident and they're just being thorough with their investigation. Leave it to the professionals. You're not Miss Marple, much as I know you love a good Agatha Christie novel.' He smiled lovingly at her and stroked her arm.

'Mmm,' she replied noncommittally, knowing full well that the temptation would be too great. 'Now, how about you drink your tea and pass me my wine in the process. I don't want to disturb Daisy now that she's asleep.'

Ted sighed in despair but dropped the subject for the time being. He reached over and picked up her glass of red wine and handed it to her, kissing her as he did so. 'Does this mean that we will have to wait until she's woken up before it's my turn to get close?' he grinned, shifting himself along the sofa towards her and leaning in for a leisurely kiss.

'Well...'

The much anticipated, and forecasted, deluge of snow had finally arrived. When Kitty and Ted awoke the next morning they could tell that snow had fallen even before moving from the snuggled warmth of the bed. The pure whiteness of the snow reflected a crisp brightness through the gaps in the curtains and external sounds absorbed by the snow and muted.

Kitty wriggled contentedly into the softness of the bed and offered no protest at Ted's offer to go and make them coffee. He pulled on his navy, thick, cotton robe which now resided at Kitty's house, along with a few of his other accoutrements for when he stayed over, and swished back the curtains.

'Wow!' he exclaimed at the sight which greeted him. It was not the moderate layer he had been expecting but deep snow drifts, six foot high in places. 'I don't think we'll be going anywhere today,' he commented.

The scene was reminiscent of paintings of winter landscapes. The view from the back of the house over the garden and subsequent farmland was beautiful. The soft morning sun was rising, creating a sparkly looking carpet which extended far off into the distance and snow drifts were ruffled gently against hedgerows. The church spire was just visible against the sky as a protruding snowy spike down in the village.

Kitty was dozing when she heard a high pitched mew from Daisy and opened her eyes just as there was a thud, followed by scrabbling, and a gingery, whiskery face meowed close up to hers, accompanied by loud purring at the pleasure of seeing Kitty.

Daisy melted Kitty's heart and she tickled the little fur ball under the chin which resulted in an increased volume of purring - astonishingly so for something so small - and the kittens paws rhythmically padded with delight into the duvet.

'Am I interrupting your love-in?' joked Ted, appearing with a tray crammed with mugs of coffee and two steaming bowls of porridge topped with blackberries.

'Well…' laughed Kitty, pushing her pillow up behind her, watching as Daisy pounced and jumped around the bed as she stalked imaginary prey.

By the time they had finished their porridge, played with the kitten and drunk their coffee, Daisy had exhausted herself and curled up into a tiny ball and was sound asleep.

'Finally. I thought she'd never go to sleep. Now I have you all to myself.' Ted reached over and started softly kissing Kitty's neck.

'I can't. Not here. Not in front of Daisy.' Kitty wriggled.

'Seriously?' Ted rolled his eyes but was not deterred. 'Right. Into the shower. Now! Or is that too close to her as well?' he jested.

'I think that will be fine,' she acquiesced demurely.

A while later, Kitty was clutching Daisy to her chest in an attempt to soothe and warm up the confused kitten by the AGA in the kitchen. 'Poor thing. Look at her.' Kitty was trying hard not to laugh. She had taken Daisy out for her first experience of snow and had placed her carefully down onto the back door step which she had duly cleared for the kitten. Naturally inquisitive, Daisy had cautiously put her tiny paw forward and dabbed at the snow down from where she had stood on top of the step. Intrigued, and a little boldly, she had stepped forward, realising too late that she could not feel solid ground beneath her, there had been a flash of ginger as she had tumbled forward into the snow and disappeared. Fortunately, with the pride of a mother watching her offspring attempting to walk for the first time, Kitty had been observing closely and immediately scooped the bedraggled bundle of fluff up.

At that moment the phone rang, attempting to also quell his laughter, Ted answered it, explaining to a bemused Kim as to what he was laughing about and then passed the phone over to Kitty. He carried on with making more coffee for them, but looked up when Kitty gasped. 'No! But why? I know he's an unpleasant and mendacious character, but I wasn't expecting that! Why do they think that?' Despite himself, the conversation piqued Ted's curiosity.

Kitty put down the phone and gently placed the dried and now sleeping kitten into her fleecy bed tucked to the side of the room.

'Well?' asked Ted.

'You are *never* going to believe this!' The gold flecks in her brown eyes shone brightly. 'Andrew's been taken in for questioning!'

'Andrew? For what purpose?'

Kitty sighed impatiently and rolled her eyes. 'To do with Zeno! I told you there was more to this than it being an accident.'

'How does Kim know? Are you *sure* it's not hearsay?' he replied, dubious.

'One hundred percent. Kim has had the police round again asking more questions, this time about Zeno and Andrew and what the relationship between them is. Apparently, Zeno felt well enough to speak to the police and has started to remember events of that night, but there are still some parts he can't yet recall. Anyway, Kim's going to visit him at the hospital later so she may know more after that. I think I'll just give Bella a call,' she said picking up the phone, despite Ted's protestations for Kitty to keep out of it, no matter what they personally thought of Andrew, and to refrain from having anything to do with the case.

Taking herself off into the sitting room to update Bella, she eventually exhausted the subject and went to find Ted, who was in the kitchen starting to wrap himself up in the necessary garments in order to protect himself from the below freezing temperature outside.

'Come on. Get your coat on. We're going for a long walk and then I'll buy you lunch at the pub,' he said referring to the rustic delights of The Speckled Goose in Wynenden. 'And before you say you can't leave Daisy after her "trauma" in the snow, I can confirm that she is not in the least bit scarred by the experience. You were so long on the phone that she woke up. We've had a long play, she's had some lunch and as you can now see,' he indicated with his index finger towards the sleeping ball, 'is asleep again. So we are safe to go. And before you ask, yes, she has used her litter box and she has drunk some water.'

Kitty laughed, amused by Ted's commentary and wrapped herself up warmly for the walk.

They took the extended route to the village; round the back of Wynenden Park, over the farm and parkland belonging to it, then looping back through to where the boundary eventually abutted the land Andrew Battle had purchased from Bastien's parents. It was slow going through the deep snow, but exhilarating to feel the fresh, crisp, air biting across their faces as they walked. By the time they reached the pub Kitty was worn out and in need of refuelling. Her cheeks glowed from the cold and exertion and she began to un-peel her outer layers immediately she stepped over the threshold into the heavily beamed, low ceilinged, 16th Century building. The fires were burning merrily in the fireplaces and, given the blocked roads and snow drifts - which the local farmers and Estate workers were currently busy snow-ploughing in an attempt to make them passable for some vehicles - it was relatively busy. Seemingly other village residents had also thought that a walk to the pub was a good idea too.

'Hi Hetty,' called out Kitty.

Hetty smiled warmly, but her face was as pale as the snow outside and there were dark circles under her eyes.

Kitty deliberated upon what to have to eat and settled on a hearty vegetable and lentil soup with the expectation of having the blackberry and apple crumble with custard for pudding. Having placed her order, Kitty chatted to Hetty who was not her usual effervescent self. Apparently the pub, despite the weather, had had a steady flow of customers from immediately the pub had opened at 10 a.m. with a flurry of customers wanting coffee; the hardy posse who had turned up for the farmers market, only to find that it - unsurprisingly - had been cancelled due to the inclement weather.

Kitty couldn't help but earwig into snippets of conversation and, like a radar, honed in on one particular discussion regarding Andrew Battle but which turned out to be mere hearsay and gossip. She inclined her head in the direction of the conversation to Hetty and said. 'I guess you've heard?' Hetty nodded.

'Come on Kitty, interrupted Ted, determined that their lunch would not be dominated by yet more debating - on Kitty's part - about Andrew. 'Let's take our drinks over there and sit by the fire whilst there's still a table free.' He picked up their coffees and one of the sparkling waters and, trailed by Ella at his heel, strode across to it.

'Thanks Hetty,' said Kitty, picking up the remaining glass of water and joining Ted, scowling at him as she sat down.

'What?' he asked innocently.

'You know what,' she replied.

'Let's not ruin this lunch by getting into an argument. I know what you're up to, trying to snoop around. As I've said before, you are *not* Miss Marple, so please, please, leave it alone.'

Kitty bristled. She didn't like being told what she should, or shouldn't, do.

Ted reached across and took her hand, stroking it with his thumb as he held it. His skin was soft and smooth, something which always surprised Kitty, given that Ted took a literal and very hands on approach at work.

She decided it would be churlish to sulk and spoil their time together, so smiled at him, but inwardly resolved to not leave the matter alone.

CHAPTER ELEVEN

Further snow fell on Sunday, as a consequence the school where Kitty worked, fifteen miles away, took the decision to close for at least the next three days; the roads were treacherous and lanes partially blocked.

On Monday morning Kitty completed as much work as she was able to without access to the files and paperwork sitting on her desk at school, there came a point where she could do no more, she'd cleared her e-mails and with little else coming in, she took herself off for a long, bracing - albeit at a slow pace - walk, enjoying the fresh air as she went.

Upon her return she lit the fire in the sitting room, curled up on the sofa with a mug of hot chocolate and snuggled Daisy into her lap, who in response purred contentedly, eyes closing, purring quietening as she drifted off into a contented nap. Kitty watched the flames as they flickered, weaved and sparked whilst she contemplated on what she knew surrounding Andrew, Zeno and the developments over the weekend, of which she knew no details. Outside heavy grey clouds loomed darker as the afternoon wore on. She knew that Kim had seen Zeno on Saturday, who had already confirmed that he remembered Andrew being present in the gym, but not why, other than a vague memory that they had argued. Andrew wasn't a member of the gym, his being the only membership application that Kim had so far refused to approve, fearing that his rudeness, arrogance and tendency to grasp any and every opportunity to accost someone with whom he felt could be of use to him, would inevitably have members leaving in their droves. There was, therefore, absolutely no reason why Andrew should have been at the property, let alone inside the building. Whilst his pride had taken a temporary dent at the rejection, he appeared to have brushed it off and moved on, like water off a ducks back. Perhaps that was what he was angry about and had decided to take it out on Zeno, surmised Kitty. But why would he argue with Zeno rather than Kim? And why outside of the gym opening hours?

A break from snowfall overnight and with Tuesday morning offering a clear, bright and sunny sky, Kitty decided to attempt to drive to the gym and nosed her car cautiously along the snow-ploughed lanes, compacted snow and ice glinting and twinkling in the sunshine as she went. Kitty arrived at the gym slightly flushed after an unpleasant encounter with a patch of black ice which had caused her to slide - albeit slowly - into a verge. She parked in the partly-cleared, virtually empty, car park and got out to inspect her car for any damage; fortunately none was visible. She hoicked her sports bag onto her shoulder and picked her way cautiously across the car park in her ancient black snow boots, stamping off the snow on the doorstep as she pushed the door to the building open.

Kim was on reception, but apart from her it was eerily quiet, no usual Tuesday morning hubbub as members moved between classes, gym and changing rooms. With only a skeleton staff in that day, many unable to access the rural location safely, Kim was covering and rather enjoying it. She looked more cheerful and happier than the last time Kitty had seen her, hardly surprising given that they now knew that Zeno was going to make a full recovery.

Boots off, trainers on, bag locked up, Kitty pushed through the door into the gym; there was one other member, along with Venka who was busy giving the equipment an additional cleaning down - not part of her usual remit but she disliked not having anything to do and had found time on her hands after a smattering of clients had cancelled their sessions due to the inclement weather and driving conditions.

Kitty smiled and said hello to them both, then began her warm-up on the treadmill adjacent to the one which Venka was cleaning. 'How are you Venka?' she enquired pleasantly.

Venka smiled, the bright pink stripes in her short hair seeming particularly vivid against the backdrop of whiteness from the snow on the other side of the panels of glass. 'Hello Kitty. See any polar bears on your way here?' she joked. Her face was lit up with a wide smile, but it looked forced, deep frown lines evident, despite the smile.

'Oh, only a couple,' bantered Kitty back. 'I guess, apart from yesterday and today, you've been run off your feet more than usual, what with having to cover Zeno's clients too?'

Venka's smile faltered and she chewed her bottom lip. 'Poor Zeno. I've been so worried about him. It's such a relief to know that he is going to make a full recovery.' She brightened a little as she said this.

'It certainly is. I've no idea why Andrew Battle was here that night. I can't imagine what they would have been arguing about. I mean, I wouldn't have thought that their paths would cross, would you?'

Venka shrugged, turned and went to clean another piece of equipment on the other side of the gym. Kitty frowned. Had she upset Venka? Perhaps she was more distressed about Zeno than she was letting on, mused Kitty?

Her thoughts were interrupted by the swish of the door. Looking up to see who was reflected in the windows, Kitty could see Ariadne and glanced over her shoulder to say hello. She closed her mouth before uttering anything; Ariadne and Venka were deep in a whispered conversation. Ariadne's eyes flicked up, saw Kitty looking at them, hesitated, then smiled.

The three of them were now alone in the gym. Ariadne strolled over and stepped onto the cross-trainer next to Kitty. 'I thought this would be a good time to come,' she commented. 'Nice and quiet so that I can relax and enjoy my workout. Venka's going to give me a P.T. session as her client has cancelled.'

Kitty didn't know Ariadne particularly well, having only met her a handful of times, and she was still in awe of, and a little intimidated by, the stunningly beautiful and talented actress, but tried not to allow her feelings of inadequacy and being star struck to get in the way of trying to see the real person, as opposed to the persona Ariadne presented to the public.

They politely conversed intermittently until Kitty had finished her warm up and moved on to some free-weights and strengthening exercises. She observed how Venka was training Ariadne, who was clearly already very fit, in the hope of picking up some tips. This was the first P.T. session Ariadne had had with Venka but they seemed naturally in tune with one another, working well as trainer and client.

Whilst Kitty was carrying out her post-workout stretches a head popped round the door. It was Bella, rosie-cheeked from her walk to the gym from home. 'Just to let you know I'm here. I'll wait for you in the juice bar, take your time. Oh. Hello Ariadne. Would you like to join us for coffee when you've finished?'

Perspiration was speckled across Ariadne's face from the intensity of her training, but she managed to gasp. 'Thanks. See you in a while.'

Showered and changed, Kitty joined Bella in the otherwise empty juice bar, spa-type music playing softly in the background, and discussed, from what they knew, Zeno's accident, neither able to come up with a plausible explanation as to why Andrew could possibly have been at the gym, let alone late at night. Kim managed to join them but was also unable to shed any light on the matter. Zeno either couldn't remember, or wouldn't say, what they had been arguing about. They changed the subject when Ariadne joined them, flushed from her session. Kim was pleased to see Ariadne looking a little less tired and gloomy than recently and there appeared to be a hint of a spark back within her.

Ariadne had barely sat down when Venka hurried into the room. 'Sorry Kim, I need you at reception.'

The remaining trio chatted for a while until they had finished their coffees and juices then left. Bella gratefully accepting Kitty's offer of a lift home, she'd found the walk through the snow to the gym more arduous than she had anticipated.

'She's nice,' commented Kitty, as they buckled up in the car.

'Who? Ariadne?'

'Yes. So... normal and not at all what I had expected.'

'She is nice. It feels as though the more time she spends with us mere mortals the nicer and more relaxed she becomes with us. When I first met her a few years ago, I felt that she came across as rather full of herself and with a sense of superiority, but that was probably from me having pre-conceived ideas about her. Anyway, initially I couldn't understand why Sophie - who is so sweet - would have a friend like her. I know they were at school together, but that's no reason to stay friends. Sophie kept insisting on how lovely Ariadne genuinely was and now I agree with her. I don't think Ariadne lets her guard down easily - or quickly - with people she doesn't know, or know terribly well, but she seems to have warmed to you Kitty, and Venka too by the looks of it.'

'I don't know why either. But from our limited interactions she's been nothing but pleasant to me,' responded Kitty.

Once she'd dropped Bella off outside the shop in Monhurst, Kitty turned her car around and headed back in the direction of home along the main road to Wynenden. Fortunately the snow ploughs and gritting lorries had been out again in the interim so Kitty felt a little more confident in driving at a slightly faster snails pace than she had done earlier that morning. At the last minute Kitty decided to pop into the shop in Wynenden for some additional provisions and drove past the turning on her right which would have taken her home, and carried straight on. Seconds later a great hulking four-wheel-drive vehicle came careering up behind her, swerved across to the other side of the road and sped past.

'Moron!' shouted Kitty, at the ludicrously irresponsible driving, glimpsing - who she thought was - Andrew behind its wheel.

She drew up and parked in front of the shop behind the same vehicle which had passed her so recklessly moments earlier. She contemplated whether to stay in the car until the driver had exited the shop, assuming that the shop had been the destination and not the pub or one of the other houses, but curiosity got the better of her. If the driver *had* been Andrew Battle, Kitty wanted to see how he was responding to Betty's inevitable interrogation.

The bell above the door pinged as she opened it. Betty didn't pause for her customary welcome, instead she continued on with the barrage of questions she had for Andrew. His sapphire blue eyes flashed dangerously but he remained - unusually for him - tight-lipped, much to Betty's frustration, who was proven to be an expert in provoking or teasing out titbits of information from customers, whether they realised it at the time or not. Andrew managed to pay and extract the change for his purchases then, without uttering a word, picked them up, placed them in the crook of his black leather-clad arm and turned to leave.

During Betty's persistent attempts at extracting a few words from Andrew, Kitty flicked through a magazine to make it look a little less obvious that she was trying to eavesdrop. However, Kitty was unable to hear what Betty's last comment to Andrew had been but clearly, whatever it was, had pressed a button within him and he erupted.

He pointed his index finger close to her face and yelled at her. 'Shut up you stupid old woman! You have no idea what you are talking about. Shut it, or I will shut it for you!' With that, he slammed out of the shop leaving Betty stunned and Kitty startled.

'Are you ok?' asked Kitty as Betty sank back onto the stool which she often perched on behind the counter.

'Oh. I feel a bit shaky.' said Betty, her voice quavering, face going pale.

'You sit there. I'll go and make you a cup of tea. Just point me in the right direction.'

Tea made - with extra sugar for the shock - Betty's colour had begun to return by the time Kitty handed the piping hot drink to her. Betty sipped it cautiously, her hands still trembling as she did so. 'Thanks love,' she said. 'Do you think I should report him to the police?' she looked expectantly at Kitty.

'It's up to you really. Whatever you feel is best,' replied Kitty, unwilling to be responsible for such a decision.

'I'll see how I feel later on then.'

'What was it that you said to make him explode like that?' asked Kitty, curious.

'I don't know really. I was asking him about Zeno and when he said absolutely nothing to me I felt a bit cross. I think perhaps I went too far. I told him he was a disgrace, that even if he weren't guilty of harming Zeno then he would be guilty of something else like that, and thank goodness he wasn't married or a father because he would be a poor excuse at either. I think I was a bit mean. I didn't intend to be, my mouth just ran away with itself.' Her brow furrowed as she said this.

'Don't worry Betty. It's probably not the first time something like that has been said to him.' Once Kitty was confident that Betty felt a bit better and had regained her composure a little, she drove home and settled in for yet another cosy afternoon by the fire and to mull over the mornings events.

An inordinate quantity of snow arrived over night which brought the locality to a virtual standstill again and ensured that the snow ploughs and gritters had yet another busy day ahead. Kitty remained cocooned in her snowy paradise, only taking brief forays out for walks, she enjoyed the sense of calm and peace which snow always seemed to give her.

So it was not until the Saturday morning that she ventured out in her car in the hope that the roads to the gym would be passable in order for her to have an early morning workout prior to meeting Bella at Wynenden Farmers Market, which, despite the inclement weather, would still be going ahead.

She nosed her car cautiously down the treacherous lane to the main road where she turned left then first right. A short distance ahead of her she could see a police car parked on the right hand side and slowed down further in order to pass without incident. The car was parked outside Andrew Battle's house. As she drove past she could see more police vehicles parked on his drive, which seemed to have been cleared of enough snow in order to do so. Kitty frowned. What had he done now? Was he being arrested for assaulting Zeno? Or perhaps attempted murder? Frustratingly, when she arrived at the gym neither Kim nor Venka nor any other members were there. As she worked out she turned the puzzle over in her mind, debating what could possibly have warranted such attention from the police, hoping that it wasn't an indication that Zeno had taken a turn for the worst.

She showered and quickly changed then drove back to the village via Andrew's house where there was still a lot of police activity. Fleetingly she thought she glimpsed the tall, solid figure of D.I. Allix, but couldn't be completely sure.

By the time she arrived in the village the road which looped around the village green had been cleared of enough snow, by some kind volunteers, to make it passable for vehicles. There were a surprising number of cars already parked in the village hall car park and Kitty proceeded with caution to manoeuvre her car into a narrow space on the far side of it, fervently hoping that neither she, nor anyone else, would slide into the car on the thick ice. When she'd locked up she picked her way tentatively around the random mounds of hardened snow towards the village hall entrance, arriving with a sigh of relief at having not slipped over and hurt herself on the way.

Inside it was busy, but not to the same extent that it had been recently. Kitty had assumed that, like her, people in the village would have had enough of being cooped up at home all week and feel the need to get out. Certainly the elderly of the village, whom Kitty imagined may have felt isolated and lonely over the previous few days, had made a stalwart effort to turn up, a large number of them had already commandeered "their" table even though the market had only just opened.

Kitty scanned the room looking for Bella, not seeing her she leisurely wandered from stall to stall admiring the delights on offer and made a few purchases. She was just about to sit down when she heard Dezo's jolly voice greet her from behind. She turned and tried not to look startled by his incongruous outfit; an oversized black fur trappers hat which encased his head and face so much that he was barely visible, a brown mink fur coat - a size too large she estimated and which, to her, made him look like what she imagined a cross between a large brown bear and a yeti would be. Completing the ensemble was, what she could only politely describe as "striking", a pair of bright red snow boots. Standing next to Dezo was Ditzi who in complete contrast looked effortlessly glamorous and stunning in a black and fuchsia-pink ski jacket, tight-fitting black jeans, black sheepskin winter boots, a pale pink cashmere hat with a white fur-like bobble, matching pale pink cashmere gloves and scarf, casually wound around Ditzi's neck, her long blond hair cascading down over it.

Ditzi was smirking as Kitty kissed them lightly on the cheeks. 'Don't say it. Just don't say it!' she laughed. Kitty raised her eyebrows and tried not to smile. 'He looks ridiculous! But kind of endearing, like a big brown cuddly bear.' She tucked her arm into Dezo's fur clad arm and wriggled up to him.

'Well, I like it,' replied Dezo, pretending to be offended but unable to resist smiling broadly.

'At least it's vintage fur. I wouldn't let him buy any new fur. And yes, you are as gorgeous as always darling.' She kissed the top of his nose and Kitty felt that she could almost hear him purr with delight.

'What do you think then Kitty?' he asked with a twinkle in his eye.

'Um,' said Kitty searching for something tactful to say. 'It's very... Unique.'

Dezo laughed loudly. 'Very diplomatic. Now, can I get you two ladies a coffee?'

'Assuming you don't mind it if we join you Kitty? added Ditzi.

'Not at all. I'd be delighted. Oh. And here's Bella,' said Kitty, as her friend appeared simultaneously with Bread Man who was laden down with large trays of the days offerings.

'Hello,' Bella called as she diverted off to join the lengthening queue. 'Can I get you anything whilst I'm here?' she offered, then making a mental note of what their requests were.

Meanwhile Dezo headed off with his coffee order. Ditzi and Kitty sat down and peeled off their outer layers now that the hall had warmed up significantly. Ditzi, naturally, was wearing a simple, but gorgeous, mid-grey, round-necked, cashmere jumper. Kitty glanced down at her own faded, well-worn blue jeans and navy wool jumper and wished that she could look as effortlessly elegant as Ditzi always did.

It wasn't long before Dezo returned with their coffee and Bella with the bread. Kitty recounted what she had seen on her way both to and from the gym, but they were interrupted by Betty who looked as though she would burst if she didn't pass on whatever snippet of gossip she was now in possession of.

'Hello Betty,' said Kitty pleasantly. 'How are you after last Tuesday?' Dezo and Ditzi looked questioningly at Kitty.

'I'm fine thank you Kitty, but you will *never* guess what has happened now!'

Kitty refrained from commenting, fairly convinced that the reason for Betty's unwarranted attention was to inform them all about the police presence at Andrew's house, as she did not wish to potentially open a gossip equivalent of a can of worms should this not be the case.

'It's Andrew!' said Betty triumphantly.

'Oh? Really?' replied Kitty, cautiously.

'Yes! He was taken away by ambulance earlier this morning!' She looked expectantly at them.

'An ambulance? What makes you think that?' asked Bella.

'I have my sources,' replied Betty secretively, tapping the side of her nose.

'I saw the police, but no ambulance,' added Kitty, without thinking.

'Police? I didn't know about that! Why? What were they doing?' Betty enquired eagerly.

Kitty shook her head and shrugged, cross that she had let slip.

'Well, I'll leave you to it,' said Betty making a hasty exit in order to re-join the group gathered at the long table, keen to impart this new nugget of information to them.

'*If* she's correct, I wonder what's happened? Paramedics and police make it sound like something serious.' said Bella, giving Kitty a meaningful look.

'Yes, indeed,' she replied quietly.

CHAPTER TWELVE

'I can't believe it. I really cannot believe it.' repeated Audrey.

'Me either,' agreed Kitty. They were standing at the back of the church having coffee after the morning service and, like many of the congregation, had been shocked by the announcement the vicar, the Rev. Jeremy Haslock (also vicar of St Nicholas Church Monhurst), had made at the start of the service. Andrew Battle was dead.

'We both know from personal experience what an unpleasant character he could be but he was still relatively young at 38 so it's still sad, just as it is when anyone dies.' Audrey paused. 'I can't help but speculate that there is more to it.' She pursed her red-glossed lips in an attempt to prevent the lid of her own pandoras box of memories from popping open, the news of Andrew's death was beginning to stir them up, memories she had hoped that she'd locked away for good.

Kitty squeezed Audrey's arm comfortingly. She knew, as did most of the village, what Andrew had done to Audrey's family. He had been truly odious at times and Kitty doubted if many, or in fact anyone, would miss him now that he was dead, which in itself was a pretty sad state of affairs.

'Would you like me to stay with you today?' offered Kitty, prepared to forego her much look forward to lunch at Bella's house.

Audrey shook her head and patted Kitty's arm. 'No. Thanks very much, I appreciate the offer, but I'll be fine.' She needed time alone to mentally process what had happened and its inevitable repercussions.

'Okay. Well, I will give you a call later anyway just to check on how you're doing. I can come over at anytime if you need me to.'

'You're a good friend,' said Audrey, smiling at Kitty. 'It's funny, we've only known each other for what? Eighteen months? And yet, it feels as though I have known you for years.'

Kitty smiled back. 'The feeling's mutual Audrey.'

Audrey nodded. 'You're a very kind person Kitty. When I launched myself onto you asking for help you gave it, even though you didn't know me. Many would have, and indeed did, run a mile to avoid me, but you didn't and I will be forever grateful for that and even more so because of the friendship we have developed.'

Kitty blushed at the compliment. 'Thank you Audrey, that's very sweet of you to say so.'

'Now, enough of this sentimentality,' said Audrey. 'I wonder,' she hesitated, 'if Andrew *didn't* die from natural causes, nor committed suicide, could he have been murdered and if so, by whom?'

'If it was murder the police are going to have their work cut out trying to find out who was responsible for it. I imagine there's rather a long list of people who could have done, or may have wanted to do, it,' she corrected herself, 'or rather have liked him disposed of. He upset so many people. Oh, I meant to say that I think I saw D.I. Allix at Andrew's house when I drove past yesterday, which I thought was rather interesting.' said Kitty.

Kitty and Audrey both knew, and respected, D.I. Allix from their entanglement in previous cases. He had always been very professional, kind, serious, very good at his job and had been - and perhaps still was - assisted by the exceedingly efficient, slightly fierce, D.S. Molly Windsor.

'Well, if he's on the case they stand a good chance of getting to the bottom of what happened to Andrew and by whom, always assuming that foul play was the cause of his death. Anyway, I'd best be off, I can see Betty eyeing me up and about to make a beeline for me. I really don't feel like being dragged into a conversation with her at the moment - we know what she'll want to talk about...'

'You go. I'll head her off. Take care of yourself. I'll call you later.' Kitty took Audrey's mug and moved purposefully towards Betty in order to head her off and give Audrey the opportunity to leave the building before Betty could accost her. Kitty, out of politeness, spent a little while chatting to Betty before excusing herself as she wanted to get home and have a play and a cuddle with Daisy before abandoning her for the afternoon. Ted would be picking her up before too long once he'd finished taking Ella for a long walk before leaving her at his house for the rest of the day. Neither he nor Kitty were confident enough just yet to leave Daisy and Ella on their own together for a prolonged period of time, unsure of what disaster might greet them upon their return.

Ted squeezed Kitty's leg affectionately once he'd parked the car on Bella's drive. 'Don't be upset with me. I just don't want anything to happen to you. I love you.' This was the result of him having said to Kitty en-route that he wanted her to keep out of Andrew's business, to not go snooping around but to leave it to the police.

His sparkling blue eyes looked beseechingly at her. She sighed. He had rather popped the balloon of her inquisitive excitement over the matter but she could't stay grumpy with him for long, he was so kind and thoughtful and she knew that what he had said had come from a good place.

She smiled. 'Oh, okay. You're forgiven, but you will have to find a way to make it up to me later.' she said with a twinkle in her eyes. 'We can agree to disagree.'

'Hmm.' he replied, suspicious about her last comment but decided to change tack. 'There are several ways that I can think of to make it up to you…' he grinned and slid his hand further up her thigh.

She batted him away playfully. 'I didn't mean that! Though I suppose it could be an option.' She winked mischievously at him and opened the car door. 'Come on then. Let's go in.'

He got out, came around the car to the passenger side, opened the door wider, took her hand and pulled her to him for a leisurely kiss.

A car horn beeped at them and Kim's head popped out of the front passenger window. 'Leave it out you two,' she giggled.

Kitty grinned before asking. 'No Matilda?' as Kim and Seb got out of their car.

'No. The lure of lunch and a playdate with Jemima over at Harry and Sophie's was too tempting so she's abandoned us.' Kim was torn between the rare opportunity of a relaxed, child-free, lunch and the guilt from missing an afternoon with her daughter, but it was made easier in the knowledge that Matilda worshipped the ground that the older, by two years, Jemima walked on and that the feeling was mutual. They would undoubtedly be having a fantastic time together.

Knocking on the front door to Bella's Edwardian red-bricked home, they waited in the chilly air, the grey sky heavy with expectant looking snow clouds.

Dave opened the door, his grey hair neatly trimmed, blue-checked shirt and beige chinos perfectly pressed. He smiled and the creases around his eyes crinkled at the pleasure of seeing the four waiting on the door step. He welcomed them into the warmth of the hall, took their coats - delicious cooking aromas wafting their way through from the kitchen - then ushered them through into the sitting room where the fire was crackling merrily in the fireplace. Seb and Ted immediately stood astride in front of the fire, warming their backs against the heat from it.

'You do realise that by standing there you are preventing the heat from coming into the room,' said Kitty rolling her eyes at them.

'Gosh, no! The thought had never crossed my mind, you've *never* said that before,' jested Ted in response.

The door bell rang and Dave hurried off to answer it. Moments later he returned with Jennifer, her dark chestnut locks looking particularly rich and glossy that day, long curls tumbling over her snug-fitting, amethyst-coloured cashmere cardigan and cream silk blouse, complemented by a moss-green coloured pencil skirt which accentuated her curvaceous figure.

The chink of approaching glasses could be heard and Bella appeared carrying a tray laden with finely engraved crystal champagne flutes and a chilled bottle of champagne.

'Great minds think alike,' said Kim, proffering the bow-wrapped bottle she had brought as a gift.

'Fabulous, thank you very much. I'll go and pop it into the fridge.' Bella hurried off with it, along with the handmade chocolates from Kitty and the flowers from Jennifer, leaving instructions for Dave to open and poor the bubbly.

She returned with a large platter filled with delectable looking smoked salmon blinis and pimento peppers filled with a herby cream cheese.

'Cheers everyone,' said Bella raising her glass of fizzing golden liquid. 'It's great to have you all here. Our first get together of the year.'

Enthusiastically they devoured the canapés, sipped the champagne - all except Ted who was drinking a non-alcoholic ginger beer and conversed convivially.

'Still no Mia and Fred?' enquired Jennifer, in reference to Bella's best friend from school and her husband who lived in a converted barn on the edge of Monhurst just off the Monhurst to Brookhurst Road, Brookhurst being the village where Dave lived.

Bella shook her head. 'Sadly not. They're actually off skiing for three weeks in Austria and not due back for another couple of weeks. A good excuse to hold another lunch once they have returned,' she replied, simultaneously handing the remaining canapés around before slipping out to the kitchen to finish preparing lunch, leaving Dave in charge of replenishing their guests glasses.

Fifteen minutes later she popped her head round the door - having refused offers of help - and announced that lunch was ready.

The ensemble followed Bella through to the dining room where the table was laden with dishes of piping hot vegetables, crispy crunchy roast potatoes, gravy and roast lamb, the aromatic sweet smell of the rosemary it had been roasted with, filling the room.

'Mmm. Yummy!' exclaimed Kitty. 'This looks and smells delicious Bella. I love the way you've laid the table.' she added in reference to the crisp white table cloth, matching napkins adorned with miniature sprigs of fresh rosemary and hawthorn tied up with a thin strip of red ribbon, beautifully engraved crystal glasses accompanied by an antique dinner service consisting of plates and serving dishes which had been passed down on the maternal side of Bella's family. The service itself was made of a white hybrid hard-paste porcelain, the rims of which were decorated with a delicate blue ribbon and bow pattern and which dated from circa 1820. To complete the setting was a silver cutlery service which Bella had also inherited, and a few small - fragrance free - votary candles in glass holders scattered in an aesthetically pleasing manner across the table, their gently flickering flames adding to the ambience.

The food tasted as good as it looked and smelt and the merry gathering whiled away a delightful Sunday afternoon together. Bella and Kitty were itching to discuss what may, or may not have, happened to Andrew, but every time one of them attempted to bring the subject up either Ted or Dave - who had both anticipated that their respective partners would try to do this - immediately cut in and changed the subject, studiously ignoring the glowering looks the pair gave them as a result. It was only once they were back in the sitting room cosily ensconced by the fire with coffee, that Bella finally succeeded. She was nestled on one of the sofa's next to Kim. Kitty and Jennifer sat opposite, neither of whom had been in church that morning and hence had not heard the announcement the vicar had made with regard to the demise of Andrew. In fact, the pair had been unaware that anything had happened to Andrew at all. Between the two of them Kitty and Bella (even though she only knew because Kitty had messaged her once she'd got home from church) enlightened their friends whilst the men kept their distance at the far end of the room, keen to avoid being dragged into a debate on the matter.

'Does Dave know anything about it?' asked Kim.

Bella shook her head. 'Not that he's saying. He says he's not currently working on the case. I think D.I. Allix is in charge of it.'

'Maybe it was natural causes? I suppose, unless the cause of death was obvious, they'll need to investigate?' said Kim.

'Well there was an awful lot of police activity at Andrew's house when I drove past yesterday.' said Kitty.

'I guess we'll know soon enough. I imagine there will be an autopsy, but if that doesn't reveal the probable cause of death I suppose the police will want to question quite a few people,' added Jennifer.

'But don't you find it suspicious that in such a short space of time Zeno was seriously injured - allegedly by Andrew - and now Andrew has been found dead?' said Kitty.

'Possibly,' replied Kim. 'But Zeno is still in hospital, so he has a cast iron alibi. Coincidences do happen.'

Bella pursed her lips and looked at Kitty, unconvinced.

At that moment they were interrupted by Seb suggesting that it was time he and Kim departed in order to retrieve their daughter from Sophie and Harry.

Surprised that it was so late - 5 o'clock - Jennifer, Ted and Kitty left at the same time. A blast of freezing air greeted them when the front door was opened, the late afternoon was dark, clear and crisp, with stars twinkling brightly in the inky-black sky.

'You free this week?' whispered Bella to Kitty.

'Only on my day off on Wednesday. Coffee? My place?' suggested Kitty.

'Perfect. I'll see what I can extract from Dave before then,' she paused, 'though, I am not holding out much hope.'

'You're right there,' whispered Dave from behind her, making Bella jump. He winked at Kitty who had seen him overhearing their conversation as he waved the others off.

'Come on Kitty it's freezing out here and you're letting all the cold air into the house,' called Ted from the car.

With further profuse thanks for a most convivial afternoon, Kitty clambered up into Ted's four wheel drive and waved as they left. Jennifer meanwhile cautiously picked her way along the slippery, icy drive to her own house which was located further up the green.

'Ahh,' sighed Kitty. 'That was such a fun afternoon and I am so full from all that scrummy food, I doubt I'll need anything else to eat tonight. Oh, please could you drop me off at Audrey's on our way to pick up Ella, then pick me up on the way back? I just want to check on her to make sure she's ok. I'm assuming that you are staying over tonight?' she added.

'Yup to both,' he smiled.

Meanwhile, at Bella's house, Dave was patiently trying to persuade his partner to not go snooping around. She in turn was doing her best to look convinced by what he was requesting, whilst knowing full well that she would not be heeding his advice.

'Please just listen to me. I know that look of yours which says "I'm listening, but I'm going to ignore what you've asked". I love you. Maybe I don't always show it. But I do and I don't want anything happening to you.' He held her shoulders as he said this and looked deep into her eyes.

'I know. Now,' she said, briskly changing the subject. 'How about you give me a hand clearing up?'

CHAPTER THIRTEEN

Kitty's heart had sunk at the sight of the mountain of work stacked up on her desk when she had arrived at work on Monday morning but determinedly proceeded to spend the day ploughing through it. The light, airy, open-plan office which the administrative staff shared was unusually quiet and free from the normal chit-chat which tended to ebb and flow throughout the day, all of them focussed on clearing the backlog of work as swiftly as possible.

As Kitty was preparing to leave, Mary - the Headmasters' Personal Assistant - walked in looking glum. Ever efficient and generally with a pleasant and cheerful disposition, the stress of the afternoon now, however, hung over her like a black cloud.

'I'm sorry to say this,' she said to Kitty and her colleagues, Liz and Jane, 'but we're closing the school again tonight. There's another snow storm heading this way, so for reasons of safety we will be closed again tomorrow but remain hopeful that we will be able to re-open again on Wednesday.'

There was a collective groan of frustration.

'Anything we can do to help?' offered Liz.

'No. Thanks for the offer. It's all under control. The parents will receive automatic e-mails and text messages tonight and will also receive updates tomorrow morning once we know how the storm has played out. The teaching staff have already been putting work up onto the school portal for the children to access and work through at home. As I can walk here from home I'll be here tomorrow anyway.'

'Ok. Thanks Mary.' said Kitty, gathering up the remaining files from her desk so that she could work through them at home the next day.

The first flurries of snow started to flutter down as Kitty drove home through the dark evening, the windscreen wipers swished intermittently as snowflakes landed and splattered across it. Several gritting lorries passed her at intervals driving in the opposite direction, grit spewing out from behind them as they went, doing what they could to prepare the roads for what was to come, the air temperature had already dropped to well below zero and snow was now settling on the verges.

The entrance gate to Kitty's property was still propped wide open by clumps of snow from the previous week. Inside the house there was a faint glow of light emitting from the lamp in the hallway which was controlled by a time switch.

Juggling her keys, handbag and pile of files, Kitty stamped her feet on the doorstep to rid them of snow. She fumbled to open the door, struggling not to drop her accoutrements outside as she did so, just managing to push the door open before they tumbled to the floor. She called out to Daisy as she removed her below-knee-height, low healed, tan leather boots, eager to see her little furry companion, simultaneously feeling guilty for abandoning her for the whole day. In fact, she had felt so guilty that she had telephoned Ted in the morning to ask if he could pop in and check on the kitten. Ever the accommodating one, he had duly made a diversion at lunchtime in order to do so.

'Hello darling,' cooed Kitty as she scooped the blinking kitten up, who immediately started to purr loudly, nuzzling her head into Kitty's neck. Their mutual love-in was interrupted by the landline ringing.

'Hello?' answered Kitty, as Daisy clambered across her shoulders and continued to rub her head against the back of Kitty's neck.

'Hi Kitty. It's Audrey.'

'Hello Audrey. How are you?' enquired Kitty, who had been concerned about her friend after she'd popped in to see her the previous evening, it had been blatantly obvious that news of Andrew's death had been stirring up deeply-buried and distressing memories within Audrey.

Audrey cleared her throat, her voice sounded thick as though she'd been crying. 'Fine.' She hesitated. 'I had a visit from D.I. Allix today.'

'Oh?' said Kitty in surprise.

'He was very kind, as he always is. Well, you know what he's like. But D.S. Windsor,' said Audrey referring to his trusty, clearly very ambitious, colleague and though nondescript in appearance had a tendency to come across as rather fierce, 'was rather interrogative in her manner. Unnervingly so, which made me clam up.'

'Oh dear,' responded Kitty.

'Yes. Well. She was asking me lots of questions such as "where was I on the night of Andrew's death" and so on. Neither of them specifically stated that Andrew had been murdered, though by their line of questioning I came to the conclusion that he must have been, but that is pure speculation on my part. I can only assume that they have me down as a suspect.'

'What? No. I'm sure they don't,' replied Kitty, fleetingly wondering if Audrey was, then berating herself for even allowing such a thought to pop into her head. Audrey would never hurt anyone. Would she? 'So what was it that you might have told them if D.S. Windsor hadn't made you clam up?'

Audrey hesitated. 'I. Well. No. Nothing really.'

'Are you sure?'

'Um…' she hesitated again. 'Perhaps we could get together and have coffee together sometime this week?'

'Sure. Yes. What about tomorrow? I'm working from home, I could walk over, it would be nice to get some fresh air during the day.'

'Okay. Thanks. That would be great. I'll be here, working from home too. The snow is such a pain,' she added, changing the subject to talk about the disruption and ensuing logistical nightmare the snow had been, and still was, causing for her cleaning company.

After Audrey had rung off, Kitty peeled Daisy from her shoulders and kissed her little head. 'Intriguing,' she whispered into the biscuit smelling ginger fur, then put her down and placed a small handful of dried food into Daisy's bowl for her supper.

Red cheeked and glowing from her long walk across the fields, feeling virtuous both from the exercise and from having risen very early in order to complete a substantial quantity of work before she went out, Kitty was ready for a late morning coffee.

She sat in Audrey's recently re-vamped kitchen; the whole room had been gutted and the previously stark white kitchen - white floor, units, work-surfaces and furniture - had been removed and in their place was a pale cream limestone floor, cherrywood units, a painted-wood centre island in a soft green colour, and pale cream with splashes of gold flecks, granite worktops. The rest of the furniture, except for the sofas in the conservatory area which were a pale green colour, similar to that on the kitchen walls, was made of maplewood and glass. The room now felt as though it had some personality to it and, a previously absent, sense of warmth, life and homeliness and not the sterile ambience her late husband had insisted upon.

Kitty moved from her perching place on a stool by the vast centre island and followed Audrey over to the sofas. The sun glimpsed in and out from behind the clouds, snatches of sparkles in the crisp white snow twinkling as it did so.

Audrey fiddled with the handle of her bone china mug, debating how much to tell Kitty. 'The thing is,' she began, 'I don't know whether to say anything or not and, if so, who to first. The last thing I want to do is to get an innocent person into trouble.' She looked anxiously at Kitty, her normally bright, green eyes, dulled with worry.

'Why don't you tell me what it is you are concerned about and then we can work out what to, or not, do?' said Kitty, her investigative antenna twitching alertly.

Audrey gazed contemplatively into her mug, took a sip of coffee, placed the mug down onto the glass table in front of her then fiddled with her fingers. Taking a deep breath, she looked up at Kitty and said. 'I know it's not him. He wouldn't. But it's odd and maybe he saw something which could help the police. I don't want to get him into any trouble and I'm worried about him anyway.' She looked beseechingly at Kitty.

'Why don't you tell me what it was that you saw,' Kitty replied gently.

'Well. I. Okay. I was driving home after work on Friday evening, a bit later than usual, and drove past Andrew's house. And he was there, tucked in by the hedge on the opposite side of the road. I only saw him because I braked for a fox which had run out in front of me.'

Kitty nodded encouragingly.

'Why would he be there? It's weird. It makes no sense.'

Who? Thought Kitty impatiently.

'What possible purpose or reason would he have of being there?'

'Who?' blurted out Kitty, unable to contain her curiosity any longer.

'Bastien.'

'Bastien?'

'Yes.' Audrey nodded. 'So you can see why I'm not sure what to do. He's been through so much, what with his parents and Dolly dying in such a short space of time. He's really struggling. If I say anything to the police they'll want to question him. I don't know how, or even *if*, he'd cope with that. He's so vulnerable at the moment.'

'I see,' replied Kitty thoughtfully.

'Given his run in with Andrew the other week, it won't look good for him,' added Audrey.

'Hmmm,' Kitty pondered. 'We are working on the assumption that Andrew's death was not from natural causes or self-inflicted, but there's been no confirmation that it *was* a suspicious death,' she said, even though her gut feeling was convincing herself otherwise. 'Hitting someone on impulse, and in public, is very different to a deliberate, pre-meditated attack. Would he really be capable of that?'

Audrey knew how deeply the pain of losing both of his parents, combined with the anger and resentment he felt towards Andrew over the sale of the land, ran in Bastien, but decided to refrain from saying so.

'You could always speak to Bastien? Confront him as to why he was there? And then decide whether to go to the police or not?'

'I suppose so.'

'Anyway, why did the police want to speak to you?'

'I'm not sure really. I suppose because of what had happened in the past. I imagine if they have reason to believe that Andrew's death was caused by, or as a result of, someone else, then they will need to speak to those with whom he had dealings, both past and present. You too I imagine.'

'Oh.' Foolishly, this hadn't dawned on Kitty. She thought of Andrew as an annoyance. One which had to be tolerated but preferably ignored. 'I don't see what I could offer that would be helpful to them,' she said, though the thought disquieted her.

'I didn't either, but it's good they're being thorough.'

'So why not speak to Bastien and then, *if* Andrew's death is confirmed as having been as a result of foul play, you could speak to D.I. Allix on his own? Unless of course in the meantime Bastien gets in touch with the police voluntarily?'

Audrey's face brightened. 'Yes. That sounds like a good solution. Thanks Kitty.'

Kitty trudged back home along the middle of the road which was absent of vehicles, her feet crunching on the compacted snow and ice as she went. She had not gone far when a four wheel drive vehicle approached from the direction in which Kitty was heading. She side stepped onto the footpath, snow so deep that it threatened to spill over the tops of her boots and waited for it to drive past, assuming that it was indicating left in order to turn down the lane it was approaching. Instead, it drew to a halt alongside her. The passenger window slid down.

'You alright?' called the cheery voice of Ditzi from within. 'Need a lift?' she offered.

'Hello Ditzi. Thanks for the offer but I'm fine.'

Ditzi glanced at her watch. 'Tell you what. Why don't you hop in and come and have some lunch with me? I've got soup warming in the bottom oven of the Aga, there's more than enough for two, then I could either drive you home or you could continue on with your walk. What do you think?'

Tempted, Kitty hesitated, feeling as though she ought to get on with her work but then reasoning that she could complete what needed to be done later on, so willingly accepted Ditzi's invitation and, despite her protestations about the snow she'd bring into the car, got in at Ditzi's insistence. They proceeded at a cautious pace, pulling up in front of the gates as they started to swing slowly open, moments later they drew up in front of the house which looked even more stunning covered in a thick layer of snow.

Kitty had not been into Ditzi's kitchen on her previous visit and couldn't help exclaiming. 'Wow!' when she walked in. It was vast. Approximately the same size as the combined ground floor area of an entire set of terraced houses, she estimated and, like the rest of what she had seen of the house, reeked of understated luxury and expense. 'This is incredible,' she added.

Ditzi blushed. 'Thanks.'

Kitty gazed at the acres of marble, granite and handmade units and touched one of the chrome handles. It felt smooth to the touch, an indented ripple detail at one end elevating each bar from the ordinary to the extraordinary. 'These are beautiful,' she commented. 'The detailing is amazing, they're so tactile, I feel like I could stroke them for hours!'

'Thank you. I love them. I tried to resist buying them but for me they add an interesting level of detail and I felt that they were perfect for the kitchen.'

Ditzi, dressed in yet another gorgeous - this time in an ice blue hue - cashmere jumper, busied herself serving the soup, warming some bread and laying the table on the far side of the kitchen in an orangery style extension which she and Dezo had added. The light flooded in and through the glass Kitty could see paths, some cleared of snow, leading off in various directions. Further away, off to her right, she could see a wrought iron gate set into a high wall which offered a glimpse through to a walled garden - something Kitty had always dreamed of. Ditzi chatted enthusiastically about her new found passion, explaining that she had absolutely no horticultural experience and was devouring as many books on the subject as she could.

'I was on my way back from the gym when I saw you,' she said, changing subject. 'I fancied a change of scenery, or rather some human company,' she added. 'Apart from

Dezo, I've seen no one all week and he's been ensconced in his studio working on one of his projects for the majority of that time, but today he's gone to see Zeno.' Before hastily saying. 'He's prone to do unexpected things, it's the creative in him.' she explained upon seeing Kitty's quizzical look. 'Anyway,' Ditzi continued, 'I insisted that all our staff stay at home this week. I don't want any of them risking themselves in this weather, so it's been very quiet here but I should have realised that the gym would be quiet too. Ariadne was there having a session with Venka, though neither of them were particularly chatty. Venka in particular looked shattered. I guess covering Zeno's clients, as well as her own, is taking its toll. Fortunately Kim had time for a quick coffee though.'

Kitty listened as she ate her soup, which was delicious; lentils and vegetables. Ditzi was animated as she chattered away, her whole face alive and glowing.

'Have you every been married Kitty?' Ditzi asked, suddenly switching subjects again. 'If you don't mind me asking?'

Kitty smiled. 'Not at all.' She recounted the tale of her failed marriage, it felt a long time ago, in the dim and distant past and she now felt little sadness toward its demise.

'And,' Ditzi hesitated, 'children?'

Kitty's face clouded and she shook her head. 'Sadly not.'

'Oh. I'm sorry.'

Kitty shrugged. 'It was not meant to be and it's certainly not going to happen now.' Gloomily she thought about the perimenopause she was convinced she was going through. 'How about you?'.

The sadness Kitty felt seemed mirrored in Ditzi's face. 'No. It's not happened yet. But I'm always hopeful that one day it might.' She didn't mention the two miscarriages she'd had, the latest one just six months ago.

'I'm sure it will. You have youth on your side. Unlike me,' Kitty joked, in an attempt to lift the air of gloom which now hung over them.

'The police were here earlier this morning,' said Ditzi, keen to steer away from the topic of babies.

Kitty's ears pricked up. 'Really? What did they want?'

'Oh, it was about Andrew Battle. D.I. Somethingorother and his rather fierce looking colleague, whose name escapes me, came.'

'Female?'

Ditzi nodded.

'I expect that was D.S. Windsor. She does come across as rather terrifying, but seems to be very efficient and diligent in her job.'

'You know them?'

'I've come across them,' replied Kitty, refraining from going into details. 'So what did they want?'

'To speak to Dezo. Andrew had been very persistent in trying to persuade Dezo to invest in one or other of his projects. I didn't like him and Dezo certainly wasn't going to part with any money. He felt that Andrew was a very unscrupulous character. Anyway, he wasn't really able to offer anything of interest to the police.'

'Like what?'

'I don't know. An insight into the details of Andrew's business dealings I suppose. It did make me wonder if they are treating Andrew's death as suspicious.'

'Really?' Interesting, mused Kitty.

'They were also asking questions about how we felt Andrew had been perceived locally, along with whether we knew of anyone in particular who might have had an issue with him.'

Oh bother, thought Kitty, that means I'll definitely be on their list. But the idea of what she might in turn be able to glean from the detectives during their visit brightened her up. 'Did you, or they, mention anyone specifically?' she asked.

'Umm,' Ditzi tried to recall. 'No, I don't think so. Sorry. I can't remember.'

'Not to worry. Anyway, I'd better be going. I've still got more work to do,' said Kitty. 'Thanks so much for lunch. It was delicious and I've really enjoyed being here with you. Perhaps I could return the favour sometime and you could come over to my place?' Ditzi looked delighted at the invitation.

Despite Ditzi's best efforts to persuade Kitty to let her drive her home, Kitty insisted that she wanted to walk back and tramped back through the snow digesting their conversation as she went. Something was niggling away at the back of her mind but she couldn't put her finger on it. So engrossed was she in her thoughts that she arrived home before she knew it.

She had barely taken her boots off, cuddled Daisy, and settled back down to work, before there was a knock at the front door. She padded through to the hall and opened the door, only to see D.I. Allix. His kind but serious face had a smile on it and the wrinkles around his eyes crinkled. He had to duck his tall frame to get through the doorway and Kitty led him through into the kitchen, pushed aside her work which was spread across the table and offered him a seat. Immediately, Daisy started clambering up his leg, her little paws sinking their claws in as she did so, like a climber using crampons to scale a great height.

'Sorry,' laughed Kitty, reaching over to remove her. 'She does love people.'

He smiled. 'It's fine. She's very sweet.' He lifted the little kitten up and put her onto his lap, stroking her head and tickling her under the chin. He accepted Kitty's offer of a cup of tea and they chatted casually until she sat down. Meanwhile, Daisy curled up and fell asleep on his lap.

'I'm assuming that you are here about Andrew Battle?' said Kitty, before D.I. Allix could say anything.

'Yes, I am,' he confirmed.

They briefly went over Kitty's previous experiences with Andrew, of which D.I. Allix was already well aware, and then discussed more recent events. Kitty included details of the evening at the pub and the altercation she had witnessed in the village shop between Andrew and Bastien.

'Apart from that, I can't think of anything specific which may be of use to you. You already know about his failed attempts to cajole Dezo into investing in one or more of his business schemes.'

D.I. Allix looked at her in surprise.

'I've just had lunch with Ditzi and she told me that you'd been there to see Dezo this morning. What happens to his company now? Andrew's I mean. And the developments? More specifically, the one in the village where work hasn't actually started yet?'

'That's something his solicitor will deal with,' replied D.I. Allix non-committally.

'And Bastien? Have you spoken to him yet?'

D.I. Allix smiled, remembering from previous experience how inquisitive Kitty could be.

'I am assuming that Andrew's death is being treated as suspicious or you wouldn't be asking questions? What did the autopsy results show?' She persisted, despite being aware that she was crossing a line.

He paused, weighing up his response. 'There are, shall we say, some unanswered questions surrounding his death. And that's all I am prepared to say. Now,' he said lifting the sleeping kitten from his lap. 'I am afraid I'm going to have to move you,' he murmured softly to Daisy, whose sleepy eyes blinked open, then closed again. 'There,' he said placing her gently into her bed. He turned to Kitty. 'Thank you for the tea Kitty. I'll be in touch if I need anything else.'

Kitty showed him out and went straight to the phone and dialled Bella's number.

'Guess what?' said Bella immediately, skipping any pleasantries.

'I was going to say the same to you! You go first.'

'I've just been speaking to Kim. You remember I was telling you that Andrew was buying Florence's old house on the other side of Monhurst? And that Kim was doing everything she could to buy it instead?' she continued breathlessly, not pausing for a response from Kitty. 'Well, apparently, Andrew had managed to push it forward and his company had exchanged contracts on the property. Kim was furious, but then her solicitor told her today that the company, Andrew's that is, has been left to his heir!'

'What?!' squeaked Kitty. 'You mean he has offspring?'

'Yes!'

'But who? I mean. Who on earth is it?'

'Now that I don't know. I suppose it's hardly surprising given the way he got through women. I wonder how many there are? Anyway, Kim is doing her utmost to find out more with the intention to offer whatever sum might be necessary in order to secure the property for herself.'

'Gosh. The plot thickens!' replied Kitty.

'So, what was it that you wanted to tell me?' asked Bella.

'Oh. It seems rather dull in comparison,' replied Kitty. 'I've just had D.I. Allix here. I couldn't get much out of him, other than the fact that, and I quote "there are, shall we say, some unanswered questions surrounding his death"!'

'Curiouser and curiouser,' replied Bella.

'Also. I saw Ditzi this morning. D.I. Allix had been to see Dezo this morning, apparently because Andrew had persistently tried to cajole Dezo into investing in his business. I don't suppose,' she paused, 'you've managed to glean any information from Dave have you?'

Bella snorted. 'No chance. He's being annoyingly tight lipped about it. He's not working directly on the case but I am sure he knows something. One of the things I love about him is his integrity and discretion, but sometimes it can be really infuriating. Like now!'

Kitty laughed. 'Can't you use your more persuasive tactics?' she joked.

'No!' giggled Bella. 'Anyway, I'll keep my ears open and see what gossip is being bandied around by Sharon. Nine times out of ten there's not an ounce of truth in what she says but very occasionally she hits upon a nugget of truth.'

Kitty suggested that she walk down to the shop in Wynenden the next morning to see if she could glean anything of interest from Betty as well. Because Wednesday was her regular day off during the week, it meant that she could do as she pleased and would confer back with Bella afterwards.

CHAPTER FOURTEEN

Kitty always felt that there was something magical about the light reflected from snow, be it from daylight, by moonlight or by starlight and often wondered if these feelings were triggered by happy memories from childhood. Consequently, she had left the bedroom curtains open overnight so that she could wake up naturally as dawn broke, when the morning light began to reflect off the snow and into the bedroom. She awoke that morning with a sense of peace and calm and luxuriated in being able to remain snuggled up in the warm cocoon of her bed, eventually, though very reluctantly, heaving herself out of bed and into the shower. Washed, dried and with a freshly laundered pair of slim cut stretchy jeans pulled on, she muttered disconsolately to herself at the effort it had taken to tug the zip up, gloomily resigning herself to the fact that the perimenopause was beginning to lumber her with the dreaded middle-aged spread. Perhaps it really was time to see her G.P. to discuss her options? Maybe H.R.T would help? She resolved to telephone the surgery later in the day to book an appointment.

The eager little face of Daisy cheered her up, such adoration and enthusiastic mewing could not help but do so. Though Kitty was attempting to train Daisy to not sit on laps at mealtimes - on the whole with a degree of success -

Daisy had managed to sneak round this rule by clambering up onto Kitty's shoulders whilst she made breakfast, purring and snuggling into her neck then refusing to move, clinging on to Kitty like a limpet, she liked to believe that it was because the kitten had missed her overnight. As a result Kitty's resolve was weakening over time, rather enjoying having a warm furry neck warmer, so the early morning ritual remained.

Startled by how late it was, and with Bella due in a couple of hours, Kitty got ready for her walk to the village shop on her gathering information mission. Protected by her winter outer garments Kitty strode as briskly as it was possible to do so through deep snow, taking the short route into the village, and arrived warm and glowing.

'Morning Betty,' she called out as she picked up a basket from just inside the door.

Betty, the curls of her tightly permed grey hair bobbing up and down, reciprocated then continued with her conversation to an older lady who was ensconced in an enormous black, full-length, padded coat, topped with a hand knitted pillar-box-red bobble hat, the petite frame of her face looking a little incongruous underneath it.

Selecting a carton of whole milk, then casually browsing the array of biscuits on offer, provided Kitty with the opportunity to eavesdrop in on their conversation. Gleefully she realised that they were debating the contents of Andrew's Will, though they seemed to have come to the bizarre conclusion that he had left some of his assets to a local donkey sanctuary. As if! thought Kitty. She didn't for one minute believe that Andrew had cared about animals, he certainly hadn't seemed to care about people unless they were of use to him and, once they had stopped being of use, were then discarded like rubbish tossed into a bin.

The bell above the door pinged and Hetty entered; large scarf wrapped around her neck but no coat, hat or gloves. She must be freezing, thought Kitty, even if she has only run along from her room at the pub a few doors away. Hetty muttered a generalized "hello", then scurried over to the fridge to get some milk. Her nose was bright red and looked sore, face so pale it appeared to have taken on a grey-like hue and her eyes appeared sunken into dark sockets, definitely not the bright and chirpy Hetty that people were used to seeing.

Kitty's attention was drawn away from her observations of Hetty to what Betty was now saying. '… anyway. I don't like to speak ill of the dead, but he was not a nice man at all and it can hardly be a surprise that someone has done him in.'

Kitty frowned. Did she know something? There was a big sniff from beside her as Hetty reached across for some chocolate biscuits, then wiped her eyes and nose with the back of her hand.

Kitty could see tears welling up in her eyes. 'You ok?' she whispered, out of Betty's earshot. Hetty nodded. But it was clear to Kitty that she wasn't. Hetty hastened over to the till, dropped some change onto the counter and left even before Betty could ring the items up.

'Oh,' said Betty, surprised by Hetty's behaviour.

'I think she's got a bad cold, or maybe a touch of the flu and doesn't want to pass it on,' said Kitty in an attempt to appease the two women, hoping that it would prevent them from being distracted away from their deliberations about Andrew.

Betty looked dubiously down at the coins in front of her before ringing the two items Hetty had paid for into the till, she retrieved the two pence change and popped it into the charity box attached to the counter. She then pumped some hand sanitiser from a bottle underneath the counter onto her hands and vigorously rubbed them together. That's new, mused Kitty, since when did Betty become hyper-sensitive about germs? Kitty turned back to the biscuits, selected a packet of double chocolate cookies and went across to look at the magazines and newspapers, flicking through a copy of Country Life as she continued to eavesdrop.

Betty's companion pumped her for more information. 'Well,' said Betty lowering her voice slightly and looking furtively around, despite there only being the three of them in the shop, 'don't spread this around…'

Kitty snorted with laughter at the irony, hastily turning it into a faux coughing fit. Betty glanced at her, then turned back to continue her conversation.

'Bastien has been taken in for questioning. Now, I don't want to cast aspersions, but there's no smoke without fire.' She folded her arms across her chest with an air of self-satisfaction.

Bastien? Hmm, if it were true then it was most interesting, thought Kitty tucking the nugget of information away for future contemplation. What never ceased to surprise Kitty about Betty was her ability to switch from using the most basic phraseology to being incredibly eloquent, Kitty's contemplation was interrupted by the sound of the shop bell pinging again. This time it was Bastien himself who walked in. Betty's cheeks tinged a faint colour of red from embarrassment, like a small child caught taking a biscuit when it had been told not to do so.

'Bastien,' she exclaimed brightly. 'How are you? What can I do for you? Anything I can help you with?'

Bastien looked rather startled and slightly alarmed by Betty's unexpected eagerness to assist him. He muttered his thanks but turned her firmly down and hurried off to the far side of the shop in order to escape any further attempts to engage him in a conversation.

Kitty popped a newspaper into her shopping basket and went to choose something from the small selection of local fruit and vegetables on display which conveniently afforded her an excellent vantage point from which to observe, not just Betty and her companion, but Bastien too.

A heavy silence hung in the shop, Betty shuffled a couple of plastic biros pointlessly around the counter in order to look occupied whilst simultaneously watching Bastien. Bastien, in turn, was swiftly grabbing his provisions, desperate to make a hasty exit.

With reluctance Kitty went to the till to pay for her meagre purchases, feeling she could not reasonably prolong her visit any further. She paid, popped the items into her small rucksack and left. Moments later Bastien hurried out, turned and headed along the icy pavement towards home.

Kitty had only just managed to get in through her front door before she heard the crunch of car tyres crackling over the icy bumps in the drive, it was Bella.

The late morning sunshine shone brightly through the large glass panes of the garden room where Kitty and Bella went to sit to drink their coffee. Daisy snoozed peacefully, sprawled across the limestone floor enjoying the warmth from the underfloor heating. They exchanged the news from their respective fact finding missions. Bella's visit to the shop in Monhurst had proved fruitless - no one had come in or out whilst she was there and Sharon - unusually for her - had not been in a chatty mood. Bella had come to the conclusion that Sharon must have had a disagreement with her husband Ron, who ran the post office part of the shop, because the pair had glowered at one another during her brief foray into the shop.

'We don't seem to have got very far.' said Bella 'But I am intrigued about his Will.'

'Yes. Me too,' replied Kitty. 'However, I don't see how we can find out who the beneficiary or beneficiaries are until probate is granted.'

'I suppose not. Not unless Kim's solicitor is able to reach an agreement for Kim to take over the purchase of Florence's cottage. Whether that's even legally possible before probate is granted I've no idea and that's always assuming the beneficiary, or beneficiaries, agree.'

'Why don't we go to the pub on Friday night to discuss it?' suggested Kitty. 'We could go to The Orchard. I think it's Hetty's turn to work there this weekend. She may well have overheard something about it whilst working? Whether she'd tell us is another matter. Though,' she added, 'if Hetty's got flu, or as hideous a cold as she seemed to be suffering from this morning, she may take a few days off to recover.'

'Well, let's go anyway. You not seeing Ted?'

Kitty shook her head. 'No. He's going on one of his rare "boys" weekends. He gets together with his three school friends and they go hiking up a mountain or something. How much of that they'll be able to do in this weather is debatable,' she rolled her eyes.

'Depends on which part of the country they're going to.' said Bella.

'Um. I think somewhere in Wales. Surprisingly the snow doesn't appear to have been as heavy there as it has been here, but I'm still dubious. However, I am sure that they will have a good time no matter what.'

A while later Bella took her leave and Kitty curled up on the sofa by the fire she'd lit earlier in the sitting room and had a nap with Daisy, the combination of warmth from the fire and her earlier fresh air and exercise having made her feel soporific.

Even though there had been quite an astonishing quantity of snow for the year already, more snow fell over night. Consequently the school took the decision to remain closed for the remainder of the week. So, other than being able to log on to the school system and deal with what was accessible, there was little else Kitty could do, in terms of work, which she found frustrating and she remained ensconced in the house with Daisy, who was naturally delighted to have the constant companionship.

Fortunately Ted was still able to get through in his four wheel drive on Thursday night as pre-arranged and they spent a very pleasant evening together. Ted had not only thoughtfully brought provisions with him to stock up her fridge, but also all the ingredients required in order for him to cook a delicious supper for them both.

On Friday morning Kitty finally ventured out for a walk to ascertain whether the roads would be passable and safe enough for her to drive to the pub in Monhurst that evening. She set off over the fields through the Wynenden Park

Estate and arrived at the gate which lead onto the Wynenden to Monhurst Road, adjacent to the cordoned off land where Andrew had intended to build - in her opinion - far too many houses, and which was adjacent to Bastien's home.

She saw a hunched-over figure walking slowly across the land, accompanied by an ancient, arthritic yellow Labrador. It was Bastien.

'Morning,' she called cheerily, waving.

Bastien looked up, hesitated, then muttered something which Kitty couldn't hear but took to be a greeting.

'How are you?' she persisted.

He shrugged.

'Are you ok?' she continued, with not an entirely altruistic motive. 'What with everything that has happened. You know. With Andrew.'

He scowled at her and said nothing.

'I had the police visit me. I think they're speaking to lots of people. It's not like Andrew was Mr Popular around here...' she let her words hang in the air.

He shifted a little, kicking the snow with his right boot, and emitted a grunt.

'I assume they'll want to speak to you too,' she hinted, hoping that he would take the bait and respond. 'Given...' she trailed off and waved her hand across in the direction of the land Bastien was standing on; his former family land.

'Got what was coming to him. Serves him right. Nasty, conniving, underhanded, mendacious, dishonest individual. Want me to go on?' he asked, not waiting for a response. 'He was a piece of shit and the world is better off without him.'

Kitty was taken aback by the ferocity with which Bastien had spoken. 'So, do you have any idea as to what happened to him?' she asked.

'How would I know?' he fired back, a little too quickly she felt. Bastien's normally hunched figure and nondescript demeanour suddenly stood tall, bristling with animation, his oversized ears appearing to waggle from underneath his dark-green woollen beanie.

'Oh,' replied Kitty, non-plussed. 'It's just that you said he'd got what was coming to him, so I assumed you'd heard something?'

'Well he did and I haven't. The person you should speak to is Venka. She came out of his house that night.'

Momentarily at a loss for words, Kitty stood there with her mouth open in surprise. Before her eyes Bastien visibly deflated and shrunk back into himself, shoulders rounded and hunched.

'Sorry,' he muttered apologetically. He turned and walked off, back over the land towards home, with his Labrador, George, hobbling dutifully behind him.

Kitty couldn't help but feel that she had missed an opportunity and was cross with herself that she hadn't been quick-witted enough to probe further, to ask how he knew that Venka had come out of Andrew's house on the night he died, even though she already knew the answer because Audrey had told her that she had seen Bastien standing opposite Andrew's house that night.

She watched Bastien retreat, then turned back to the gate which opened onto the road, unlatched it and stepped cautiously forward, looking out for cars as she did so. Would the development make this walk impossible? Make the road so busy that it would be far too dangerous to even attempt to cross it? Could the development be stopped now that Andrew was dead? Or had it reached the point of no return? Kitty's mind was like a washing machine stuck on a spin cycle, questions looping round and round. Had the cause of death been discovered yet? Was it from natural causes? self-inflicted? If so why? Or as a result of someone else's actions? What had Andrew and Zeno been arguing about? Was Venka involved? Or had Bastien said that to deflect attention away from himself? If so, why? How was he involved? So deep in her thoughts was she that Kitty bumped into Venka who was coming out of the shop with Valentina - the little tot bundled up in a bright-pink padded snow suit accompanied by an electric-blue woollen bobble hat. Valentina's blonde hair was pulled into a low ponytail which protruded from underneath her hat and which swished about as she jumped excitedly about, enthusiastically telling Kitty that they were on their way to the playground to make snowmen.

'Sorry.' apologised Kitty. 'I was deep in thought,' she offered as an explanation.

'No problem,' replied Venka tightly, voice strained, face and body exuding stress and tension.

'Are you alright?' asked Kitty.

Venka nodded and turned to Valentina, but not before Kitty had seen tears welling up in her eyes. Kind hearted, often ferocious in demeanour - except with Valentina - Kitty thought that Venka looked worn down by life. Was she exhausted from her temporary additional workload? Or was there more to it?'

'Say goodbye to Kitty,' Venka murmured softly to Valentina, who dutifully did as she was told.

With yet another bounce, a broad smile and a wave from Valentina, Venka held firmly onto her daughters hand and prepared to cross the road, leaving Kitty with even more to mull over.

Once back at home she set about cleaning the house as a distraction. Her trusty, and much appreciated, cleaner had been unable to come for a couple of weeks due to the perilous road conditions and every room was in need of a spruce up. She found the process therapeutic but, no matter how hard she tried, she was unable to retrieve whatever it was that was lurking at the back of her mind. A nugget of information which she was convinced was relevant to what had taken place between Zeno and Andrew. Frustrated, she finished cleaning then heated up and ate some leftover soup, after which she settled down to watch a film with Daisy, before long they were both fast asleep.

CHAPTER FIFTEEN

It was slow progress driving to The Orchard pub in Monhurst. Even though the lane from Kitty's house to the main road had been snow ploughed it had not been gritted, consequently the compacted snow had become like an ice rink. She was already feeling out of sorts having woken, momentarily disorientated, from a couple of hours sleep on the sofa to darkness, bar a faint glow from the dying embers of the fire. Now, as she pulled the car slowly to a halt in the pub car park, she was perspiring from the stressful journey and already feeling anxious about the return journey; too much sliding and slipping along with a near miss with a hedge in her lane had shaken her and there would be the added complication of tackling the incline up the lane home. Would her little car even make it, she worried as she tugged her navy wool coat tightly around her, pulling the collar up to try to prevent the biting wind from snapping at it. Shivering, she pushed the pub door open and was immediately embraced by the warmth from within. Surprisingly it was fairly quiet, just a dozen or so other people. Kitty was pleased to see that Bella had managed to get them a couple of the deep comfy chairs by one of the fires, which was burning merrily in the fireplace.

'Are you ok?' asked Bella. 'You look a bit. Well…'

'Grumpy?' offered Kitty.

'Something like that.' Bella raised an eyebrow quizzically and listened sympathetically whilst Kitty recounted her journey whilst simultaneously taking her coat off and draping it over the back of the chair.

'You're welcome to stay at mine tonight if you don't want to drive back?'

'Thanks Bella, but I'll need to get back for Daisy.'

Bella laughed and rolled her eyes. 'That kitten is like a surrogate child!'

'Well, you can't blame me! You have to admit she *is* pretty cute,' smiled Kitty. Daisy had brought out her maternal side and meant the world to her, mutual giving and receiving of love for one another - albeit for different reasons - was a joy.

'True. Anyway,' said Bella, pushing a steaming glass of red liquid across the table towards Kitty. 'This should warm you up. It's a hot, spiced juice. Bit like mulled wine without the alcohol, which is what I've got,' she indicated to an almost identical looking glass and contents. 'Hetty said it's very good and as it's a cold winters night it seemed appropriate. If it's revolting, I'll get you something else.'

Kitty took a cautious sip. 'Actually,' she said, 'it's rather nice. Thanks. Cheers.' She took another sip. 'So, what have you been up to?'

'I have news!' grinned Bella.

'Great! So do I!' exclaimed Kitty in reply.

Bella lowered her voice, then lent in towards Kitty. 'I saw Kim this afternoon when I went to the gym, Venka had been "invited" to go to the police station for questioning today.

'But I only saw her this morning with Valentina,' interrupted Kitty.

'It was this afternoon. She phoned Kim in a bit of a state because she had no one to look after Valentina. Kim was working but arranged for Seb to look after Valentina as he was already at home looking after Matilda. Apparently Venka was there for three hours. Mysterious, huh?'

'Indeed,' replied Kitty thoughtfully.

'So, what was it that you have to tell me?' asked Bella.

'I bumped into Bastien today.' She recounted her conversation with him, finishing with, '… so if he told the police what he knew about,' she glanced around to double check that there was no one within earshot, 'Venka, that may be why she was interviewed. Of course the real question is, why was she at Andrew's house in the first place?'

'Intriguing,' replied Bella thoughtfully. 'Perhaps, she was there to give Andrew a P.T. session? As his membership application to join the gym was rejected.'

'Hmm. Possible I suppose.' said Kitty, annoyed that she hadn't thought of that herself. 'Anyway,' she said, changing the subject. 'I don't suppose you've had any luck getting anything out of Dave yet have you?'

'Nope,' replied Bella, tightly.

'Another drink?' offered Kitty thinking it wise to pause the conversation.

'Yes please.'

Kitty went up to the bar. It felt strange, she reflected, because the last time she'd been there, Andrew had been very much alive. Whilst she hadn't liked him it still made her feel a little sad that he had died, it would have to be a hardhearted person to not feel some empathy towards the situation. Kitty watched Hetty quickly and efficiently serving other customers in her usual engaging manner, it appeared that her cold had quickly passed, she thought, noticing that Hetty still looked pale, exhausted and as though she had the weight of the world on her shoulders.

'Kitty?' Hetty looked at her questioningly.

'Oh. Sorry, Hetty, I was lost in thought. Mulled wine for Bella please and is there any chance that I could have a hot chocolate with whipped cream and marshmallows please? It just feels like the perfect night for one.'

'No problem,' replied Hetty. 'How was that?' she asked, nodding towards Kitty's empty glass.

'Delicious thanks. Really nice. I imagine it's proving quite popular in this weather?' She chatted on whilst Hetty deftly prepared the drinks. 'I was just thinking about the last time I was in here, Andrew was here. It feels peculiar knowing that he'll never be in here again.'

Hetty chewed on her bottom lip as she rang up the till.

'I imagine he was a very good customer,' added Kitty, aware of Andrew's propensity for alcohol.

'Uhh,' muttered Hetty, before serving the next customer, though not before Kitty had seen tears welling up in her eyes.

'There you are.' said Kitty as she placed the drinks onto the table. 'I think I've just unwittingly upset Hetty. I only made a passing remark about Andrew.'

'I suppose it's the shock. Whether you liked him or not, he was a real character in these parts. What, or who, are people going to moan about and campaign against now?' pondered Bella out loud.

'Oh I'm sure they'll find something, or someone.' smiled Kitty. 'Now. Tell me. What's going on in your life Bella? It seems like an age since we've had a really good catch up even though it was only a couple of days ago.

What's really happening between you and Dave? You don't seem very happy?'

Bella shrugged and sighed. 'Oh I don't know. One minute things are great. The next they're not. I don't know if it's me, or him, or both of us. Neither of us seems to want to commit, it's like we keep going around in the same repetitive cycle. How long do we keep on like this? Do we make a go of it and move in with one another or break up? But for good this time. I can't keep carrying on with this on/off thing we've been doing.' She let out another deep sigh and looked beseechingly at Kitty, wishing that she would wave a magic wand and resolve her problems.

'Shouldn't you be saying all this to Dave? Or have you already?'

Bella shook her head.

'Maybe you should?' suggested Kitty gently. 'I can't provide you with any answers, but it seems to me that the two of you are at a crossroads in your relationship.'

They continued to chat, consuming more drinks as they did so, until closing time. Kitty hugged Bella, who then walked gloomily home, whilst Kitty braced herself for the drive home, relieved when she finally crept safely onto her drive without incident.

Kitty tossed and turned all night, fidgeting, twitching and becoming more frustrated the more often she woke up, which in turn prevented her from falling back to sleep again quickly. At 4 a.m. she gave up, made herself a cup of tea and went back to bed, taking a somniferous, but purring, Daisy with her for comfort. Daisy's soothing, rhythmic purring calmed Kitty as she stroked her soft fur and eventually she too drifted back to sleep. She awoke with a start at 7 a.m. feeling a little refreshed, then panicked when she couldn't see Daisy beside her, concerned that she may have rolled onto the kitten whilst they were both asleep. She sighed with momentary relief when she saw the small ginger form curled up on the chair by the window, until she realised that Daisy was asleep on the new cashmere jumper she'd purchased online in the sales recently. Kitty hopped out of bed, scooped Daisy up, retrieved the jumper and then padded barefoot down to the kitchen. Her stomach felt a little unsettled and she regretted having so many hot chocolate's with whipped cream the previous evening.

Doubting very much that Bella would make it to the gym that morning, despite them having tentatively arranged to do so the previous night, Kitty decided to go anyway. It was deserted, Kitty had the gym all to herself. To begin with it was nice, but after a while it became a little boring being on her own. After a quick shower and change she briefly chatted with the receptionist before heading outside into the strong sunshine and clear blue sky. Kitty could hear the drip, drip, drip of icicles beginning to melt, which dangled down from the roof. As she crossed the car park a four wheel drive vehicle drove in at a swift pace. She waved to the driver, but it was not reciprocated, the car came to a halt outside the offices rather than the members car park.

Kitty frowned. Why would he park over there when the main car park was deserted?

The drivers door opened and Dezo got out. Kitty waved again. He hesitated, waved back and walked around to the passenger side of the vehicle and opened the door.

'Oh!' uttered Kitty out loud in surprise as Zeno stepped down from the vehicle, his six foot, darkly-clothed frame partly silhouetted against snow banked up against the lower part of the building. He looked thinner, she thought, though it was rather difficult for her to tell from a distance. She got into her car and started the engine, drumming her fingers on the steering wheel. Why on earth was Dezo driving him home? She edged the car slowly towards the exit, observing the pair in her rear view mirror as she did so. Zeno opened the door leading up to his first floor flat whilst Dezo retrieved a bag from the boot. Zeno turned and said something to Dezo who looked up, nodded, then followed Zeno inside, closing the door behind him.

Kitty drove on autopilot, puzzled by what she'd just witnessed. A slip on black ice made her snap back to the present and turn her full attention back to the road just as she approached the end of Stream Lane before turning right. Shortly afterwards she drove past Andrew's house on the left hand side. There was no evidence that the police had ever been there. Andrew's cars were still parked on the drive, covered in snow, if you were not aware of his fate you would never know that there was no one in residence. What secrets could the house tell? Could it reveal what had happened that night? An idea flitted across Kitty's mind but she brushed it aside. No. She definitely couldn't, she told herself.

She parked in the village hall car park and continued her contemplations as she walked around to the entrance of the building.

'Hi!' said a voice, interrupting her flow of thoughts.

'Oh. Hello.' She started, seeing Ditzi. Ditzi's green eyes looked bright but Kitty could see that, even though she had tried hide it, her makeup could not fully conceal the large bags and dark splurges underneath them.

'How are you?' Kitty asked as they walked in together.

'Fine. Thanks.' replied Ditzi.

Kitty never believed a woman who said she was "fine" because it frequently meant the complete opposite. 'I've just seen Dezo,' said Kitty. A look which Kitty couldn't decipher flitted across Ditzi's face. 'At the gym.' she added for clarity. 'With Zeno. It's great that he's well enough to be discharged from hospital and so nice of Dezo to give him a lift home.'

'Yes,' replied Ditzi tightly.

'Busy today,' commented Kitty, deciding it prudent to change the subject.

'Mmm,' replied Ditzi distractedly.

Kitty was relieved when Bella turned up, having felt uncomfortable by the awkward silence which had fallen between herself and Ditzi.

Bella sat down and let out a groan.

Kitty smirked. 'Feeling a little rough this morning are you?' she teased.

'I blame you for this,' grumbled Bella.

Ditzi looked quizzically at them.

'We went to the pub last night,' explained Kitty.

'And she kept plying me with mulled wine,' added Bella.

'I didn't make you drink them,' laughed Kitty. 'Though I do think I overdid the hot chocolate, whipped cream and marshmallows.' She patted Bella's hand and ignored the dark scowl Bella gave her. 'She'll be fine once the caffeine kicks in,' added Kitty to Ditzi.

'I just can't drink like I used to. I only had three or four glasses during the whole evening. But it feels like I've been out on an all-nighter, which I haven't done since my youth! Oh, I forgot to say yesterday,' said Bella, 'that I bumped into Ariadne at the gym. She wasn't in the best of moods, I think she had been expecting a session with Venka and really wasn't best pleased when she was told that Venka wasn't there, some kind of communication mix up I think. It was just as well that Kim was covering reception because Ariadne really had a go at her.'

'I hope she's okay,' said Kitty. 'I wouldn't have thought that Ariadne would have a go at Kim given they are good friends.'

'Maybe that's why she felt she could, knowing that Kim is a kind person and would let it go.' reasoned Bella.

'Mmm. Possibly,' replied Kitty.

'Anyway,' said Bella changing the subject, 'I'm going to need another shot of caffeine to keep me going. Would either of you like another?'

Whilst Bella was fetching their beverages, Kitty leaned closer to Ditzi and whispered to her. 'Are you ok? Really? Can I do anything to help?'

Ditzi shook her head, tears pricking at her eyes. 'No. Thanks.' she murmured.

Just as Bella was returning with their drinks, Betty launched herself at them. Her grey hair, usually heavily permed, looked rather loose and wild that morning and her face was alight, bursting to pass on what she termed as "news".

'Have you heard?' Betty blurted out excitedly.

'Heard what?' replied Kitty cautiously.

'About Venka!' Betty exclaimed.

Bella opened her mouth to say that they had but Kitty kicked her from underneath the table making her yelp. A sixth sense had made Kitty feel that Betty was not in possession of factual information but was actually fishing for gossip.

'What about her?' asked Kitty, ignoring Bella's scowl.

'She's been arrested!' Betty bristled with self-importance.

There was a stunned silence before Kitty gathered herself. 'Arrested? How do you know that?' she asked.

'Well...' Betty looked furtively around, as though she was about to impart a top secret piece of information, when in fact the reality was that she had already been spreading the "news" since she had first caught wind of the alleged discovery. 'I saw her being driven away by what's-her-name, you know Kitty, that person who works for D.I. Thingumy.'

'Do you mean D.S. Windsor?'

Betty nodded. 'Yes. Her. Anyway, I was walking over to see my friend Violet, you know, the one who lives in Wynenden Close, not far from the house you rented, where Venka and Valentina now live .' Betty digressed.

With resignation the trio waited for Betty to finish her monologue and get to the point. Experience had taught them that, once Betty was in full flow, it was futile to interrupt or attempt to hurry her along.

'... so there you are. Can you believe it! I wouldn't have thought she was the type to commit murder. And what about her poor little daughter? Who is going to look after her whilst her mother is locked up?'

Kitty bristled with indignation. Betty had gone too far this time. 'Firstly,' she said in a stony voice, 'do you know for a *fact* that Venka has been arrested and charged? Or are you making assumptions based purely upon seeing her in D.S. Windsor's car, which, I might add, could have been for any number of reasons? Secondly, has it even been confirmed by the police that Andrew's death was caused by anything other than being from natural causes? As far as I am aware they haven't confirmed the cause either way and thirdly, what happened - assuming what you have said is correct - to innocent until proven guilty?'

'Well,' plundered Betty, clearly not having expected such a response. 'I…'

'Don't you realise how damaging and dangerous such a rumour could be? What about poor little Valentina? How do you think your gossip could effect her? And Venka's reputation? She has to live in this village and people always assume the worst. No smoke without fire and so on, when there may not be an ounce of truth at all in what you are saying.' Kitty could feel her blood boiling with anger and it was taking every ounce of self-control to prevent her from shouting at Betty.

'I…' Betty blushed and at least had the decency to look shamefaced.

'Perhaps,' continued Kitty, 'it would be a good idea if you squash these rumours quickly, before any more damage can be done?'

'Yes. Umm…' Betty turned and went off with the air of a wounded animal about her.

The three sat momentarily in silence.

'Gosh,' said Ditzi.

'You certainly told her,' added Bella.

Kitty shifted uncomfortably. 'Do you think I went too far?'

'Well. No. But the delivery was a bit, well, intense? And are you one hundred percent sure that Venka hasn't been arrested?' asked Bella.

'Umm. I don't actually. I only know what you told me yesterday. Nothing else.'

'Poor Venka has got her reputation to think about and Valentina too. All of us are aware as to how damaging scurrilous rumours can be and the impact they can have. I don't think any of us know what the cause of Andrew's death was. Ultimately, the only ones who truly know what goes on behind closed doors, are the individuals themselves, despite what others may presume.' said Ditzi.

'True,' replied Bella.

Kitty nodded, scrutinizing Ditzi's face. There was heartfelt meaning to what Ditzi had just said, she was sure of it, and Ditzi was avoiding her gaze.

CHAPTER SIXTEEN

Kitty was missing her best friend Libby who lived with her family on the edge of the village but was currently spending two months in the Far East and Australia. James, Libby's husband, had had to go out there on business. Rather than go alone, they had made the decision to go as a family with their children, Henry (almost 10) and Alice aged 8, an opportunity too good to be missed they had felt and fortunately the school was in agreement.

Often on a Sunday Kitty would go across to their house for lunch with them, sometimes with, sometimes without, Ted. On top of that she and Libby would regularly meet up and spoke on the phone every day. A month into their trip and with Ted away for the weekend, Kitty - who usually relished her own company - felt lonely and disgruntled.

On impulse, she grabbed her bag and decided to drive to the farm shop on the other side of the village and en-route check that all was safe and well at Libby's house; a large detached house built in the Tudor period, set within 10 acres of land.

The farm shop was a single-storey, recently converted, barn. It was light, airy and had a warm, welcoming atmosphere. Full height glass double entrance doors opened into a long rectangular space. On the left-hand side and straight ahead, was the retail area selling an impressive array of produce, much of which was locally produced and, at this time of year, also included apples and pears picked the previous autumn from Seb's smallholding. The remainder of the visible space consisted of a kitchen and small cafe area selling light refreshments. The limited menu, which included freshly made cakes and soups every day, was excellently executed and therefore proved very popular in the area with a brisk turnover of business and was particularly busy at weekends.

By the time Kitty had arrived it was mid-afternoon and all the tables were occupied. In the far corner she saw Hetty sitting on her own at a table for two nursing a large mug of something hot. Kitty hesitated, then weaved her way around the other tables towards her.

'Would you mind if I joined you?' she asked.

Hetty looked up. Her green eyes were red-rimmed and, since the last time Kitty had seen her, the dark circles underneath them had developed into a deeper purply/black hue. She smiled weakly. Her demeanour absent of her usual bright, happy, fizzing-with-energy self. 'Yeah. That's okay,' Hetty responded politely.

Kitty sat down on the wooden chair opposite Hetty and wriggled out of her navy padded jacket. Immediately a teenage girl who was waitressing that day, came over to take Kitty's order and she quickly scanned the menu which was written on a small, free-standing, chalk board in front of her.

'Um,' she said. 'A hot chocolate with marshmallows, no cream and a piece of carrot cake please. Hetty, can I get you anything?'

'No. Thanks. I'm fine,' she replied, her voice strained.

Kitty chattered away to fill in the uncomfortable silence which had fallen between them, hoping that by doing so she would be able to engage Hetty in conversation. She paused when the waitress returned with her order, swiftly took a bite of the carrot cake; deliciously moist, light, sweet but not too sweet - the cream-cheese topping giving just the right balance of acidity.

'You look sad,' said Kitty when she had finished her mouthful.

Hetty looked up from contemplating the contents of her mug. Her eyes began to well up and a big fat tear slid down her cheek. She brushed it quickly away, sniffed and shrugged.

'Can I help in any way?' enquired Kitty gently.

Hetty shook her head. 'No. It won't change anything.'

Hetty's inner pain was visibly etched across her face, whatever the cause, Kitty felt sure that Hetty was hurting deeply.

'Sometimes just talking can help. About whatever it is which is making you sad. I'm happy to listen and I promise that I won't tell another soul,' reassured Kitty, genuinely concerned.

Hetty's fingers fiddled with the handle of her white mug, contemplating what, if anything, to say. She opened her mouth. Then closed it. Then opened it again. 'It's. I'm.' Another tear slid down her face but Kitty remained silent, giving Hetty the space to voice whatever she did, or did not, want to tell Kitty. Conversations around them provided enough noise to ensure that no one could overhear Hetty's soft voice.

'I. I am sad,' she said, wiping more tears away as they trickled faster down her cheeks. 'And I can't tell anyone why.' She looked beseechingly at Kitty. 'No one would understand.'

'I might. And if I can't, I am very empathetic. What is it that you feel you can't tell anyone?' Kitty's heart beat a little faster, intrigued.

'About. About,' she sniffed again, her nose running. Kitty retrieved a fresh tissue from her jacket pocket and proffered it. Hetty took it, blew her nose then crumpled the tissue up, picking at the edges of it, small scraps fluttering onto the table as she did so. She took another deep breath, paused, released a long out-breath, then, looked directly at Kitty. 'About.' She gulped. 'Andrew.' She whispered, looking quickly away, apprehensive as to Kitty's reaction.

Though Kitty was startled by Hetty's words, she swiftly regained her composure and opened her mouth to reply, but before Kitty could say anything a loud voice called out her name from the other side of the cafe. She turned and inwardly groaned.

'Cooee! Kitty!' It was Betty, waving at her and making a beeline for them.

Bloody typical, thought Kitty, of all the moments. She glanced back at Hetty and could see that her emotional shutters had come down, the moment had passed.

Kitty rose and swiftly walked towards the rapidly approaching Betty in an attempt to prevent her from accosting Hetty as well.

'I wanted to apologise for yesterday,' said Betty loudly, then lowered her voice. 'About what I said. You were right. Venka hasn't been arrested and I am doing all I can to make it right.'

Kitty tried not to show her surprise. She knew that, deep down, Betty was kind at heart but often got carried away. However Kitty had never heard Betty make such an abject apology for her gossiping.

'Well. Good. Thank you for your apology, though it's not me you need to apologise to. However, I do apologise if I came across as a little brusque in my delivery yesterday.'

'Oh.' It was Betty's turn to look surprised. 'I don't think you have anything to apologise for. I. Well. I get carried away sometimes.'

Kitty smiled at Betty, relieved that the air had been cleared between the two of them.

'I'll leave you to it then. Bye.' Betty turned and went off to resume her shopping.

Kitty returned to Hetty who was by now putting her bright pink jacket on in preparation to leave. Bother, thought Kitty in frustration. It was tantalising to have received such a nugget of information regarding the root cause of Hetty's sadness, but to not know the relevance or context of it.

'Thanks,' said Hetty.

'I haven't done anything. But if you ever want to talk, I'm here for you. I mean it.' Kitty smiled and squeezed Hetty's arm in a show of comfort Hetty nodded and hurried to the exit, desperate not to have to engage in conversation with anyone else.

Kitty sat at the table drumming her fingers against her mug in frustration. What had Hetty been about to tell me, she wondered?

CHAPTER SEVENTEEN

After a couple of very busy days at work Kitty relished the prospect of having a day to do as she pleased on her mid-week day off. She'd not seen Bella since her relationship crisis meeting with Dave the previous Sunday, nor had she seen Ted after his boys weekend away and was looking forward to seeing him that evening

A few minutes before 10 a.m. Kitty pulled into the Oast Gym car park. She frowned. Strange, she thought, as she reversed her car into a parking space. Why is the car park so empty? The schools were in term, as far as she was aware fitness classes were going ahead and the roads were no longer blocked or impassable. So why were there only a handful of vehicles?

She stamped her feet on the mat to dispose of slush from her trainers and pushed the entrance door open. Tara greeted her with a cheery "hello" and a smile.

'It seems quiet today,' commented Kitty as she signed in. 'Where is everyone? Have classes been cancelled today?'

Tara's smile faltered momentarily, then she replied in a pleasant, but measured, manner. 'No. Classes are all going ahead as scheduled. Perhaps the snow we've had has disrupted members routines?' she suggested.

'I suppose it's possible,' replied Kitty, dubious.

She deposited her bags and coat in the empty changing room then headed into the gym for her workout. Bar one other member, it was deserted. What *is* going on? Kitty wondered again, mystified. Motivational music beat in the background as Kitty went through her routine, pushing herself hard in the hope that it would energise her for the rest of the day. Sweat was dripping down her by the time she finished, making the prospect of a hot shower with an icy blast of cold water at the end to make her body tingle, was most appealing. A couple of members were in the changing area when she emerged wrapped in a big fluffy white towel. Kitty smiled and retrieved her belongings from the locker then went into one of the spacious cubicles to get dressed. She was deep in her own thoughts when her attention was caught upon hearing mention of Venka and tuned into the conversation.

'… so Trish said that she isn't going to come to a gym which harbours a murderer,' said one of the women.

'That's what I'd heard too. And the others aren't coming here either until she's been sacked or they'll leave,' replied the other.

'They have *got* to do something. I mean, fancy having someone like that working here. Didn't they check her out before they employed her? I bet she was the one who attacked Zeno and not Andrew. Two crimes committed. What does that say about the management?'

Kitty heard the changing room door shut as the pair left, leaving her open-mouthed in shock from what they'd said. Was that the reason why the gym was so quiet? Were members boycotting it because of Venka? Based purely on unfounded gossip and rumours. Kitty could feel her blood begin to boil, furious at the situation. Poor Venka. Poor

Kim. Did she even know what some members were saying? Should she mention it to Kim? This could be devastating for both Venka and Kim. Had Betty, by spreading her gossip, created an enormous ripple effect? Kitty hurriedly finished getting changed whilst she deliberated and only partly dried her hair because she was due to meet Bella in the gym juice bar momentarily.

Apart from Bella and Kitty, the juice bar was deserted. Bella sipped her coffee whilst Kitty recounted the conversation she'd overheard, Bella's eyes grew wider as she listened to her friend.

'That's terrible,' said Bella once Kitty had finished.

'What do you think we should do? Do you think Kim is aware of the rumours?' asked Kitty.

'I don't know,' replied Bella. 'If she doesn't, then she must be wondering why daily attendance figures are down.'

'You know Kim better than me Bells,' said Kitty, using her nickname for Bella. 'Maybe you should speak to her? If it were me, I would want to know. Wouldn't you?'

Bella nodded thoughtfully. Kitty sipped her green juice silently, the fierceness of it - she'd opted for no fruit but extra ginger - bit at her throat, not entirely convinced that she liked the taste of it, but feeling that it had to be doing her some good.

'I'll go and find her after my workout. Her car was parked by the offices so she's around somewhere. I don't think there's anything else we can do, other than try to help nip the gossip in the bud, possibly too late, but we can try.'

'Okay,' replied Kitty, relieved that the onus was not going to be on her to tell Kim, though she felt an element of guilt from the fact that she had not burst out of her changing cubicle and confronted the members as soon as she'd overhead them. 'Anyway, how was your meeting with Dave? Did you manage to resolve anything?'

Bella looked glum. 'Not really. We've agreed to take yet another break. Not what I wanted, but he was very persistent. I feel like we either have to commit to one another and live together, or go our separate ways for good. He doesn't want to sell his house and is being stubborn about it. I obviously don't want to sell mine, having just moved in. As a compromise I suggested that we both rent out our houses and buy one together, then we can both put money in for the deposit and take out a joint mortgage. It could then be paid off equally by us each month and, in theory, there would still be excess rental money from both our properties, even having taken into consideration potential maintenance and taxation costs.'

'Seems like a sensible compromise. What's the problem?'

'"Financially a risk", according to Dave,' Bella sighed. 'I've done the figures and yes, there is a risk, but it is minimal. We are both very lucky to own our houses outright, nor have any loans or debt. Even if he retired early and I never worked again we'd get by and of course there would always be the option to sell one, or both, of the properties.'

Kitty frowned. To her it didn't sound as though Dave had any intention of committing long-term to Bella.

'I know I like my independence, as does he, and I know that we are both a little commitment phobic from our experiences of previous relationships, but it feels like we are treading water going nowhere.'

'Does your relationship *have* to go anywhere?' asked Kitty.

Bella looked puzzled. 'What do you mean?'

'If you both love each other and you both enjoy spending time together, does the next step have to be the traditional moving in together or getting married? Can't you both commit to being in a longterm relationship but live in your own houses? And, for example, stay over at each others houses when you like, either on specified days or on an ad hoc basis?'

'Oh.' replied Bella non-plussed. 'That seems very...' she searched for the right word, 'bohemian.'

'Maybe. But there's no rule to say that you couldn't. You'd still be a couple, perhaps taking holidays together, spending weekends together, or whatever works for you both.'

'Mmm. It's something to contemplate.' Bella brightened a little. 'Since when did you become such a radical thinker?'

Kitty laughed and waved her empty glass at her. 'Must be the juice affecting my brain.'

Bella grinned back. 'Well,' she said reluctantly, 'I'd better go and do my workout, then find Kim before she leaves to pick up Matilda from nursery or wherever she is today.'

Kitty stood up and gave her friend a big hug. 'Take care. Let me know how it goes with Kim and everything else.'

'Will do. Speak soon.'

They parted in reception and Kitty hurried home for a quick lunch and a play with Daisy before heading out to the scenic little town of Rye in East Sussex for the afternoon.

CHAPTER EIGHTEEN

Kitty parked in the Market Place car park adjacent to the railway station in Rye. The area was functional and barely gave a hint as to the picturesque delights which awaited visitors in the ancient town with its cobbled streets and eclectic array of historic buildings.

She walked up one of the steep cobbled paths which led up to the High Street. Even though Kitty had visited the town on numerous occasions it never ceased to amaze her that she could find something new to discover, or an historical gem she'd never noticed before. Timber framed Tudor period buildings nestled next to ones from the Georgian and Edwardian periods, creating a beautiful and eye catching ensemble. Whilst the shops no longer sold the wares which would have been on offer decades and centuries previously, there was still a pleasing array; clothing to hats, kitchenware to an old fashioned sweet shop, an excellent deli offering - amongst other things - local cheeses, a bookshop, numerous antique shops, gift shops and an admirable art gallery which had, it was believed, been established by Trust Deed in 1957 by the artist Mary Stormont, or possibly earlier.

In recent years Kitty had habitually begun her visits to the town with a visit to the small, but perfectly curated, chocolate shop. Not, however, one which sold chocolate to be eaten, but to be drunk. Approximately 20 different percentages of cocoa were on offer from which to choose, to consume either hot or cold, additionally there were three varieties of ice cream milkshakes to be tempted by, along with a small selection of tea, coffee and alternative cold drinks.

Kitty decided to opt for an 85% with oat milk hot chocolate and whilst she waited for her beverage to be made, she thought back to previous times, pre-pandemic, when the alternative to a takeaway drink was to perch on one of the stools inside the shop and sip the hot chocolate from a white bowl. Eagerly she took her drink and wrapped her hands around her reusable mug to warm them up, then walked back up towards the High Street where she began to browse in shop windows as she went. Kitty was so engrossed in admiring a sapphire and diamond ring in the window of a small antique jewellery shop, that she gave a little start when she heard her name being softly spoken from behind her. She glanced round and saw long, long hair which flowed down from beneath a navy cashmere beanie and a pair of sapphire blue eyes - similar in colour to the central stone of the ring Kitty had been looking intently at - peered back at her. Wound around the lower part of the woman's face and neck, from nose downwards, was a chunky-knit navy cashmere scarf. It took a moment for Kitty to realise that it was Ariadne.

'Hello,' said Kitty. 'Sorry. I didn't recognise you under all that cashmere.'

Ariadne laughed and tugged her scarf down a little, revealing a big smile. 'My disguise is working then,' she grinned, hastily pushing the scarf back up. She glanced furtively around to check that no one, other than Kitty, had recognised her, even though the town was fairly quiet - a Wednesday afternoon in the middle of winter - the tidal-wave of summer tourists long gone and a brief respite before the onslaught began again in a couple of months or so.

Despite Ariadne's so called "disguise", her whole being oozed glamour which in itself drew attention to her. From her beautifully cut navy pea-coat, to her skinny jeans and long, navy, suede, spikey-healed boots - not the most practical of foot-wear for tackling cobbles with though fortunately for her these were absent in the high street.

'I had one of those earlier,' said Ariadne with a nod towards Kitty's thermal mug, guessing where she'd been. 'I tried the 100% with soya which is definitely an acquired taste!' she joked. 'Mind if I accompany you?' she asked.

'Not at all,' replied Kitty, surprised and rather over-awed.

Amicably they strolled along together, chatting, dipping in and out of shops, whiling away the afternoon. Kitty couldn't quite believe that she was spending the afternoon in the presence of, what she perceived to be, a Hollywood Mega Star, but found that as the minutes ticked by she felt more and more relaxed with her. Ariadne came across as so normal, so down to earth.

'Do you fancy stopping for some tea and cake?' suggested Ariadne once they had weaved their way around the town, including a visit to the church and surrounding streets such as Mermaid Street, past Lamb House; where E F Benson had lived for a while and where he had drawn inspiration for his renowned Mapp and Lucia series of books.

'Why not,' replied Kitty. 'Where do you fancy?'

'I don't know. Where would you recommend? Preferably somewhere quiet.' added Ariadne, who was relishing the anonymity.

'Um,' pondered Kitty, wracking her brains as they paused on the edge of Church Square. 'I'm not sure really. It's so quiet here at the moment that I feel we'd be ok in any of the cafes. How about we see if the old tea shop just down here is open? Or we could sit outside the cinema? I think we're both wrapped up enough and its outdoor area is tucked back from the street, I very much doubt that any one else will be sitting outside in this weather.'

'Whichever offers the most privacy is fine by me. Let's have a look shall we?' replied Ariadne.

The old tea shop with its low beams and window filled with a delectable display of cakes looked inviting, however there were a number of people seated at tables throughout the shop. In contrast, there was no one sitting outside the independent two screen cinema which was located within the Old School House.

Ariadne tucked herself out of sight of the street as best she could whilst Kitty ventured inside to make their order. Inside were approximately half a dozen people waiting in the cafe area prior to watching a film. The windows were above standard height which precluded them from seeing Ariadne.

'Here we are,' said Kitty, placing down two plates; one with a slice of lemon drizzle and one with a slice of coffee and walnut cake on. 'Which would you like?' she offered.

Ariadne chose the lemon drizzle, moments later a friendly member of staff brought out two pots of Earl Grey tea. The young woman carefully placed them down onto the table along with cups, saucers, a jug of milk and some sugar, then looked up. Her mouth dropped open in recognition of whom she was serving, stunned to see Ariadne, blushed, smiled nervously, then hurried back inside.

'Oh dear.' said Kitty.

Ariadne shrugged.

'Don't you find it irritating to not be able to go anywhere without being recognised?' asked Kitty, curious.

Ariadne sighed and shrugged again. 'Yes, sometimes, but I always try to be pleasant. I remind myself that without the paying public making the choice to go and see my films, I'd be out of a job. It's as simple as that. The fact that I am well known is the price I have to pay for being so fortunate and having had such a successful career, one which has provided me with financial security and opened up many doors to opportunities I could never have imagined possible for me. It would be churlish of me to complain, rather like biting the hand which feeds me so to speak. It doesn't mean to say that the persistent intrusion into my private life isn't challenging though.'

Kitty nodded. 'But isn't being tucked away here in the countryside too quiet for you? After all, I am assuming, you must have a very full social life in both L.A. and London and probably all over the world?'

Ariadne wrinkled her nose. 'I can't deny I haven't enjoyed my life in L.A. in the past and I do enjoy going out and having a good time, but the allure of that lifestyle has waned over the past couple of years. Perhaps it's because I am getting older?' She said, pausing to sip her tea. 'And maybe it's also because I have stopped deluding myself and accepted that many of the people with whom I have associated myself with aren't genuine friends. I feel they have only been around me because of what they have perceived I can offer them access to, often a stepping stone to something bigger and better for themselves. I doubt many would actually be there for me in a crisis. In fact,' she corrected herself, 'they haven't, apart from four people who I have been able to count on,' reflected Ariadne sadly.

'There are people here, apart from Sophie, who'd be there for you, if you let them. Offer support if you need, or needed, it,' said Kitty.

Ariadne nodded. 'Yes. I am starting to realise that.'

'Do you think you'll spend more time here? Put down roots? Even buy a house?'

Ariadne hesitated. 'I'm considering it. I...' she stopped. 'We'll see.'

Kitty's curiosity was piqued and she flicked through her memory for properties she felt might appeal to Ariadne, but decided that now was not the moment to offer suggestions. Instead she changed the subject. 'Are you enjoying your P.T. with Venka?' she asked.

'Definitely. She is getting me into shape.' Ariadne smiled broadly.

'How's she coping?' asked Kitty. 'With everything going on, covering for Zeno and... other stuff?'

'Fine, as far as I know,' replied Ariadne, before deflecting swiftly by asking. 'How's your kitten?'

When they became too cold from sitting outside, they walked back to their respective vehicles to warm up, darkness had fallen and the temperature along with it.

Driving cautiously up Wynenden Farm Lane towards home, Kitty saw a shadow ahead, the moonlight reflected off the snow into areas usually swallowed up by the darkness of night. She slowed the car and saw a red bobble on a hat move just as a figure stepped backwards into the hedge in an attempt to obscure themselves from Kitty's view. A frisson of nerves rippled through Kitty and she gulped. The beam from the car headlights swept across a dark leg as she turned the car left into the entrance to her drive. She braced herself and peered intently into the frost laden foliage, then let out a sigh of relief; it was Hetty. But what was she doing hiding amongst the trees and hedge in a temperature of -5 degrees celsius? wondered Kitty, feeling rather bemused.

She lowered the window a fraction and called out to her. 'You ok Hetty?'

The figure hesitated, then stepped forward.

'Would you like to come in?' suggested Kitty, nodding towards the house. 'Or I could drive you home if you'd prefer?' she offered. 'Or both.'

'Um,' replied Hetty.

'Tell you what. Come in whilst you decide and I'll pop the kettle on.' Kitty eased her car onto the snow covered gravel drive, gathered her bags and got out. 'Brrr. It's freezing out here. Quite literally,' she commented, as she led the way to the front door, Hetty following in her wake.

'Here we are,' said Kitty, stamping her feet before taking her boots off in the hallway. Not for the first time was she glad that she had installed underfloor heating beneath the stone floors downstairs as warmth seeped through her socks. Hetty followed suit and they went into the kitchen.

A joyful Daisy was standing in the middle of the room waiting expectantly for her owner, mewing an enthusiastic greeting.

'Oh, she is *so* adorable!' exclaimed Hetty, immediately dropping to her knees to tickle and stroke the kitten, who in response cranked up the volume of her purring to demonstrate her pleasure at the attention.

'I think so,' replied Kitty proudly, as if receiving a compliment on a newborn baby. It always fascinated her the way pets could draw even the most reserved of people out of themselves and Hetty was no exception.

'Tea?' offered Kitty, as Hetty, now crossed legged on the floor, continued to tickle and cuddle a very appreciative Daisy.

'Yes please.'

With the tea brewed, Kitty said. 'Let's go through to the garden room,' and led the way through from the kitchen, carrying both mugs. She put them down on to a side table then sank into one of the sofas. Hetty, cuddling Daisy, resumed her position on the floor and propped herself against the back of the wall and glass opposite Kitty.

Kitty sipped her tea and watched Hetty's animated face as she kissed, tickled and played with the energised ball of fluff.

'I would love to have a kitten,' commented Hetty. 'It must be so nice to snuggle up with her all the time. To have a little living being there when you need her.' Tears welled up in Hetty's eyes. 'But I can't possibly have one in my room at the pub. It's a nice place to live, but its not my home, it doesn't feel like home and I've got no prospect of every owning a house and making it feel home. Particularly now.' She looked miserably at Daisy, who was curled up on her lap preparing for yet another nap.

'Particularly now? Why? What's happened Hetty?' Kitty reached over, picked up Hetty's mug of tea and passed it to her.

Hetty took it gratefully and sipped whilst contemplating what, if anything, to say. 'I've got no family,' she said eventually, 'but I have some good friends. It's just... They wouldn't understand, so they don't know. And we both wanted it kept private.'

Kitty waited, intrigued.

'I.' Hetty glanced at Kitty, then looked away. 'I'm not sure *anyone* would understand.'

'Try me,' suggested Kitty gently, smiling encouragingly at Hetty, who in turn glanced quickly away.

There was another prolonged silence, Hetty weighing up the pros and cons in her head as to how to respond. Eventually she spoke.

'It worked well for us both. Fun. No commitment. And he was kind. No one else saw, or wanted to see, that in him.'

Kitty frowned. Who? To whom was she referring?

'In-between his relationships, and occasionally during. It worked for us. He was a good listener. He made me laugh, feel happy, and also hopeful about the life ahead of me. He was a good friend and the sex, well, he had a lot of energy,' she blushed and snatched a glance at Kitty, who in turn was transfixed by what Hetty was telling her. 'He really did give me hope. And he helped me out, both as a friend and financially. I was saving for a deposit to rent a nice flat or - and that was my ultimate dream - to buy a little house. He gave good advice too. I simply don't know what I am going to do without him.' She looked beseechingly at Kitty.

'I'm sorry,' replied Kitty. 'Whoever it is that you are referring to sounds as though he was a good friend to you.

But what has happened? Has he found someone else? Moved? Fallen out with you? I don't understand.'

Hetty paused. 'He's. He's,' tears flooded down her cheeks. 'He's not here anymore.'

'Oh Hetty! I'm so sorry. How awful for you.' Kitty knew from bitter personal experience what it was like to be abandoned by someone you had believed cared deeply about you. She got up and lowered herself on to the floor next to Hetty and hugged her. Hetty's tense body gradually relaxed into Kitty's arms, then she wept, great, loud, body-wracking sobs. Crying in a way that she hadn't been able to since he'd left. Crying until she felt exhausted, her face red and puffy.

'Is it anyone I know?' asked Kitty, gently. 'Perhaps you could speak to him? Even if it is over between you two it may still help to bring some kind of closure?'

Hetty looked at her, startled. 'I thought you'd guessed?'

Kitty frowned and shook her head. 'No. I…' then it dawned on her. It couldn't be? Surely not? 'You don't mean…' her voice trailed off.

Hetty nodded.

CHAPTER NINETEEN

Kitty sat in a stunned silence whilst Hetty shifted nervously on the floor, studiously focussing on Daisy.

'You're. You are disgusted aren't you?' Hetty uttered haltingly.

'No. Not at all,' replied Kitty. 'It's just that it is rather a shock. I mean. Andrew. Why him of all people? The person you've just described to me was the polar opposite to the one I, and many others, have encountered.'

Hetty shrugged. 'At first I felt the same as you. But one night he was the last customer in the pub, I was on my own, feeling down about splitting up with my boyfriend and we somehow connected. He talked. I talked. He revealed a completely different side to himself. After that we would occasionally chat after hours. There was nothing physical then. It was good to be able to be honest about how I felt about my life and I believe he felt the same.'

Kitty listened intently, then asked. 'Do you often feel that you have to hide how you are truly feeling? That you can't be honest about what's going on in your life?'

Hetty nodded, simultaneously chewing on her bottom lip. 'Yes. I've always been the people pleaser. Bringing people together. Making them feel better about themselves. Trying to help other people resolve their problems. But in doing so, I've come to realise that I neglect myself, shut things away and ignore my emotions. Don't get me wrong, I love the potential that, in some tiny way, I may bring a little light into other peoples lives, that's why I adore my job so much.' She looked at Kitty, hopeful for some kind of validation.

Kitty smiled. 'You do. You come across as bright and bubbly and customers love that, I know I do.' She paused. 'But I find it sad that you feel you had no one to turn to other than Andrew and quite frankly I am surprised that he could be so understanding. From my perspective he always came across as ruthless, heartless even. The fact that he had turned his back on his family, including his mother who is apparently living hand to mouth and struggling day to day, is just one example.'

Hetty opened her mouth, then shut it. Then opened it again. 'I'm not going to go into detail. It's private and Andrew trusted me and I am not going to betray him.' Her voice wobbled as she spoke and tears pricked at her eyes again. 'But what I will say, is that there was more to it than met the eye. Stuff from his childhood few knew about and that's the way he wanted it. So, yes, he could come across as heartless, but to me he wasn't. He was ruthless in business, pushing boundaries and could be unethical - I called him out time and again on his actions - he'd had no moral guidance as a child, no foundation, so saw nothing wrong in his behaviour, in pushing the law to the limit. But, believe it or not, he was beginning to soften, to at least comprehend that his actions could have consequences on a much deeper level.'

'Really?' Kitty was highly sceptical.

Hetty nodded. 'Yes, you may not believe me, but he did.'

'But if the two of you connected on such a level, why was he dating so many other women? Why didn't you become a couple?'

'Wrong time really. When we first got to know one another three years ago, I was only 22 and he was 35, ridiculously the age difference seemed too great then, besides he was very focussed on work and playing the field. I also thought that it wouldn't be long before I was off doing something with my life, somewhere else in the world...'

'You still could. But what stopped you doing so back then?'

Hetty pursed her lips, then blew out. 'Money. Lack of self-belief. Low self-esteem. A sense of duty and responsibility. Things Andrew has really helped me with. Helped me to believe in myself.' She shrugged and looked at the floor as tears streamed down her cheeks again. 'What am I going to do without him?' she cried. 'I've lost my best friend.'

Comforting her, Kitty held Hetty in a tight hug until her sobs had subsided. 'You'll be ok. It's a cliché I know, but time does help to heal, maybe not completely, it could take weeks, months or even years. Grieving is a very personal, very individual experience. But one thing I can guarantee is that you will always have the memories you shared with him, no one can take them away from you and if he encouraged you and helped you to build up your self-esteem and self-belief then, even if the memories fade a little, he will have helped you more than you currently believe.'

Hetty wiped away the snot running down from her nostrils with the back of her hand and gave a noisy sniff.

'I suppose so,' she replied thoughtfully.

'Did you only ever meet after hours in the pub?' asked Kitty inquisitively.

'No. We'd also meet at his house. Very occasionally he'd take me out for dinner, but miles away from here to minimise the risk of bumping into anyone either of us knew. I felt that it would affect my work in the pub, you know, if people thought that we were together, and he wanted to keep himself on the market for other women.' She smiled at a memory. 'But I was the one who really knew him. The others thought they did, but they didn't. He wasn't into serious relationships. Many of them wanted commitment which only made Andrew run a mile. The fact that I wasn't looking for that - and the sex was great - made us a perfect fit.'

'Perhaps I'm out of touch with modern life, but if you got on so well, could confide in one another, enjoyed each others company and had a great sex life, isn't that what would be called a relationship?'

'Maybe, but usually when Andrew was with another woman - be it for weeks or months - we didn't have sex. There were a few exceptions, but there was an unspoken understanding between us and none of his other women knew about me.'

Kitty looked thoughtfully at Hetty, carefully formulating her next question. 'I guess if it worked for you both that's what counted. When was the last time you saw him?' she asked in an attempt at a casual manner.

Hetty looked down at Daisy and tickled the soft, white, fur under her chin.

'I…'

There was a sudden slam which made them both jump. Daisy leapt off Hetty's lap and skittled through to the kitchen.

'Hello?' called a voice. 'I'm here.' It was Ted.

'We're in here,' called out Kitty getting up off the floor, slightly irritated by his unintentional bad timing.

Ted's cheery face appeared, a momentary glimpse of surprise flicked across it when he saw Hetty who had also scrambled to her feet.

'Hello Hetty. Nice to see you,' he said pleasantly. 'How are you?'

Kitty frowned at him and shook her head. A look he failed to interpret.

'Ok thanks Ted. Well, I'd best be off. No it's fine, I'll walk, but thank you,' she said in response to Kitty's repeat offer of a lift home.

'Not at all. I won't hear of it. I'll run you back,' said Ted.

'No, really, it's fine Ted, but thank you anyway.

'I'll do it,' interjected Kitty, hoping that it wouldn't be too late to pick up the thread of their interrupted conversation.

'Nope. You stay here in the warm. I've still got my coat on and Ella's in the car so I've got to go out again to fetch her anyway.'

'Well. If you're sure. Thank you. And thanks Kitty.'

'Anytime.' She hugged Hetty tightly.

Hetty nodded.

Ted picked up the ferociously mewing kitten who was standing by his feet and who, until that moment, had failed to attract his attention, he kissed the top of her head and murmured that he'd be back shortly.

Kitty lay down on the sofa in the garden room to mull over what Hetty had told her. Daisy immediately jumped onto her and kneaded Kitty's stomach with her tiny ginger paws, purring loudly.

'Supper's ready,' said Ted softly to the still sleeping body he had returned to.

'Mmmm,' mumbled Kitty, blinking, confused.

'Are you feeling ok?' asked Ted as she came too. 'It's not like you to fall asleep early in the evening.'

Kitty slid herself up into a sitting position, careful to ensure that Daisy was not disturbed, and rubbed her eyes.

'Yes. Fine. I had no idea I was so tired. One minute I was awake, the next…' her voice trailed off.

Ted could see that Kitty was distracted and was worried that there was something wrong, despite her protestations that there wasn't.

Having assured Hetty that she could trust her, that anything Hetty told her would be in confidence, Kitty had to refrain from telling Ted, though she wished that she could confide in him. Her promise also meant that she couldn't tell Bella.

Kitty awoke on Saturday morning having slept for hours and felt less exhausted than she had over the previous couple of days. She rolled over to snuggle up to Ted but found his side of the bed empty and the duvet tossed back. She sank back, rubbed her eyes and stretched again. There was a loud, high-pitched, squeaky mew followed by a flash of ginger as Daisy leapt up onto the bed and landed on Kitty.

The faint rattle of crockery grew louder as it approached up the stairs, then Ted appeared in the doorway with a tray laid with Kitty's breakfast. She shifted herself up and tucked another pillow behind her.

'Ooh, lovely,' she said as he placed it onto her lap; a bowl of porridge, some toast and a camomile tea. Hungrily she spooned a mouthful of porridge in and then came to an abrupt halt. 'You're dressed,' she frowned. Usually, if Ted stayed over on a Friday night, they would snuggle up and have breakfast together in bed before he went to work for the morning. 'Why?'

He smiled. 'Have you seen the time?'

She glanced at the small silver clock on her bedside table which had belonged to her mother. '9 o'clock!' she yelped. 'How did that happen?!'

He laughed. 'You were sound asleep and I didn't want to wake you.' He kissed her lingeringly full on the lips. 'I'll see you at lunchtime. Take it easy, have a nice relaxing morning.'

She resumed munching on her breakfast. 'Bloody menopause,' she muttered under her breath, resolving to go online when she got up and book an appointment with her G.P. to discuss her options, having failed to do so the other day. She'd heard stories from friends who were at the same time of life as her; the fact that doctors currently received little or no training on the menopause - which affected every single woman later in life - meant that the advice a G.P. was able to offer varied wildly from one doctor to another, even from within the same practice. What Kitty found just as shocking was the number of perimenopausal women who were misdiagnosed and instead treated for depression, when, in general, they weren't depressed but were suffering from low moods due to their oestrogen levels falling which also affected the body in a multitude of different ways.

Kitty herself had gone onto a menopause website recommended to her, one which had been set up by a G.P. who specialised in the menopause and was fact based. It had been a real eye opener for Kitty and made her realise just how much misinformation circulated on social media and in the written press, so it was hardly surprising that a vast number of women were confused or very concerned about taking HRT. Some of the stories she had read were completely inaccurate and not at all based on scientific fact - scaremongering at its worst - the upshot being that many women weren't in the position to be able to make an informed choice for themselves.

Gloomily Kitty sat in bed and contemplated the implications; that she was getting old.

Her mobile pinged, it was a message from Bella. 'Oh bother!' exclaimed Kitty at the reminder that she was supposed to have been at the gym with her and was now almost an hour after they had pre-arranged to meet. Hastily she replied, apologising and arranging to meet Bella at the farmers' market in half an hour.

Twenty minutes later, with her breakfast accoutrements abandoned in the kitchen sink, Kitty kissed Daisy and hurried out of the house into the chilly air, the sky mottled with clouds, sunshine intermittently appearing from behind them.

'Sorry!' she said breathlessly, hastening over to Bella who was waiting at the entrance to the village hall. 'Woke up late and forgot,' she grinned.

Bella kissed Kitty's cheek then tucked her arm into Kitty's. 'Forgiven. Just this once though,' she winked.

'Gosh it is busy today,' commented Bella when they had finished their shopping - even Bread Man had beaten them that day. 'I can't see any tables available.'

'Venka's got two spare seats, over there,' said Kitty pointing to the far side of the hall. 'Let's ask if we can join her and Valentina?' suggested Kitty.

Valentina squealed with excitement when she saw Kitty and Bella heading in her direction and slithered off her chair to give them a hug, her little arms wrapping themselves around Kitty's legs, clinging on like a limpet. Eventually Kitty managed to extricate the bubbly little girl and sit down, only for Valentina to try and scramble up onto her lap. She scooped the brightly dressed girl up and listened as she chattered happily away whilst simultaneously twisting the fringe of Kitty's navy wool scarf around her little fingers. She looks so like her mother, thought Kitty.

Today Venka's hair was as bright a red as the top of a matchstick and she looked less tired than when Kitty had previously seen her.

'Good news about Zeno,' commented Bella, placing their drinks down onto the table.

'Yes. I'm very happy that he's out of hospital and back at his flat,' replied Venka.

'Is Dezo still fussing around him like a mother hen?' asked Kitty.

Venka laughed. 'Apparently so. He's doing his food shopping for him and pops in most days after his workout.'

'I gather from Ditzi that Dezo can be a little bit full-on when he has a "pet project" as she calls his whims. All coming from a good place even though it is a little strange.'

'Hmm,' added Bella.

They looked quizzically at her.

'"Hmm" what?' asked Kitty.

'Well.' Bella stopped and looked at Valentina who was nodding off to sleep on Kitty's lap, scarf fringe wrapped around fingers, gently sucking her thumb and stroking the wool on the end of her nose.

'Well what?' said Venka to Bella.

'It *is* a little odd. Unless there is something we don't know about.'

Kitty frowned. 'Such as?'

Bella gave a little shrug.

Then the penny dropped as to what Bella was alluding to. Kitty's eyes opened wide. 'Don't be ridiculous. He adores Ditzi.' She lowered her voice. 'And besides he's not, you know…'

'Interested in men?' added Venka.

'Maybe,' replied Bella. 'But no one really knows what goes on behind closed doors. Just saying.' She shrugged again.

'No. I don't believe it. I hope you've not said this to anyone else?' reprimanded Kitty sternly.

'Kitty! You ought to know me better than that.' Bella scowled at her friend.

'I think I'd better get Valentina home. She was up at 5 a.m. so it's hardly surprising that she's tired,' said Venka rising from her chair, unwilling to be drawn in further on the subject.

They waited until Venka and Valentina had departed, then Bella leaned towards Kitty and, in a fierce whisper, said. 'I take exception to you believing that I would spread this around. You know me better than that. I merely made the comment on the spur of the moment and I wouldn't have done so if it were anyone other than you and Venka sitting here.'

'Sorry if I offended you Bell's, but I can't believe you said something like that in front of someone else, let alone Venka, or have you forgotten what good friends she and Zeno are? Don't you think that she'll tell him? And he in turn might tell Dezo. What then? Think how it could affect our friendship with Ditzi, apart from them all believing that we - or rather you - are a gossip and spreading hurtful rumours about them?'

Bella looked crestfallen. 'Oh no!' she exclaimed. 'Here come Dezo and Ditzi,' she added, blushing deeply.

'This won't be awkward then,' muttered Kitty under her breath.

'Mind if we join you ?' asked Ditzi cheerily.

'Not at all.' replied Kitty. 'Lovely to see you both.' She smiled at them but could almost feel the heat radiating off Bella in her embarrassment.

Dutifully Dezo went off to purchase tea and coffee for them whilst Kitty chatted to Ditzi. Bella tried to smile, even though her insides felt like they were in the grip of a vice, and just about managed a weak smile when Dezo sat down, furtively glanced at Kitty, who narrowed her eyes back at her.

'What?' asked Ditzi. 'Am I missing something?' she smiled.

Kitty looked at Bella, who in turn looked beseechingly back at her.

With a groan of resignation, Bella put her head in her hands.

'Bella? Are you alright? What's wrong?' Ditzi looked alarmed and Dezo's face was etched with concern.

Bella lifted her head. There was nothing for it. She would have to confess.

'I'm sorry,' she started, looking from one to the other.

'Sorry? For what?' asked Dezo.

Bella blushed again, more deeply and vividly than Kitty had ever seen her friend do so before.

'I.' She hesitated. 'We.' She indicated to Kitty who scowled, hoping that Bella wasn't about to drag her into what she felt was a misplaced accusation, 'were talking to Venka just now. Chatting. And I said what good news it was that Zeno was home. And, well, we were puzzled as to why you have been going to see him so much Dezo, not that it's any of our business. But then I, and I can't believe I said it, or rather implied that perhaps there was, something… you know…' she tried to clear the frog in her throat, 'um, else going on…' her voice trailed off and she hung her head in shame, fearful to look at them.

'Going on?' said Dezo, a hard edge to his voice. 'Like what?'

Ditzi clutched her husbands hand tightly.

'Um…' gulped Bella. 'Like an affair…' Tears welled up. 'I am so, so sorry. I know there's nothing like that going on. It's so obvious that you two adore and are devoted to one another. I've no idea why I said something so unkind and unwarranted. Please, please forgive me,' she begged. She looked pleadingly at them.

Kitty didn't know what to do with herself or where to look, so embarrassed was she by the conversation.

Bella would have preferred it if they shouted at her, or at least said something, but there was just silence.

'Go on,' murmured Ditzi to Dezo encouragingly, softly, squeezing his hand. 'Tell them. It's time they knew. Time everyone knew. It's what you want.' She looked down, avoiding both Bella and Kitty's gaze.

CHAPTER TWENTY

Once they had reconvened to the vast kitchen at Wynenden Hall, Ditzi distracted herself by making hot drinks for the four of them whilst Bella and Kitty sat ensconced in one of the large, comfy white sofas in the orangery, which the kitchen opened into. Despite her wonderment at the stunning kitchen, Bella, like Kitty, was on tenterhooks waiting impatiently to find out what Dezo was going to tell them. She was trying hard not to jump to conclusions, but her mind was whirling with possibilities; was he actually having an affair with Zeno? Was his marriage a sham and just for show?

'Dezo,' said Ditzi, as she placed the drinks down onto the glass coffee-table which was equidistant between the two sofas. She patted the seat next to her. Dezo, who had been pacing nervously around, did so with reluctance but obediently sat down next to his wife. Beads of perspiration bubbled on his bald head and he brushed the sweat away from his brows with the back of his hand. A protracted silence ensued, Kitty and Bella gripped their mugs in anticipation, whilst Ditzi plucked at the bottom edge of her cashmere jumper, giving the impression that she was deep in contemplation.

Several times Dezo cleared his throat, on each occasion he gave an involuntary twitch to the left side of his neck. His usual overtly-confident and jolly persona had vanished.

'It's not something I'm ashamed of,' he started nervously, snatching a fleeting glance at Bella and Kitty. 'I never realised. Not really,' he continued, 'but I suppose I wasn't surprised once I had got over the shock.' He paused, searching for the right words. 'Perhaps, on some level deep down, I knew.' He half shrugged as though to convince himself. 'I. We,' he corrected himself, 'wanted to be sure before,' he looked at Ditzi, who in response slid her hand across and held his right hand tightly, 'before I told Ditzi. I didn't want to hurt her. She is such a darling to me, but I couldn't ignore it. This is something we - Zeno and I - are in for the long-term. For the rest of our lives, which of course will, and does, affect Ditzi. It will have a huge impact on her. On us. But. Well,' he placed his other hand over hers, stroking it and gazing into her eyes.

Bloody Hell! Thought Bella and Kitty, stealing a glance at one another. Never in a million years would they have believed that Bella's wild accusation would turn out to be spot on. How could he do that to Ditzi, they wondered? She was so devoted to her husband.

'My feelings for him were. Are,' he corrected himself, 'overwhelming. I never expected, nor have experienced such an intensity of emotion, on a different level to anything else I have ever felt before and so completely different to how I feel about Ditzi whom I absolutely adore and is my world. She has been amazing. Beyond supportive. Just incredible. I am, so, so blessed to have her as my wife. She's been so open to this relationship. I really can't express how deeply I love her and for the compassion she has shown towards me.' His voice was thick with emotion and he brushed a rare tear from his eye.

Bella and Kitty were stunned. They had felt sure that they were open-minded individuals, but they were both struggling to get their heads around the implication of what Dezo was telling them. What was going to happen? Would the three of them live together? How could Ditzi remain so calm? Because of their own previous experiences of relationships they both felt that, if they were in her position, the situation would prove to be too much of a massive challenge. Irrespective of who their spouse was having an affair with, they felt as though it was the worst kind of betrayal.

'For the time being Zeno is going to stay in his flat. Ditzi has been generous and kind and has said that he is welcome here anytime, that he's part of our unit. The three of us.' He smiled with adoration at Ditzi.

Bloody Hell, thought Kitty again. Was this a joke? The circumstances sounded more like a scenario for a book or storyline for a film.

'So now you know,' he finished and looked from one to the other. 'My hope is that the everyone will be welcoming and accepting once they find out.'

'He's shocked you hasn't he?' said Ditzi softly.

They shut their open mouths which had dropped open again, then nodded.

'Do you think people will get used to the idea? In a few weeks I would hope that we'll be old news. I want to protect Ditzi from gossip as much as possible. Kitty? Bella?' he asked.

'I,' stuttered Kitty. 'Bella. What do you think?'

She narrowed her eyes at Kitty. 'I,' she said tentatively, choosing her words carefully. 'I'm not sure how. Um. Open-minded people are in these parts...' her voice trailed off. What Dezo had said had stirred up the feelings of loss that she still felt about her late husband. For her, marriage was supposed to be for life, but Bella understood that, ultimately, it didn't matter what anyone else thought, if Ditzi felt comfortable with the set-up, then it was no one else's business.

Dezo frowned. 'I know it's shocking, but it's not unheard of. Not that extraordinary.'

'Not that unheard of?!' exploded Kitty, whose anger had been bubbling away for the past few minutes, memories of how her husband had treated her forced at full throttle to the front of her mind again.

Dezo and Ditzi looked shocked by the ferocity of her outburst.

'Having an affair. With a younger. *Much* younger person. Of the opposite sex to your wife, whom you claim you are so devoted to, and then expecting her to welcome him in and accept the pair of you as a couple. You know,' she waved her hand wildly around, 'doing it here. In her home. Her house. Your marital home. I doubt if there is *anyone* in the village who will understand,' she shouted, red faced from fury.

Dezo and Ditzi stared wide eyed at Kitty's outburst. There was a deafening silence. Then Dezo chuckled.

'I can't believe I forgot,' he chortled. 'I'm so sorry. I thought I had. Didn't you darling?' He looked at her and she nodded. 'I'm not having an *affair* with Zeno. Each to their own and all that, but it's not my thing, Zeno is my *son*.'

'You're son?' uttered Bella eventually.

He nodded. 'Yes. I had no idea until Zeno contacted me a little while ago, long before he was attacked at the gym. Apparently his mother had told him at a very young age that his father wasn't around and he had always assumed she'd meant dead. It was only a couple of years ago, when he finally saw his birth certificate, that he discovered who his father was. However, it had my birth name on it, rather than the name I changed it to, so he spent a lot of time researching and trying to find out more about me and wondering why he kept hitting a dead end. Finally, he managed to discover that I had changed my name by deed poll, and subsequently that I was not only alive, but was living in Wynenden. It must be a one in a several million chance to find us both living in the same county, let alone almost the same village.' Dezo paused, allowing his words to sink in before continuing. 'He then contacted me. Naturally I was very suspicious to start with - lots of opportunists out there - but we both did DNA tests and the results came back proving that he was, beyond doubt, my son. His mother died some time ago so I will never be able to ask her why she didn't tell me that I was a father. I've missed out on so much of his life.' He looked away sadly. 'I was 34 when he was born and still pretty irresponsible and had other issues too. Perhaps that's why she didn't tell me?' He looked thoughtful, contemplating this.

'Gosh,' stuttered Kitty, sweating from embarrassment by her outburst. 'I am *so* sorry for what I have just said. Please forgive me?'

'Oh Kitty,' said Ditzi, 'there's nothing to forgive. Our fault entirely. Given what you thought Dezo was implying, I feel you were rather restrained.' she joked.

'Thank you. I do feel such a fool. I am so sorry.' she repeated.

'It's me who should be ashamed,' interrupted Bella. 'I'm the one who implied that you and Zeno were having an affair. I am so very sorry too. I really am.'

Dezo smiled broadly. 'Think nothing of it. It's forgotten. Now, why don't I put some bacon into the Aga and make us bacon sandwiches for lunch? It's about the only thing I am good at cooking! Thank goodness Ditzi is a wonderful cook or I would have to live off nothing else!' He put his arm around her, pulling her tightly to him and kissed the top of her head tenderly.'

He walked towards the fridge, turned his head and asked. 'So. Do you think people in the village will accept us as a family? Or do you think it will be too shocking for them?' he winked, beaming a dazzling smile at them.

Whilst chewing on her last mouthful of a particularly delicious bacon sandwich; crisp and crunchy bacon, tomato ketchup, a touch of rocket all nestled within a soft sourdough roll fresh from the farmers' market, Kitty's phone began to ping with messages. She ignored it, but when it had pinged twice more she went and rummaged in her bag to retrieve it.

'Oh no!' she cried.

'Everything okay?' asked Bella.

'Yes. No. Bother. I completely forgot that I was supposed to be meeting Ted at home for lunch.' By now it was 2.30. 'What an idiot I am!' She slapped her forehead and rolled her eyes, quickly texting back to say that she was ok and would be back shortly. 'Apologies, but I'm going to have to go.'

'You have nothing to apologise for,' smiled Ditzi.

'Thank you for a delicious lunch,' she said as she kissed Dezo, Ditzi and Bella in turn. 'And for telling us your news. I will spread the word when appropriate moments arise as per your wishes. Bye.' She hurried out of the kitchen followed by Ditzi.

'Thank you,' said Ditzi, giving Kitty a big hug.

'For what?' asked Kitty, surprised.

'For being lovely. For being understanding.'

'Not at all, you are too kind Ditzi. Take care of yourself. Let me know if there is anything I can do to help, or even if you just want to talk. You're amazing.' She gave Ditzi's arm a little squeeze then left.

Kitty was curled up on the sofa in the garden room next to Ted, Daisy tucked into the crook of his arm asleep.

'... so that's it. Bit of a surprise wouldn't you say?' She had just recounted to him the events of her day so far.

Ted nodded. 'Nice for them both to have discovered one another, even if it is 28 years late. I imagine it is going to provide plenty of fodder for the gossips around here for a while. Still, I suppose it'll take their minds of speculating about Andrew's death. And, of course, there'll be those who ridiculously abandoned the gym because of rumours about Venka, who will come back hot on the trail of gossip about Dezo and Zeno. Do you think Kim knows yet?'

'From what Dezo said, Zeno is planning to tell to her today. Kim's been so good to him - almost like family - and he wants her to be one of the first to know, to not hear it second-hand.'

He nodded. 'Sounds like a wise idea. Anyway, I've been meaning to ask, are you ok? It's just that you have looked a bit peaky recently and you don't seem to have been yourself these last few weeks.'

Kitty flushed and looked away. Time to confess. But would he still love her?' she thought irrationally.

'There's something I've not told you,' she began hesitantly, seeing him frown in concern. 'You're right. I've not been feeling myself. I've ignored it for a while and I know I've been a bit, um, hormonal,' she gave a slight grimace at this understatement. 'I didn't want to say anything in case. In case.' Tears pricked at her eyes.

'In case what?' he asked softly, stroking her knees soothingly.

She gulped. 'In case you don't love me or find me attractive any more.' He looked alarmed and she braced herself. 'I. I. I think the menopause has begun.' She couldn't bring herself to look at him again for fear of the look she'd see.

There was a long pause.

'Is that it? Nothing else?' he asked.

She shook her head.

'Phew! You had me worried there. And why would I love you less or not be attracted to you because of that? You're still the woman I love.'

'Really?' Relief flooded through her.

'Yes. Of course, you silly thing. Come here.' He scooped his arm around her and cuddled her, careful not to disturb the kitten nestled in the crook of his other arm.

Kitty promptly burst into tears and sobbed, eventually blowing her nose to alleviate the sniffing.

'It must be horrible for you. I gather that there are many symptoms of menopause. I really hope that you aren't suffering too much, but perhaps that's a stupid thing to say?'

She looked at him in astonishment. 'How do you know anything about the menopause?' she asked.

'My sister,' he smiled, pleased with himself. 'She's perimenopausal - it's not termed the menopause until a full year has passed since the last period - so she's been telling me all about it, though I imagine every woman experiences it differently.'

'Wow! You have got to be the only male on the planet who knows anything about it. I'm seriously impressed. And you're okay about it? I've been meaning to make an appointment with my G.P. to talk through my options, you know, HRT or not or whatever.'

'Good idea. Just make sure you see one who is clued up on the subject.'

Kitty laughed. 'Your sisters advice again?'

He grinned.

Sunday morning heralded a joint benefice service at St Nicholas Church, Monhurst. The church was full and included Bella, Kitty, Seb, Kim and Matilda, Jennifer, Ditzi and Dezo - who was braced for the worst should word have got out regarding his son - and, surprisingly, Bastien, amongst the congregation. The topic of discussion over coffee afterwards was not, however, regarding the relationship between Dezo and Zeno, but about Andrew. The Rev. Jeremy Haslock had announced at the beginning of the service that Andrew's funeral would take place a week on Monday at All Saints Church, Wynenden at 2 p.m. What no one knew, other than the vicar, was who was making all the arrangements for it? A debate between Sharon and Betty started immediately the service was over, speculating as to who would, or would not, make an appearance at the service. Kitty watched as Dezo and Ditzi slipped away, followed shortly afterwards by Bastian and then Jennifer, the latter having been most allusive over the past couple of weeks.

Extracting themselves as well, Bella and Kitty hurried past Jennifer's house on the way to Bella's.

Handing Kitty a mug of steaming hot tea, Bella put her mug of coffee on the side table adjacent to the sofa and flopped down onto it opposite Kitty who was seated on the other side of the fireplace. The fire burned merrily, the room feeling toasty warm compared to the chill outside.

'That's lasted well,' commented Kitty, nodding towards the fire, logs only half burnt.

'I asked Dave to light it before he left this morning,' replied Bella.

'Oh?' Kitty raised an eyebrow.

Bella grinned.

'Well? Out with it. What's going on? Last time we talked it was all off between the two of you?'

'Now, don't go getting big-headed,' smirked Bella, 'but I listened to what you said, about not having to follow convention if it didn't work for us. And I talked about it with Dave. It feels like the right fit for us, that we have our own version of "normal" for our relationship. We won't live together - but that doesn't mean to say we couldn't in the future - we stay over at each others houses if we want to, keeping a few of our things permanently in one another's homes. We'll take holidays together if we feel like it, go away for weekends and so on. It feels so good and such a relief that we have found a way forward, as a result we are getting on much, much better. It's as though a pressure, or a weight, to conform has been lifted and we can now just enjoy being us, in our own version of togetherness and it doesn't matter what anybody else thinks about it. So, thank you for your advice Kitty.' She beamed at her friend.

'That's fantastic! I'm really pleased for you both.'

Still beaming, Bella changed the subject. 'What do you think about the announcement in the service about Andrew's funeral? Are you going to go?' she asked.

It was an affirmative from them both, curious to see who would attend, yet mystified as to who had been making the arrangements. Would anyone actually mourn his passing? Kitty knew that Hetty would, but anyone else? She was doubtful and found it sad, tragic even, that someone could manage to alienate so many people as to potentially only have one person truly mourn their death.

'What?' asked Kitty, despite knowing Bella well enough to sense when she was debating whether to tell her something or not.

Bella hesitated. 'It's probably nothing,' she started.

'Go on,' said Kitty.

'It's just. Well. When I mentioned to Dave last night, about Dezo and Zeno, he seemed rather interested.' She frowned at the recollection.

'Interested? In a normal person sort of way or in a D.I. sort of way?' asked Kitty.

'I'd like to think the former and not the later, but it's niggling away at me. My gut feeling is that he switched, albeit subtly, to work mode. You don't think that Dezo may have had something to do with Andrew's death do you?'

'Dezo? No, that thought hadn't even crossed my mind. He doesn't seem the type,' replied Kitty thoughtfully.

'Is there a type,' said Bella, 'who commits murder? Think about it, if it were your newly discovered offspring who had been attacked and seriously injured by Andrew, wouldn't you want to punish him for doing so?'

'Well,' pondered Kitty, listening to the ticking of the brass carriage clock on the table behind her. 'I suppose so. But murder?' Despite what she had said she knew that deep down, if she had a child, she would do anything to protect it. But to go as far as murder? Could anyone ever really know what they were capable of in such circumstances? Would parental instinct drive even the calmest, kindest, most violence-adverse person to that extreme? She shifted in her seat, uncomfortable with the sense that she couldn't say to herself one hundred percent that she would definitely not, let alone admit it to anyone else.

'I hope not, is all I can say. Perhaps I shouldn't have told Dave about them, I just assumed that he would already be aware of the fact.'

'He would have found out sooner or later, Bell's. If not from you, then someone else. After yesterday it's probably best that we refrain from speculating…'

CHAPTER TWENTY-ONE

There was an imperceptible sense of doom hanging over Wynenden, untouchable, but distinctly present. The heavy grey cloud which hung low over the entire village seemed to compound this sense and, despite the stillness in the air, a frisson of charge could be felt rippling throughout the village; anticipation, expectation. The day of Andrew's funeral had arrived.

Bastian, dressed in his customary black jeans, white t-shirt and navy crew-neck jumper, huddled into his navy padded jacket, shoulders hunched, the tips of his protruding ears tinged with red from cold despite it being a relatively mild day for the beginning of February. He stared moodily at the fenced off field adjacent to his current residence and former childhood home, which was due to be crammed with an overtly large number of houses - planning permission obtained with remarkable ease by Andrew. The peace and tranquility which had been present for generations, would be obliterated by the development.

He turned and plodded up the footpath into the village, kicking stones with his black trainers as he went. Ahead of him he could see a couple of cars driving towards him from the opposite direction, then indicating to turn right at the green. Following on foot was a trickle of residents also heading to the church to attend the funeral.

Kitty waited by her car whilst Bella locked hers and together they walked from the car park to the church. Inside, numbers were relatively sparse. For a man who was only 38 years old and in the prime of his life, they would have expected more than the current twenty or so who had turned up. Clearly, he'd had not had a close circle of friends, but where were those who had been employed by him? Surely, Kitty mused, they could have had the decency to show up even if they hadn't particularly liked him? And no family as yet. Would they be accompanying the coffin? Spotting Hetty, Kitty walked over and settled into the pew next to her with Bella following suit. She took Hetty's black-gloved hand and squeezed it.

'You ok?' Kitty whispered.

Hetty nodded, doing her utmost to keep tears from flooding out like a dam which had burst its banks, she didn't want the potential intrusion from other people speculating or asking questions as to why she was so upset.

The organ started playing funereal music and Kitty glanced around to see who was present; Sharon, Betty and a couple of other village gossips were squeezed in a pew together, awaiting the start of the service with anticipation. Dezo and Ditzi were there. Venka sat alone, her hair coloured with a black streak. Kim and Seb and, half hidden at the back, Bastien.

Apart from Hetty, Kitty felt that there was no one attending out of true respect for, or with a sense of loss over, Andrew. It was more like a gathering of those who wanted definitive confirmation for themselves that he really was dead and gone.

The music paused and the Rev. Jeremy Haslock requested that they stand. With the organist resuming play, Andrew was brought in, his coffin surprisingly plain and simple. No family appeared in its wake. No loved ones escorting him to the end, on to his final resting place in the churchyard.

If this was a representation of his life, how lonely had he been, thought Kitty, moved by the bleakness of what his life, or rather death, appeared to reveal?

The service was short and simple. There was no personal, heart-felt eulogy given, no weeping or wailing over a life lost and missed beyond desperation, no one present, except for Hetty, who appears to genuinely mourn his passing.

Kitty followed the small congregation who, apart from Hetty, could not truly be referred to as mourners, out of the church, along one of the paths and across the damp, trodden-down grass to the deep hole which had been dug for Andrew's coffin. She felt depressed by the futility of his life and tucked her arm through Hetty's, feeling the young woman's weight sink against her. Next to her she heard Bella whisper and glanced up. As if out of nowhere Dave had appeared, by the look of surprise on Bella's face she had clearly not been expecting him to be there. The faint lines on Kitty's forehead creased more deeply as she frowned. Why was he here? Was it related to work?

With the committal complete, the few who were so inclined strolled down to the pub where the wake, if it could really be called that, was to be held. The warmth embraced them as they walked into The Speckled Goose and apart from a couple of pub stalwarts it was empty and eerily quiet. A few sandwiches, cupcakes and biscuits sat forlornly on a table to the side, looking as feeble as the turnout in the church had been. Barely a dozen had decided to come on from the funeral so the landlord offered the first drink on the house along with unlimited tea and coffee which was already laid out on a table adjacent to the food.

Hetty looked pale, lost and overwhelmed. It hurt her that more people had not turned out for Andrew. She knew what he was, or rather had been, like as a person deep down and felt sad that others had not got to see the softer side of him. If they had, she felt sure that both the church and the pub would have been packed. But he had never allowed that to happen, feeling that if people saw a nicer, more vulnerable side to him, they would take it as a sign of weakness and he was convinced that they would see it as an opportunity to take advantage of him.

'Penny for them?' asked Kitty gently, feeling maternal towards Hetty.

Bleak eyes looked back at her and Kitty could sense the fear and loneliness bubbling up within Hetty.

'I'm here. Any time. Just call if you need me.' Kitty squeezed Hetty's arm gently in a demonstration of support.

'Thanks,' she replied in a hoarse whisper.

'You alright, Luvvie?' interrupted Betty who had bustled over unnoticed.

In a blink of an eye Kitty saw Hetty switch to her barmaid persona, one which was now attempting to smile at Betty as though she had not a care in the world. Hetty was resolutely determined that no one, other than Kitty, would ever have even the tiniest of inkling as to what had gone on between herself and Andrew.

'Fine thanks Betty. And you? How are you doing? Have a drink…'

Kitty stepped away to pour a cup of tea and get a biscuit to nibble on, it had been a long time since lunch and wafts of over-brewed coffee were making her empty stomach feel queasy.

There was a general air of dutiful attendance in the pub and, after a relatively short period of time, people started to drift away, including Bella and Dave. Bella was determined to find out why her partner had turned up unexpectedly at the burial. This left Kitty and Hetty on their own and, whilst Kitty felt exhausted and had been dreaming of putting her feet up and having a snooze in front of the fire at home, Hetty looked so forlorn that she couldn't bring herself to abandon her. The stark and depressing vision of Hetty sitting alone and bereft in her room above the pub was enough to make Kitty push her fatigue aside.

They sat in silence for a while, Kitty giving Hetty the space to talk if she wanted to. Eventually Hetty slid down from the stool she had been perched upon by the bar and said that she was going to have a lie down in her room, leaving Kitty to go home with a feeling of emptiness and concern for the young woman. She curled up on the sofa with Daisy, comforted somewhat by the warm furry purring creature, and drifted off to sleep.

When Kitty drove past Andrew's house en-route to the gym on Wednesday morning, she noticed a nondescript dark car parked on the drive - certainly not one of Andrew's - and frowned, wondering who it belonged to, an estate agent perhaps? Surely it would be too soon for the house to be put on the market, she pondered as she continued on to the gym?

The building was beginning to fill up by the time Kitty walked through the main door, many of them gorgeous looking women dressed in their expensive lycra which accentuated their beautifully toned bodies to perfection, they ambled past Kitty like gazelles on a morning stroll in search of fresh fodder. Just seeing them made Kitty's lack of enthusiasm ebb further away and feel more discontented about the snugness of the waistband of her leggings and the feeling of gloom that her middle-aged spread was expanding despite her best efforts in regularly exercising. She ignored the fact that her current propensity for consuming hot chocolate with marshmallows and whipped cream was not helping and sighed deeply as she pushed the door to the gym open and was met by loud thumping music and multiple members working out hard. Resigning herself to the fact that as she'd made the effort to come she had to work out, she told herself that the sooner she started, the sooner she'd be finished, knowing that despite her current lethargy and gloom she would feel better for having done so.

Post workout and shower, Kitty hurried past a couple of members, her body wrapped snuggly up in a fluffy towel and swiftly placed her belongings into a changing cubicle, got changed and came out to dry her hair. The two members, both clad as glamorously as each other, chatted to one another as they wiped, slicked and groomed their faces in the mirrors. Despite wearing her new, sale-bargain, cashmere jumper, Kitty felt dowdy in comparison. She switched off the hairdryer and tweaked at her cropped hair half listening in to their conversation, they changed subjects as swiftly as a dodgem car changed direction.

'I meant to say,' the blonde one said swishing her lengthy straight locks around, to her glossy, bobbed, ebony-coloured hair companion, 'you know who,' she glanced furtively at Kitty who feigned deafness to their conversation, 'is *definitely* having an affair with you know,' she lowered her voice, but not low enough to prevent Kitty from hearing her say, 'Zeno.'

'No!' cried her companion out loud. 'How do you know that?' Her eyes were bright at this morsel of gossip.

'I saw them. Together. In Dez... His car,' she hastily corrected herself in a failed attempt at being discreet.

Kitty could feel indignation bristle through her. They had to be referring to Zeno and Dezo and felt both a mix of indignant about the gossip and dread about what she now had to do. What she had promised she would do if such circumstances arose. So she did, taking a deep breath and smiled at the two.

'Who is it that you're talking about?' she asked pleasantly.

The pair looked at one another - should they or shouldn't they? their glance said.

'I suppose it's no secret,' said the blonde. 'I'm not the only one who knows. I'm talking about Zeno and Dezo, you know, the owner of Wynenden Hall.'

Kitty nodded innocently.

'They're having an *affair*.' The blonde looked expectantly at Kitty having imparted the nugget of gossip.

'An affair?' repeated Kitty. 'What makes you think that?' Her voice took on a hard edge.

If the blonde had not overdone the botox, Kitty would have been able to see the frown on her forehead, as it was nothing moved.

'Around,' replied the blonde, non-committally.

'Ah. Not from Dezo or Zeno themselves?'

'No,' she replied, as her friend shifted awkwardly beside her.

'Well,' said Kitty, keeping her anger in check but speaking with a deathly evenness, 'they are *not* having an affair.'

'How do you know that?' said the blonde, flicking her hair again, this time with an air of defiance.

'Because Dezo told me,' replied Kitty.

'Well, he would say that wouldn't he. He wouldn't want his wife to find out.'

'They are *not* having an affair,' repeated Kitty, 'because Zeno is Dezo's *son*.'

'His son!' They exclaimed.

'Yes. One hundred percent. So, perhaps you could help put a stop to the circulation of such untrue and defamatory tittle-tattle from spreading further?'

Kitty gathered up her bags - she was late to meet Bella in the juice bar - smiled at the women and left them in a stunned silence.

'What's up with you?' asked Bella, as Kitty flopped down onto the sofa opposite her.

'I've done the deed,' replied Kitty, rummaging in her bag for her phone.

Bella raised an eyebrow questioningly.

'About. You know,' added Kitty. 'So I'm just going to text Ditzi to let her know.' She quickly tapped a message into her phone and pressed send.

'Ah. I see,' replied Bella as the penny dropped.

Kitty nodded. 'Yup. In the changing room just now and...' her voice trailed off, 'those two,' she indicated with a slight tilt of her head in the direction of the two women who had just walked in.

Bella's eyes flicked across, then back. 'Looks like word is going to get around quickly,' she said, noting that they had already started talking to a group of women who were sipping their assortment of healthy looking juices.

'Do you think I should let Zeno know?' asked Kitty. 'He's started popping in here even though he's not back at work yet.'

'I'd leave it. I'm sure Dezo will do that.'

Kitty's phone pinged with a message back from Ditzi. 'Yup. Done already. That was quick.'

'I think they'll be relieved that the truth is now out in the open,' mused Bella. 'Anyway. Do you want to know what I got out of Dave?' she said with a knowing smile.

It transpired that Dave had been at Andrew's funeral in order to observe who was in attendance and report back to his colleague D.I. Allix. Bella had also managed to discover that there was to be an inquest which would take place in a few months time.

Driving past Andrew's house on the way home, Kitty could feel herself magnetically drawn to it. Distracted though she already was in contemplating his inquest and the implications of one being held, there was something about the house she was sure she was missing, but couldn't put her finger on. The car which had been there earlier was now no longer parked on the drive. Had it been D.I. Allix's? And if so, why? What was it that he was looking for?

She drove on then stopped at the shop in the village to pick up her newspaper, had a brief chat with Betty and was about to leave when the shop telephone rang. From the ensuing exclamations Betty was emitting, it was clear that word about Dezo and Zeno was spreading like wildfire.

Kitty was astonished, though she really shouldn't have been, how could she not expect such a tasty morsel of information to spread quite so swiftly? Hurriedly she left the shop, unwilling to become embroiled in a debate about them with Betty.

Feeling restless and out of sorts, Kitty had an early lunch then drove over to the small town of Tenterden to do her grocery shopping and have a wander around the delightful town with its wide High Street and tree-lined lower High Street. Despite the February gloom and greyness, the town was busy and Kitty took her time pottering in and out of the shops; purchasing a book in the book shop, having a good rummage through the antique shops and a couple of the charity shops, one in particular sold vintage and antique items in aid of a local charity.

In the distance, the bellowing of steam trains could be heard announcing their departure as they left the station to take their passengers on a journey through the Kent and Sussex countryside. Kitty knew that the following week the trains would be extra busy with parents taking their children out for a fun filled trip during half term.

The architecture of the town consisted of a broad range of buildings dating from hundreds of years ago right up to the present time, including the church, 12th Century St Mildred's. The town had become prosperous in the fourteenth century as a centre of the wool trade and many of the buildings contributed towards creating a most pleasant visual demonstration of an historic landscape. Of particular popularity with visitors to the town was the Tudor period, timber-framed tea room which had been in-situ as such for as long as Kitty could remember, but of which she did not know its previous use. The low-beamed interior exuded an essence of the past and, for those not privileged enough to reside in such an historic building, gave them the opportunity to experience and imagine, at least for a little while, what it would be like to live in such a splendid property and to ponder upon who else may have visited it over the hundreds of years of its existence.

That afternoon Kitty was not in the mood to sit still and continued to feel restless so decided to walk down to the far end of the High Street and purchase a takeaway hot chocolate from the chocolate shop which could be found within a narrow sliver of a building, identifiable by its jolly orange-coloured awning.

She strolled down the left-hand side of the High Street, past shops and along where pretty cottages were set back from the path. In the distance she could see two figures at the very far end of the street where the line of leafless trees ended.

Based solely on their body language, Kitty felt that the pair were having an argument. She squinted, they looked vaguely familiar, but she was too far away to be able to identify them. As she was about to cut across the wide grass verge and road to the opposite side, where the draw of hot chocolate was luring her, the arm waving stopped. The shorter one took the taller ones hand and drew it tenderly to her face. The taller one appeared to say something, looked nervously about, then took the hand away from her cheek.

Kitty, who was an intermittent but regular visitor to the chocolate shop, chatted to the welcoming couple who owned it whilst her drink was being made - good quality chocolate, most definitely not a high-sugar-mix imposter purporting to be of high quality. Unable to resist as always, Kitty chose half a dozen differently flavoured individual chocolate truffles and a bar of 85% cocoa from the generous selection.

She took a cautious sip of the steaming drink whilst her bill was totted up. The door behind her opened and a gust of cold air blew in around her ankles. She turned to smile pleasantly and came face to face with the couple who had, moments previously, appeared to make up so tenderly, their smiles faltered when they saw Kitty and the look of surprise on her face.

CHAPTER TWENTY-TWO

'Kitty,' said Ariadne, regaining her composure and giving Kitty a perfunctory kiss on the cheek. 'How lovely to see you again.' She twiddled a few strands of her honey-blonde hair as she spoke, her perfectly manicured long slim fingers trembling slightly as she did so.

'You too Ariadne. And you Venka.' Had she misread the signs she wondered?

Venka smiled nervously, she had the air of a child caught with her hand in the cookie jar. Meanwhile, Ariadne ordered two hot chocolates for them, then studiously perused the selection of chocolate bars. The air in the small shop invisibly crackled with nervous tension, the owners doing their best to fill the awkward silence with small talk.

Kitty attempted to leave but Ariadne, still with a smile fixed on her face, suggested that they all stroll together with their drinks, or even sit down on a bench beneath one of the trees and chat. Curiosity got the better of her so she agreed, though she got the feeling that refusing was not an option.

As a result, the trio strolled along the now quietening wide path as though this were an every day occurrence. Kitty followed Ariadne and Venka across the road to one of the benches on the other side where they sat down; Kitty at one end, Ariadne at the other, Venka perched tensely in-between. Venka flicked the lid of her drink with her nail, the rhythmic click, click, click, filling the silence.

Ariadne cleared her throat as if to speak, but remained silent. Kitty said nothing. There was something going on that much was obvious, but what? She had a few ideas but was reluctant to say anything in case she was wildly off the mark. Her propensity to take a soft approach when broaching a delicate subject deserted her, possibly as a result of her beginning to feel cold, and she blurted out that she had seen them both at the far end of the High Street when she was on her way to the chocolate shop.

By the worried glance they exchanged, it became apparent that this was what they had feared. Venka switched from flicking the side of her lid to tapping the top; fast, rhythmic, beats, exhibiting her nervousness.

It was Ariadne who took the cue and spoke, her voice wavering as she did so.

'It was stupid of me to even suggest coming here,' she sighed, 'but I. We,' she corrected, 'just wanted to enjoy a little bit of normality. I'd hoped that it would provide a brief distraction from all the stress Venka has been under recently.'

Kitty nodded. So far so logical. But?

'We've become close friends since I came back. It's hard to believe that it has only been a few weeks, it feels more like months, longer even. Venka has helped me so much, I don't just mean in terms of fitness, I mean personally, emotionally.' She smiled at Venka, her face relaxing as she did so. 'I was,' she paused, gazing into the distance as she searched for the right words to express herself, 'in a bad place when I came back. Things have been, for a while. Well. Tough,' her eyes clouded in recollection. 'Sophie has been amazing, as has Harry. It was so kind and generous of them to insist that I stay with them. Being in their flat has given me some space and time to myself whilst not feeling completely isolated, to have the choice as to whether to pop in and spend time with them or not. I. I don't know what would have happened if Sophie hadn't been there for me.' Tears welled up in her blue eyes.

Kitty's stomach lurched with fear. Was Ariadne implying that she had felt in such a dark place that she'd had the overwhelming, beyond her control, urge to end her life?

'Anyway,' continued Ariadne having taken a deep breath, 'Venka has been amazing. We clicked immediately. I felt I could trust her, which is a really difficult thing for me to do.' Ariadne looked directly at Kitty and in that moment Kitty felt humbled that Ariadne was being so open and putting her trust in her.

'I understand,' replied Kitty.

With this confirmation, Ariadne continued. 'As I said. We've become very close.' She briefly touched Venka's knee, who nodded in agreement. 'Very close indeed,' added Ariadne.

It took a moment for the penny to drop. 'Oh!' exclaimed Kitty in surprise.

'And whilst we are absolutely not in any way ashamed of our relationship we felt - particularly with everything else currently going on in the village - that it would be best to keep it to ourselves for the time being. More importantly, Venka has Valentina to think about and also the potential impact on her work to take into consideration. Because of my career, news of our relationship will inevitably blow up into a massive media circus. We need to be sure that this is for the long term before we go public.' Venka nodded in agreement. 'And then work out how best to minimise the impact it will have on us and those we care about.'

The responsibility of keeping such a secret made Kitty feel like she was holding something which could explode at any moment. One slip, one accidental or careless word and it would all blow up. She usually felt that it was a privilege to be taken into someones confidence, but on this occasion it felt like a massive burden, one she could do without at the present time.

They had had a lucky escape, if it had been someone less trustworthy their carelessness could have led to them having to deal with the consequences now, rather than later managed on their terms.

They parted company and Kitty, worn out by the events of the day, lethargically did her grocery shopping in the supermarket before heading home. As she drove distractedly through the dusk she couldn't shake the sense that half of what she had actually needed remained on the shelves in the shop.

On Thursday evening Bella telephoned Kitty, eager for them to get together as soon as possible - she had news she said - and they arranged to meet on Friday evening.

Kitty, who was relishing the prospect of the two week extended half-term holiday which stretched ahead of her, had not been home long when Bella arrived, just as Ted was leaving to meet Seb and Harry in the pub for the evening. Kitty hugged him and breathed in his fresh citrus cologne, looked up into his smiling face and received a tender kiss from him and wanted to remain in that moment for ever. She held him tighter, his toned athletic body and 6'1" height making her feel safe and comforted.

'That's my cue,' he said, in response to the firm rap on the front door. He kissed her again. 'Have a lovely evening darling.' He opened the front door, Kitty standing behind him, enjoying the warmth from the underfloor heating which was seeping through her socks, greeted Bella, then bade them both farewell before going off into the cold night.

'Brrr,' shivered Kitty. 'Come in. Come in. It's chilly out there.'

Bella extracted herself from the many layers she had put on to conserve heat, grumbling about the possibility of more snow; as far as she was concerned there'd been enough for that winter. Box ticked. Job done. And a swift move on to Spring was what she hankered after.

They went into the kitchen and Kitty retrieved plates from a cupboard whilst Bella unpacked the Indian Takeaway food she'd picked up on her way over. The delicious aroma of spices wafted through the kitchen as Kitty opened the containers, making their mouths water in anticipation. They chatted as they ate, Kitty bursting to tell her friend about Ariadne and Venka, doing her utmost to act as "normally" as possible. But Bella was too astute and knew her friend far too well and, having provided Kitty with enough time to enlighten her, asked her directly.

'Secret?' replied Kitty, feigning as much innocence as she could muster, turning her attention to the food as a distraction by helping herself to more rice, vegetable korma and garlic naan bread. 'I don't know what you mean?'

'You're looking shifty. Come on. Out with it. What's up?'

Anticipating that Bella might pick up on the fact that she was hiding something, Kitty had rehearsed an excuse in advance, one which she hoped would be plausible enough to mollify Bella for the time being. Sooner or later Ariadne and Venka's relationship would be in the public domain, but until then Kitty was determined that her lips would remain firmly closed on the subject.

'If you call the fact that I'm menopausal - or rather perimenopausal - a secret, then I am. Rather depressing really. Can't say I want to acknowledge that it is happening. It feels like such a horrible step towards the final stage of life and another reminder that I will never be a mother.' She sat there gloomily, feeling rather emotional.

'Oh.' replied Bella non-plussed. 'But we've talked about that. Have you been to see the doctor yet?'

Kitty shook her head. Her memory had turned to mush and yet again she had forgotten to book an appointment.

Knowing all too well the pain of desperately wanting to carry a child, to be a mother, yet for it to be unattainable, Bella empathised with Kitty. She too was going through the menopause but, unlike Kitty, she had been more proactive and after a great deal of research, discussions with her GP and then her gynaecologist, Bella had recently decided to give HRT a go and was now beginning to feel more like her old self, pre the stealthy onset of perimenopause. In fact, she was beginning to feel that she had a new lease of life, that a new and exciting chapter lay ahead of her rather than a gloomy decline into decrepitude.

'And that's it? Nothing else you're keeping from me? asked Bella.'

'Nothing to tell,' replied Kitty carefully. 'So. What's the big news? That you wanted to tell me so urgently?'

'Ah ha! Yes. I was speaking to Kim. By the way there's no other topic being discussed at the gym other than the one regarding Dezo and Zeno. It is literally buzzing like a hive packed full of bees in the height of summer. Anyway, she was telling me that she has heard from Andrew's solicitor.

Kitty's gold-speckled brown eyes widened in surprise. 'Really? How come?'

'Well, you know she had hoped to buy Florence's old house but Andrew pipped her at the post?'

Kitty nodded.

'And that at the time of Andrew's death he, or rather his company, had exchanged contracts on the property.'

'Uhuh,' replied Kitty.

'Well, apparently, Andrew had recently re-written his Will. It states that, in the event of his death, if the purchase had not proceeded to completion then it was to be offered to Kim for her to take over the purchase and if Kim did not wish to proceed, then the company would move forward to completion *and* this had been agreed with the existing vendor,' finished Bella breathlessly.

'Really? That is weird. I mean, why would Andrew do that? Can it even legally be done?'

'I know!' exclaimed Bella. 'I asked Kim the exact same question! According to Andrew's solicitor it is possible, though apparently he didn't go into the legal technicalities.'

'Were there conditions attached to Andrew's offer?' asked Kitty, dubious about his motives.

'No. I don't think so. So, what do you think?'

Kitty pursed her lips together then blew out. 'I don't know. I've never heard of anything like this before. If Andrew changed his Will recently and that bequest was in it, to me that could imply that he was expecting or planning to die, or feared that he might, otherwise I would have expected his company to have completed on the property swiftly and without a lengthy delay.'

'You would think so,' replied Bella. 'It is rather suspicious.'

'Have you mentioned it to Dave?' asked Kitty.

Bella rolled her eyes and confirmed that she had asked, but that he had remained suitably tight lipped on the subject and not forthcoming with information in any way, shape or form.

'So is Kim going to go ahead and buy the property?' asked Kitty.

'Yup. That's the plan, though I am assuming it will take some time to go through though, probate has to be granted and other legal matters dealt with. I believe that Andrew's company was held solely in his name and is therefore part of his Estate. I've no idea if they can keep trading or not, or even what will happen to it in the long term nor who will actually inherit the company, I imagine, his heir or heirs - but we have no idea who that is.'

Kitty digested the news in silence whilst Bella pondered upon the possible wider implications of Andrew's recent decision to change his Will.

'Are you sure that Kim has no inkling about why Andrew changed his Will to her benefit?' probed Kitty as she cleared away the supper dishes and cleaned up after their meal.

'Mmm. She's as puzzled as we are, but she did let something else slip then clammed up when I asked her what she'd meant.'

Kitty glanced up from loading the dishwasher. 'What was that?'

'Well, she implied that, whilst her intention had been to initially buy Florence's house, re-develop it and then rent it out, she was now - in theory - going to buy it on behalf of someone else. I could see that she was annoyed that she'd let that slip but wouldn't be drawn into it.'

'Gosh. I wonder what she's up to?' said Kitty pursing her lips and frowning. 'Could she have meant that she's hoping to buy it for Matilda and keep it in a Trust or something until she's older?'

'It's possible I suppose, but really I have no idea. 'Why would she be coy about it if she were buying it for Matilda? Rather intriguing don't you think,?' said Bella.

'Perhaps she didn't want to jinx the purchase until it was all signed and sealed? I wonder if Seb will say anything tonight to Ted and Harry?'

Bella snorted. 'I doubt it. You know what they're like. This wouldn't be the least bit interesting to them. Besides, if Kim wants it to remain a secret he's not going to say anything anyway.'

'Hmm. I suppose so,' replied Kitty thoughtfully, before adding, 'there must be a long list of suspects who would be happy to see the back of Andrew. Do you think it was work related? Some rival developer sick of Andrew's mendacity and underhanded ways?'

Before Bella could reply, Kitty suggested that they move through to the sitting room to continue to chat in front of the roaring log fire.

Weak sunshine filtered through one of the bedroom windows, the sky an inviting clear-blue and with Ted on his way to work after their Saturday morning ritual of breakfast in bed, Kitty settled back for a snooze, Daisy - half hidden - was fast asleep under the duvet on the other side of the bed; the gym could wait for another day Kitty felt. But the weather was too beautiful to be neglected so Kitty eventually got dressed, wrapped up warmly, left Daisy in her own bed in the kitchen and walked across the fields to the village, the morning frost crunching underfoot as she went.

Kitty felt energised and alive, humming happily as she went, the fresh air and exercise felt good. At the village hall she saw Bella sitting at a table waiting for her and waved, indicating that she would do a quick circuit to buy some provisions. By the time she reached Bella there was a cup of tea waiting for her and, despite them having spent the previous evening together, they still found plenty to talk about.

Kitty, sitting facing towards the entrance to the hall, suddenly stopped mid-sentence, lowered her voice and whispered to Bella. 'This is going to put the cat amongst the pigeons.'

Bella turned to see what Kitty was referring to. Walking into the hall together were Ditzi, Dezo and Zeno. A bold statement by the trio, demonstrating that they had nothing to hide and that they were definitely a united family unit. Admittedly Zeno - who had never visited the market before so had no idea as to what to expect - looked apprehensive, it was apparent he'd been forewarned about what might happen and looked anxiously around as though about to be thrown into a den of lions and receive a good mauling.

A momentary hush fell in the hall then, as though the volume had suddenly been turned up by the flick of a switch, the chatter re-filled the room.

The trio walked in a leisurely manner around the room, slowly, surely, chatting to one another, speaking to stall-holders, making purchases, before heading over to Bella and Kitty.

'Mind if we join you?' asked Dezo.

'Of course not. Please do,' replied Kitty amicably.

'You'll be safe with us,' whispered Bella, grinning. 'Lovely to see you out and about Zeno, and looking so well too.'

Out of the corner of her eye Bella could see that Betty and her companions, who were seated around "their" large table, were craning their necks to see precisely what was transpiring, desperate not to miss out on something. I imagine they're planning their strategy in order to have an excuse to come over, chuckled Bella to herself.

'Here we are,' said Dezo returning, handing the drinks around. There was a pause, Dezo cleared his throat. 'So,' he said, 'you both know Zeno.' Bella and Kitty nodded.

Kitty hesitated before blurting out to Zeno. 'I'm so sorry. It was me. You know. Who stirred this all up.'

Zeno interrupted her softly. 'It's ok. Really. I should thank you. It saved me or, or,' he struggled to say "dad", 'Dezo, from having to tell everyone.'

He looks wise beyond his 28 years mused Bella.

They were interrupted by, what one could only imagine the posse at the large table thought of as their "diplomatic contingency". Given that this consisted of Sharon and Betty it was actually the polar opposite. Surprisingly for the pair they appeared nervous and fluttered hesitantly on the periphery of the group. Dezo and Ditzi shot one another a meaningful look. Dezo cleared his throat again; this was what they had hoped and anticipated for, the sole purpose of them attending the market that morning, a show of family solidarity. Nothing to hide. Nothing to be ashamed of and the most sure fire way of getting the message out was by having Sharon and Betty broadcast it in their own unique way.

'Sharon. Betty,' he said pleasantly, rising from his seat to greet them. They looked a little taken aback by the welcome. 'How are you both?' he beamed at them.

Ditzi remained silent but attempted to smile. Zeno, meanwhile, shifted apprehensively in his seat, to him it felt as unpleasant an experience as having root canal treatment and at that particular moment in time he felt he would rather be undergoing it.

Dezo continued. 'You know my son, Zeno,' he said loudly enough to ensure that those seated in close proximity could hear. 'Isn't it excellent news that he is recovering so well?' Dezo ploughed on. 'I am so proud of my son and what he has achieved. Ditzi and I are delighted to welcome him into the heart of our family, aren't we darling?' He looked at Ditzi who took her cue and was suitably profuse in her response. Bella and Kitty felt sure that though Ditzi was smiling, she was covering up the strain of the previous few weeks, discovering out of the blue that your husband has an adult son had unsurprisingly been a huge shock, just as it had been for Dezo.

Zeno continued to smile nervously. Outside of work he was usually a quietly confident individual but, even though he was the one who had been determined to find his father, the reality of it still felt awkward and was taking time to get used to. His mother and step-father - both deceased - had not been big on expressing their emotions or in communicating their feelings, something which Dezo was proving to be surprisingly good at but which at times also felt over-whelming.

Betty and Sharon, who were as equally taken aback by Dezo's openness, managed to rally, burning with inquisitive questions which Dezo good-naturedly answered until exasperation eventually got the better of him. Fortuitously, they were interrupted by Valentina who had run over and leapt at Zeno - making him wince in pain as his injuries twinged - shouting excitedly, clearly thrilled to see him. The feeling was mutual, the little girl clambered up onto his lap and snuggled into him, putting her arms around his neck and holding him as tightly as a two year old whose arms could only just manage to go around his neck was capable of. He stooped his tall frame forward a little to make it easier for her to do so.

'Sorry Zeno,' smiled Venka.

He laughed, it was the first time that Bella and Kitty had seen him relax since arriving in the hall.

Dezo politely acquired a spare chair from a neighbouring table and equally politely terminated the conversation with Sharon and Betty.

Venka sat down and they all chatted for a while until Dezo felt that they had completed the task they had set out to achieve. Then the trio left, as they did so there was a noticeable whoosh in conversational volume.

CHAPTER TWENTY-THREE

The mention of Florence again had left Bella feeling unsettled. She'd done her best to push aside the terrible memories of what had happened in the past and the fact that how, without Dave's incredibly well timed intervention, the outcome could have been very different. For the past couple of years she'd merely had the occasional fleeting thought about Florence and, since that day six years ago, had never been back to the house. But now? Bella was torn between taking a leap of faith and facing whatever opening the Pandora's box might do to her, or continuing to try to keep the lid firmly closed on it. She worried about whether she had genuinely come to terms with what had happened to her or not, fearful as to what the long term consequences might be if she hadn't.

Despite trying to quash these thoughts they now continued to churn away inside her head, rather like a washing machine spinning on a fast cycle. She tucked her grey-tinged brown hair behind her ears and sighed, drumming her fingers on top of the kitchen work surface and stared unseeingly out into the garden. The robin which habitually hopped around on a bush near the back door was doing so now, its bright red breast accented against the backdrop of crisp white frost. Until today the robin without fail had always managed to bring a smile to Bella's face, but she saw nothing, only bleakness.

Like a scab being constantly picked, scratched and prodded, Bella knew that deep down these memories had now been irrevocably stirred up and she had to stop deluding herself that she had come to terms with the trauma inflicted upon her. If she didn't face it head on now she may never attain a resolution, a finality. Decisively she strode out of the kitchen, lifted her coat, hat and scarf off the stair banister where she had flung them the previous day, grabbed her keys and left the house.

Gripping the car steering wheel so tightly that her knuckles went white, she rested her forehead on them, took three deep breaths and started the engine. If she didn't go now she'd bottle it.

Bella turned left at the end of her drive, then left again onto the main road followed by the next left-hand turn. The palms of her hands started to sweat and she could feel her heart rate increasing until, by the time she had turned right into a single-track lane, her heart was pounding furiously. She slowed the car down to a crawl, then stopped. Slightly overgrown, but still accessible, was the track which led to Florence's house, tucked away in a wooded area, hidden from sight. She felt bile rise in her throat and a sense of panic rushed through her. Should she call Dave? Ask him to come with her? No, she decided, he would only try to stop her. Kitty maybe? Ultimately, Bella knew that this was something she had to face on her own and not metaphorically hide behind someone else.

The sun had slipped behind a cloud and a chill shivered down her spine. She gulped, mouth becoming dry, turned the wheel and edged the car slowly, cautiously, along the bumpy track. As the car reached the edge of the clearing surrounding the immediate proximity to the house, Bella involuntarily held her breath, bracing herself.

The house, dilapidated even six years ago, was now in a terrible state of disrepair; windows smashed - presumably by vandals - copious numbers of tiles missing from the roof, overall a sad, dejected and neglected sight. In her mind Bella had held the image of the property as it had been when she was last there and was unreasonably taken aback by the state it had fallen into. She sat for a few minutes trying to slow down her rapidly increasing heart rate, dreading yet knowing what she had to do.

The long grass was bent and curled with time, weighed down by glistening frost. Bella picked her way along a trodden down path which she presumed Andrew and his surveyors had previously made. She walked around to the side of the house and hesitated by the wooden back door which had gashes in it from where wood had rotted and fallen off over time, leaving sharp jaggedy edges imitating stalagmites and stalactites.

Apprehensively Bella turned the handle. Despite the rot and decay, the door remained surprisingly tricky to open, swollen in place by damp. But she hadn't come this far to give up at the final hurdle and with one big shove with her shoulder, she rammed the door open and tumbled into the deserted room. She stood there, her breath coming fast and furious, plumes of cold air wafting from her open mouth. A musty smell assaulted her nasal passages, she looked around at the deep layers of dust and copious cobwebs from years of neglect. She picked her way carefully through to the hallway, there was a massive crack in the wall to the left of the front door, wide enough to see daylight through. She hesitated and glanced up the staircase, memories so vivid that it could have been yesterday. Bella placed one foot onto the bottom step and as her weight went down there was a sharp splintering sound, she leapt back just in time to prevent her foot from disappearing through the deceptively rotten tread. Her heart pounded furiously and save for her heavy breathing, there was an eerie silence. Instinct was telling her to run, she hastened back to the kitchen and hurried out of the gloomy dank interior into the daylight, stopped, then frowned. Had she imagined it she wondered? She peered back through the open doorway. No she hadn't. Sitting in the decrepit sink was a mug and an old metal saucepan looking as though they had been recently used, she'd not noticed them on her way into the house, how peculiar, she thought as she tugged the door closed behind her.

Bella walked hurriedly away and didn't look back until she had reached the safety of her car. What had filled her with so much fear and trepidation mere minutes before now left her with a hollow, empty feeling. The air of dejection about the house made her feel sad; wasted lives and the ripple effect caused by one persons actions spreading out for generations. Could this also apply to Andrew? What may he have done to enrage someone enough to potentially kill him? What was the straw which broke the camels back? What, and who, would be ensnared in the ripple from his death over the ensuing years? Did Andrew's heir or heirs even know that he had been their father?

Save for the distant harsh craw of a single crow there was silence. As dankness seeped into her she unlocked the car door, slid inside, turned the engine on and maxed up the heating. Her hands no longer gripped the steering wheel in abject terror she realised, a layer of fear had evaporated and she sincerely hoped that this indicated a positive turning point for her. Yet now she felt the urgent need to be with people, to not be alone, to talk to someone about what she'd just done, preferably someone who knew what had happened six years ago and who had been there for her and understood the impact it had had on her then. Not Kitty. Not Dave - he wouldn't be objective enough she felt. Perhaps Kim, thought Bella?

At the main road Bella decisively drove straight across the crossroads into Coppice Lane. The quiet country lane took her past her friends Cressa and Jack's house, prompting her to realise that she had not seen or spoken to either of them since early January. She took the next right, right again, then left down the lane towards Kim and Seb's house. Seb's work truck was parked outside but she could see no sign of Kim's car. She hesitated, but the need to see a friendly face was so strong that she drove up the drive, parked and knocked on the front door.

Seb opened it, wiping crumbs from his mouth as he did so. His short brown hair was as unkempt as ever and his soft brown eyes exuded the warmth and gentleness they always did. He smiled broadly when he saw Bella and insisted she come in.

Matilda was sitting on her booster seat at the glass and chrome table munching a cheese sandwich which Seb had cut into squares for her, humming to herself, an almost empty bowl of spaghetti hoops next to the plate, orange sauce splattered around her mouth. She grinned and waved at Bella but a firm glance from Seb reminded her that she was not to talk with her mouth full.

Bella accepted Seb's offer of a cup of coffee and went and sat opposite Matilda, relishing the normality of the domestic scene and chatted to the little girl who, between mouthfuls, gabbled happily away to Bella, her legs dangling down, swinging them back and forth as she did so.

Seb joined them and Bella wrapped her hands around her piping hot mug, enjoying the warmth which began to diminish the chill she still felt.

Sandwich finished, yoghurt messily consumed along with satsuma segments and with her hands and face wiped, Matilda was allowed to get down from the table and happily pottered off to play with some toys, her distant chatter wafting through from the playroom as she did so.

'Are you ok Bella?' asked Seb. 'When you arrived you looked like you'd seen a ghost.'

Astute as ever in his observations, Bella told him where she had just been. If he was surprised he didn't show it, he simply listened until she had finished speaking.

'And how do you feel now?' he asked gently.

She shrugged. 'I don't know really. I suppose it has always been there in the back of my mind even though I tried my hardest to ignore it. But I feel that over time I've built it up into something bigger, scarier, than it was…'

Seb interrupted her. 'Bella, it *was* scary and incredibly traumatic for you. I doubt you could possibly have built what happened to you up into something bigger than it was. You could have died.' He took her hand and squeezed comfortingly.

She smiled weakly. 'Maybe.' she shrugged. 'After I'd been inside the house today and come out, I looked back and for a brief moment it simply looked like a sad neglected house and it didn't fill me with fear anymore. Whether that feeling will grow or not I don't know, but I'm sure it's helped me on some level.'

'I'm glad. I really hope that it has,' he smiled and gave her hand a final squeeze. 'If you want to keep going there I doubt it would be a problem.'

'Kim told Kitty that she's hopeful now that you'll be able to buy the property?'

He nodded.

'I imagine the purchase could take a while to go through, what with all the legal complications.' Bella paused. 'Kim also mentioned that you're intending to refurbish it then rent it out. It might be cathartic for me to see the work carried out, you know, negative to positive, that sort of thing?'

Seb hesitated. 'Nothing is set in stone yet,' he replied cautiously.

They were interrupted by the front door slamming closed and Kim's voice could be heard lovingly greeting her daughter. Seb leapt up, by the time he'd reached the kitchen door Kim walked in carrying Matilda who was clutching her white squishy toy dog, sucking her thumb and looking a little sleepy.

He kissed Kim and said. 'Here, let me take Tilda, looks like she's ready for her nap, aren't you chicken.' He scooped Matilda up from Kim, and the little girl immediately wrapped her arms around his neck, gave Bella a little wave before snuggling her head into the nape of his neck.

Kim retrieved the sandwich Seb had prepared her from the fridge and sat down with a heavy sigh, exhausted after a particularly intense morning at work.

Inevitably, Bella felt that she had to tell Dave what she had done. He wasn't impressed. In fact, to say that he was not happy, would have been an understatement. Whilst Bella could partially understand his reaction, she had hoped that he would be pleased she'd taken such a monumental step forward towards closure of what had been a terrible episode in her life. Instead, he had been furious and they'd had a massive row resulting in him storming out, leaving Bella bewildered as to what had just occurred, coming to the conclusion that he himself hadn't dealt with his own feelings about what had happened.

On Wednesday, having slept appallingly the night before, Bella unenthusiastically dragged herself off to the gym. She'd been tempted to cancel her coffee with Kitty post-workout, but once she'd completed her routine she felt a little perkier and even better after she had off-loaded onto Kitty.

Whilst Kitty drove home she mulled over what Bella had told her but as she approached Andrew's house she slowed and impulsively tucked her car into the old disused field gateway opposite his house and got out. Whether the urge was fuelled by pure nosiness or a gut-feeling, she wasn't sure, however the lure of the house had been growing stronger in her in recent days and now there was an overwhelming sense of inevitability. Irrespective of any potential consequences, she had to access the property.

She zipped up her navy padded jacket, looked furtively up and down the lane, listened intently for the sound of an approaching vehicle, person, or the clip-clop of horses hooves. There was silence, bar birdsong from a few birds in the hedges and trees. Kitty hurried across the road feeling a flutter of nerves in the pit of her stomach as she turned the latch on the wrought-iron pedestrian gate which was adjacent to the drive gates, it turned noiselessly. She let out a sigh of relief and stepped onto the driveway where frost still glinted in the shadowy patches where the low rays of sunshine had yet to reach.

Kitty tiptoed down the drive as quickly as she could in order to get out of the sightline of the road, pausing every few seconds to listen for approaching vehicles, then crept around the side of the house. She wasn't entirely sure what it was that she was looking for, on the one hand she felt that what she was doing was insane, but on the other the urge outweighed it all.

She hadn't considered how she would gain access to the house and not surprisingly there were no conveniently unlocked or smashed windows. Completing a full circuit of the property and feeling more confident that she wouldn't be interrupted, Kitty began to search underneath the flower pots by the back door in the hope that a key would magically appear beneath one. Sadly her search proved to be fruitless. Absent mindedly she rested a hand on the back door handle whilst she considered what if any, her options were. It gave way underneath the pressure. Astonished, Kitty pressed the handle right down and pushed. The door opened noiselessly. Nothing but the quiet hum of a vast wine fridge in what appeared to be a back kitchen or laundry room, greeted her.

She stepped onto the doormat and habitually wiped her feet on it, then crept forward through the room and into the kitchen. She was taken aback by the stylishness of the uber modern steel and granite fittings which were dominated by an enormous range along with a copious quantity of cupboards, presumably where the culinary accoutrements were hidden, she thought, as there were none on display, giving the room a rather stark, clinical feel. She felt that this was a kitchen designed for, or by, someone with a passion for cooking which was, not something Kitty had ever imagined would be of interest to Andrew. Tucked neatly under the expansive length of the black granite island was a row of low-backed black leather and chrome stools, from where there was a prime view out into the garden through the rectangular, single-expanse, piece of glass, itself mirroring the length of the adjacent work top. Some distance behind the stools was a rectangular steel table, the sort of thing Kitty imagined - having watched many a crime drama on television - would be more suitable for autopsies than for dining and around it ten, very uninviting, steel chairs.

Kitty continued her tour of the house. The sitting room was a mishmash of outdated, cheap-looking tables with ring stains from mugs and glasses, two over-sized black leather sofas - still smelling fresh and new - a mottled beige swirly old shag-pile carpet, a glass and formica cabinet and, tucked out of immediate sight behind one of the sofas, a large box of toys.

She shrugged to herself at the sight and resumed her inspection. A room at the back of the house overlooked the garden and contained an array of expensive-looking gym equipment.

As she progressed, Kitty became aware that the house was spotlessly clean and assumed that cleaners must have been organised to come in once the police had finished.

The final room downstairs was a study. Floor to ceiling bookcases lined the length of the back wall, filled with neatly labelled files, box files and building journals. A large desk offered a view out onto the driveway and to its right was a metal filing cabinet which appeared to have been forced open, the police with no key she imagined?

The top draw was ajar by mere millimetres and Kitty wrestled with temptation then reasoned that, as she was already trespassing, she might as well go the whole hog and look inside the cabinet.

Flicking through the very organised and labelled files of the draw she was disappointed, they appeared to only contain mundane invoices and receipts, likewise with the next draw. With the glimmer of hope that she could still discover something of interest diminishing, Kitty opened the final draw and found it filled with neatly filed bank statements. Her fingers hovered over the first file, then pulled it out with anticipation, disappointed by what she found - seemingly uninteresting company bank statements - whilst the funds in the company were substantial, there was nothing she could identify as intriguing within them. She let out a big sigh, put the file back and fished the last one out. When she opened it, her eyes grew wide in astonishment, inside were details of run-of-the-mill transactions but, more interestingly, they also showed substantial sums being transferred - both in to and out of - the bank accounts, to recipients and payees who did not appear to be related to the building trade, property or associated businesses. She retrieved her phone from her pocket and took several photographs without thinking about the legality - or rather lack of - what she was doing. She slid the file back into place, double checking that it was just as she had found it, then swiftly ran her eyes across the files on the bookcases again to make sure she had not missed something.

With her confidence growing, Kitty stepped swiftly, albeit quietly, up the carpeted stairs and noiselessly pushed the doors on the landing open one by one; three bland bedrooms and a bathroom. As she reached towards the final door handle, concluding that it had to be the master bedroom, it turned and the door started to open. Kitty screamed, turned and ran, the echo of reciprocal screams following her. She was half way down the stairs, hands sweating, heart pounding furiously, before her brain registered the identity of the person and stopped, legs turning to jelly and buckling underneath her, only just managing to prevent herself from falling down the remaining distance because of the tight grip she had on the bannister. Her shoulder gave a sharp tug and pain shot through it.

CHAPTER TWENTY-FOUR

'Here. Sip this,' said the person proffering a glass of water. 'You look as pale as a ghost.'

The water trembled in the glass as Kitty took it to her mouth, her shoulder was throbbing from the pain of wrenching it. She sat on the bottom step of the stairs, the figure towering over her. Kitty sipped slowly to give herself time to calm down and gather her thoughts.

'Come through here,' the person said, indicating towards the sitting room.

Meekly Kitty did as she was told and perched on the edge of the sofa nearest the door. Simultaneously they spoke.

'You first,' said Kitty.

There was a curt nod. 'What are you doing here?'

'I was going to ask you the same thing, Venka,' replied Kitty, 'given that neither of us should be here?'

Venka stared at Kitty intently, calculating her response.

'You shouldn't be here,' she said with an edge of defiance.

Non-plussed, Kitty replied. 'Nor should you. And anyway, aren't you supposed to be at work? I saw you giving Ariadne a session just a couple of hours ago. And your car is not here. How did you get in?'

'Not that it's any of your business, but I ran over and I'm on my lunch break.'

'So, why *are* you here?' persisted Kitty.

'*No.* You tell me why *you* are here?'

Recognising stalemate, Kitty reluctantly acquiesced.

'I was curious,' she replied evasively.

'About what?' Venka's eyes narrowed.

Kitty shrugged. 'I'm not sure,' she replied. And you?'

Venka gazed thoughtfully out of the window.

'I have a right to be here,' she eventually said.

'A right?' Kitty frowned.

'Yes.'

'Why? What sort of right?' retorted Kitty. Before her very eyes she saw the often brusque, strong-minded Venka crumple before her.

'Venka?' said Kitty gently. 'What is it? What's wrong?'

'Wrong?' Venka looked at her, then sighed. 'Nothing and everything,' she replied enigmatically.

Kitty silently urged Venka to explain what she meant.

Several times Venka opened her mouth to speak, then shut it, eventually saying. 'It's complicated.'

Somewhere in the depths of Kitty's mind a thought was fluttering about trying to get her attention, the same one she felt she'd been trying to recall previously, but had so far failed to do so. It felt so close, so tangible, if only her brain would get out of its fog she was sure she could grab it. The silence lengthened between them, Kitty could sense the internal tussle Venka was going through in deciding what, if anything, further to tell her.

Whilst she waited, Kitty endeavoured to relax, to allow her mind to wander through Andrew's house, mentally pausing in each room, searching for clues. Like a rare bird flitting behind one bush then to another, there was a flash of memory, but it remained frustratingly out of her grasp and sighed in frustration. She glanced at Venka again who was looking pensive, then her eyes fell upon the box of toys and, in that moment, the elusive thought burst through with clarity and she gasped aloud. No. Surely not? thought Kitty.

'What?' asked Venka apprehensively.

Should I? thought Kitty. Then blurted out. 'Valentina is Andrew's daughter, isn't she?' she said.

Venka's eyes grew wide.

'How did you know?' she whispered.

'I didn't. Not really. Not until just now. When I saw you with Valentina the other day I recognised something in her, but didn't know what. However, seeing the pink bedroom, the box of toys and the fact that you are here. It makes sense.'

Venka looked as though a great weight had been lifted off her shoulders and she slumped back into the sofa.

Meanwhile Kitty was burning up with curiosity. Venka and Andrew. Probably the most unlikely of couples Kitty could ever have imagined. Andrew had never let slip that he was a father and had certainly never acted as though he was one. And now Valentina would never have the opportunity to get to know him as she grew up, just the thought of it made Kitty well up with tears.

'I suppose you are wondering about Andrew and myself? said Venka.

'Well. Yes,' replied Kitty.

'I won't say that it was a mistake, because I have my incredible daughter and whilst she was definitely a surprise, she is absolutely *not* a mistake.' Venka glowed as she spoke about her beloved daughter, her pride and joy.

Recounting their history, she told Kitty that she had met Andrew just over three years ago in a pub a few miles away. She'd only had one drink, as had Andrew, and then she'd left, but her car wouldn't start and her mobile had run out of charge so she'd gone back into the pub to phone for a taxi, intending to arrange recovery of the vehicle the next day. Andrew had offered to give her a lift home, which she had reluctantly accepted as there were no taxis available for a couple of hours. On the way he had asked if she'd like a drink at his house - the night was still young - and that he'd call and pay for a taxi once they got to his house so that she could leave as soon as one became available, cautiously she'd accepted.

One drink led to another and before she knew it she'd cancelled the taxi and they'd both willingly proceeded to consume further copious quantities of alcohol with the inevitable result, waking up the next morning in bed beside him. It had been fun and it had happened a couple more times over the ensuing weeks with neither of them having any desire or expectation for it to be more than just a casual fling; Venka was between relationships and Andrew had made it crystal clear that he was not a commitment sort of man.

Then she'd discovered that she was pregnant with his child. He had flatly refused to accept that, or even acknowledge, Valentina was his offspring when she was born. As a self-employed single mother, the struggle had been colossal. She'd received no support of any kind from Andrew - financial or otherwise - she had put his name on Valentina's birth certificate but other than that had kept the identity of her baby's father a secret, he would have denied it anyway and she didn't want Valentina to be embroiled in any kind of public fiasco.

'However, in the past six months things had changed,' continued Venka.

'Changed? In what way?' asked Kitty.

'He wanted to be involved. To become a part of Valentina's life. Be a father to her.'

'Really?' said Kitty, astonished.

Venka nodded. 'He'd changed. I've no idea why and certainly to everyone else he was his usual outwardly vile, arrogant and obnoxious self. But to me he was civil and the way he was with Valentina was so sweet.' She smiled fondly at the memory of Andrew and Valentina's first meeting; Andrew had looked terrified and Valentina had clung to her legs.

'I only ever brought Valentina here to see him. Andrew wanted time to get to know her before he publicly acknowledge her as his daughter and I also wanted to be sure of his commitment to being a father to her, to be sure that he would not abandon Valentina at the first sign of trouble or repeatedly let her down.'

'And he didn't?'

'No. If we arranged a time for me to bring her over - neither she nor I were ready for her to be on her own with him - he stuck to it. Then he had one of the bedrooms painted pink in the hope that at some point Valentina would feel comfortable enough with him to stay overnight. And he was buying her toys. But…' Venka's voice trailed off.

'But what?'

'He was furious when I told him that Zeno knew.' She looked bleakly at Kitty and appeared to shrink into herself.

Kitty was hit by a realisation.

'So that's why Andrew went to see Zeno and…'

'Yes. I will never forgive myself. If I hadn't told Zeno, Andrew wouldn't have gone round to make sure that Zeno kept his mouth shut. I knew that Zeno would never tell anyone else, he's my best friend and I trust him implicitly. But because of me, he,' she paused, 'could have died.' Tears trickled down her face, she brushed them away with the back of her hand, then suddenly sat up ram-rod straight as she pulled herself together.

'It was Andrew who hurt him. Not you. Venka, it wasn't your fault,' said Kitty.

'He could have killed him.'

'Was that his intention?' asked Kitty.

'No! Definitely not,' replied Venka vehemently.

'How can you be so sure?'

'Whilst Andrew had not always behaved in a responsible manner, as far as I was aware he had never lied to me. He told me that Zeno stepped back and stumbled on a piece of equipment, banging his head as he fell. And Zeno has corroborated this.' She paused. 'As for why I am in the house, I can see that you are still wondering?' said Venka.

'Well. Yes.' replied Kitty.

'You may as well know. People will find out sooner or later. Andrew has left the majority of his Estate in Trust for Valentina.'

Kitty's jaw dropped open in surprise, though on reflection it made sense.

'And the house that I am renting,' she continued, 'unbeknownst to me he had bought it from the landlord and has left it to me, along with a monthly allowance for Valentina and myself until she is eighteen when Valentina will then have access to the assets he has left in Trust for her.'

'Wow!' was all Kitty could say.

'He only altered his Will a couple of months ago. He'd promised that he would look after Valentina and had made financial provisions for her, but I never imagined that he would also look after me, and so generously too.'

Who knew he had it in him? mused Kitty.

'You said the "majority" of his Estate. Who else benefits?'

Venka hesitated. 'I don't know yet,' she replied firmly. She glanced at her watch and yelped. 'I need to get going or I'll be late back at work. *We* need to go.' She hesitated before adding. 'Please keep this to yourself for the time being.'

Kitty nodded.

Back at home, with the weather set to change yet again, the sun having slid behind a heavy grey cloud, Kitty lit the fire in the sitting room, sank back into the cushions and waited for Daisy to join her. Seconds later the growing, but still tiny, kitten leapt into the air, landed deftly onto Kitty's lap and proceeded to snuggle up for a cosy afternoon sleep.

Kitty stroked Daisy's soft, furry head and gazed thoughtfully into the flickering flames which in turn had an hypnotic effect, making her drift off to sleep.

CHAPTER TWENTY-FIVE

Heavy snow fell overnight bringing a sense of calm and stillness over the village of Wynenden. Kitty could see wisps of smoke wafting lazily up through the blue cloudless sky from chimneys down in the village, the sun, gentle and golden, dazzling down onto the snow which sparkled like a carpet of flawless D grade diamonds. She found the view from her house particularly mesmerising on such days, the countryside seemed so peaceful, so serene.

Kitty was on her own, Ted had left a little earlier for work whilst it was still dark. His sense of responsibility made him want to check on his employers at Wynenden Park - Sir Geoffrey Percevall-Sharparrow and his wife Lady Susan - beforehand. Even though they were both robust and in good health at their respective ages of 74 and 73, he still felt a protectiveness towards them and it gave him peace of mind to make sure that they were safe and well and had everything they required during such inclement weather. Invariably the couple were up early, Sir Geoffrey always itching to take the dogs out for a walk as soon as dawn broke; a motley collection of labradors, terriers and unidentifiable mixes.

Reluctant to even attempt to venture out into the snowdrift ridden icy roads in her non-four wheel drive car, Kitty found that the day now lay ahead of her like a blank canvas, plans she had originally made eradicated by the weather. She was so used to being busy, always doing something or having plans in place, that for some reason the prospect of a completely empty day made her feel unsettled and restless.

Deciding that some fresh air and exercise would do her some good and help to clear her head, Kitty turned from her bedroom window and carefully walked downstairs so as not to disturb her purring neck warmer. In the kitchen it became apparent that her neck warmer did not want to move and after a bit of a tussle with Daisy biting and holding onto a clump of Kitty's hair, she finally managed to extricate the kitten and get her settled into her bed.

Wrapped up warmly, with just her nose exposed, eyes protected from the reflected dazzle by sunglasses, feet double-socked inside her thermal-lined boots, she set off up the lane before branching left and onto the footpath which would take her across the fields behind the village and afford her a stunning view of Wynenden Park in all its Georgian neo-classical splendour en-route, after which there was a gentle dip in the lay of the land down across towards the heart of the village and from where the church tower and spire could be seen from some distance away.

Due to the depth of the snow her progress was slow but steady. The freshness in the air and the exercise helped rid Kitty of the unsettled and restless feeling she had felt. In the distance, in front of Wynenden Park, she could see a cloud of snow frothing up as dogs leapt excitedly about, fluffing the snow into the air from their bouncing enthusiasm, which made her laugh in amusement.

With a sense of Déjà vu, Kitty saw Bastien and his ever slowing Labrador, George, who were behind the metal builders fence which secured the periphery of the 15 acres Andrew had - according to Bastien - swindled out of his parents. She approached the final stretch of footpath, just before it terminated at the Wynenden to Monhurst Road. He had his back to her but as she approached he turned and walked diagonally across the field. Kitty waved and called out. He hesitated, then continued his progress, eventually reaching the apex of the field, adjacent to the footpath and gate to the road, just as Kitty did, with only the high fence dividing them.

'Hi Bastien. Another lovely day today,' she called out pleasantly.

'Hello Kitty,' he replied. 'Yes, it certainly is. How are you?'

Surprised by his willingness to converse she took it as a sign that he was feeling a little better within himself.

'I'm fine thanks Bastien,' she said. 'I suppose,' she continued cautiously, grasping the opportunity which had presented itself, 'that this may be delayed for a while.' She nodded towards the field in reference to the building works.

Bastien smiled broadly.

'You could say that,' he replied enigmatically.

'Oh?' said Kitty, curious.

He smiled again. 'In fact, there will be no building works carried out here full stop.'

'Really?' said Kitty. 'How can you be so sure?' She wasn't aware of an appeal having been lodged against the planning decision, nor some other legal process set in motion in an attempt to overturn the decision, though that didn't mean it hadn't happened.

'Uh huh,' he grinned broadly, which lit up his face, ears wiggling as they protruded from his black beanie. 'I am one hundred percent sure because Andrew has left the land to me in his Will.'

'What?! He did what? Why?' Kitty was flabbergasted.

Bastien shrugged. 'I have no idea why. At least the toerag did something decent for once in his life. Anyway, I've got to get George to the vets, he's been a bit off his food.' Apprehension flitted across his face. 'Nice to see you Kitty. Bye.'

Kitty watched his retreating figure as he walked slowly back towards his house in consideration of George who was hobbling in discomfort beside him. Clicking open the wooden gate which led directly onto the road, Kitty checked for traffic then crossed over to the tarmac footpath on the other side. She hesitated, then decisively turned right towards Audrey's house, figuring it was likely that she would be working from home in this weather. She was correct. Audrey welcomed Kitty in, delighted to have an excuse to take a break from work, insisting that Kitty was not interrupting her.

Seated on the comfortable sofas in the conservatory area of the kitchen, sun streaming through the glass adding an additional layer of warmth, Kitty clasped her hands around her mug of tea.

'Bastien's looking brighter,' said Audrey. 'I saw him taking George for a very slow walk yesterday. I sincerely hope there's nothing - apart from old age - wrong with the dog, it's the only living connection Bastien has left to his parents and he's devoted to him.'

'Yes, I've just seen him too. I got the impression that Bastien is starting to feel a little better, though you and I both know from experience that grief doesn't just suddenly disappear, that it can leap out and hit you with a ferocity at any moment and is often triggered by something which may appear to be completely innocuous. Did he have much to say when you saw him?' Asked Kitty with what she hoped was an air of innocence.

Audrey shook her head. 'No. We just had a little chat about this and that.'

Kitty got the distinct impression that Bastian had already told Audrey about Andrew's bequest and tried to steer the conversation onto the topic, but failed.

'And you? Did you have a nice chat?' asked Audrey, also dancing around the subject.

'Bit like you. This and that,' replied Kitty cryptically.

There was a pause and then Audrey burst out laughing. 'You know, don't you?' she grinned.

'Know? About what?' replied Kitty cautiously.

'About Andrew leaving the land to Bastien!'

Kitty laughed. 'Phew!' she exclaimed. 'I didn't want to let the cat out of the bag even though I was convinced you would already know.'

'It will be so nice for Bastien to have the land back. It distressed his parents a great deal when they had to sell it out of necessity. Bastien was furious with Andrew that he had ripped them off.'

'So I gather, I can't say I blame him. But why would Andrew do that? Just give it back? What was going on with him? It seems so out of character and presumably, if he hadn't died so unexpectedly, the houses would have been built anyway?'

'I imagine so,' replied Audrey thoughtfully. 'You don't think…' she paused, 'Bastien knew, before Andrew died. About the Will?'

'I was wondering that myself,' said Kitty, disliking herself for even considering the implication.

Neither were prepared to voice what they were actually both thinking; that Bastien had had something to do with Andrew's death.

Shortly afterwards, Kitty took her leave and carefully picked her way along the footpath through the village. The street was deserted; no cars, no people, no animals which gave the impression that everyone had gone into hibernation.

A warming, welcome, lunch of homemade butternut squash soup, velvety in texture, deep golden-orange in colour, slipped easily down upon her return. Despite Daisy's enthusiasm to venture outside after lunch, Kitty retreated to the sitting room trailed by the protesting kitten, collapsed onto the sofa and curled up with one of her favourite Agatha Christie novels, eyes eventually drooping as she drifted off to sleep, a somniferous Daisy sprawled across her stomach.

Kitty awoke with a start from her nap, the late afternoon dusk had crept in, just a faint glow from the dwindling fire and reflected whiteness from the snow outside lit the room. She frowned, wondering what had woken her so suddenly.

A loud rapping on the front door made her jump. She deposited the still sleepy kitten onto the rug in front of the fire, then padded to the door, the time switch of the hall lamp clicking it on as she walked past. With the safety chain in place, she peered around the partially opened door to see who it was.

'Oh! It's you,' she exclaimed in surprise.

Kitty shut the door, slid the chain across to release it, then opened the door wide enough to allow the visitor to enter.

'Come in,' she invited.

The tall frame of D.I. Allix ducked through the low doorframe, wiping his feet thoroughly on the mat as he did so. Kitty led him through into the kitchen, flicking on lights and drawing curtains and blinds as she went.

'Tea?' she offered, filling the kettle up and putting it onto the hot plate of the Aga to boil.

'Thank you Mrs Muier,' he replied, giving her a smile, his green eyes emanating warmth and kindness.

'Kitty, please. Mrs Muier is far too formal and we've known each other long enough, I say this every time,' she smiled.

He chortled. 'Kitty then. How have you been?' he enquired politely whilst Kitty made the tea, waiting until she had finished to get down to business.

Daisy meanwhile was now very much awake and vying for attention and had already clambered up D.I. Allix's leg onto his lap and was purring loudly, padding her little paws up and down with pleasure as he alternately stroked her on the head then tickled her under the chin.

'I'm assuming you are here about Andrew?' said Kitty

'Yes, indeed I am,' he replied, remembering Kitty's directness.

'Do you know who killed him yet?' she asked directly.

'You are assuming that he was murdered?' he replied rhetorically.

'Was he not?'

'We are still making enquiries,' he replied noncommittally. 'But what I wanted to ask you was whether or not you had received any sort of communication from him prior to his death; a letter, an e-mail or a text for example?'

'No. Not in the least. Why would I have?'

'Had he pestered you again? About the house?'

She frowned. 'No. But now you come to mention it he had gone suspiciously quiet on the matter, apart from one incident in the pub recently. I had assumed that, after word had got out about what he was planning to do had he been able to buy this house, he was focusing on his other projects. What makes you ask?'

D.I. Allix paused. 'It would appear that he had changed his Will a few months prior to his death and made changes which appear, shall we say, out of character.'

'Ah. So you've seen a copy of his Will,' replied Kitty.

D.I. Allix spread his hand out and gave a look which implied that he had, but said nothing.

'So you will know about the rather surprising bequests and um, other stuff?' "Stuff" meaning Venka and Valentina thought Kitty, not wishing to be specific just in case there was the remotest possibility that D.I. Allix was not actually aware of the fact.

'You know?' He looked surprised. 'Precisely what do you know?'

Feeling no option other than to recount what she knew about Venka, Valentina and also Bastien, she proceeded to do so.

He frowned, puzzled as to why Venka - who had been adamant that she would tell no one about the contents of Andrew's Will for the time being in order to protect Valentina for as long as possible - had done so.'

'Are you particularly close to Venka?' He enquired.

'No. Not especially,' replied Kitty.

'So why did she tell you?' he asked, scenting that there was more to this than met the eye.

Kitty shifted uncomfortably in her chair, her cheeks pinking up.

'I… Um…' her voice trailed off and she avoided his gaze.

He studied her for a moment. 'That's ok,' he said. 'I have to speak to Venka anyway, I am sure she will be able to provide me with an explanation.'

Kitty would have been completely hopeless at withstanding interrogation. She crumpled under D.I. Allix's mild questioning and confessed to trespassing on Andrew's property, glancing guiltily at him once she'd finished.

He nodded then caught Kitty off guard by completely changing tack, asking her when she had last seen Andrew, what his behaviour had been like and so on. Satisfied with what she told him, he ended his visit by imparting an astonishing, to Kitty anyway, piece of information. Andrew had left the land which surrounded her house - of which he had procured by dubious means from Sir Geoffrey when an injection of funds was urgently required for repairs to Wynenden Park - to Sir Geoffrey and Lady Susan.

Ted *must* know, thought Kitty once D.I. Allix had left. Why hasn't he told me? And why would Andrew do that? She was convinced that there would be further surprises to come from Andrew's Will, but D.I. Allix was not forthcoming with such information.

The next day Kitty felt disgruntled that her half-term holiday plans were going to be disrupted for another day because of further snowfall overnight. It was becoming tedious, as much as she loved snow, she felt that you could have too much of a good thing, particularly when it was causing problems for Ted at work and as a consequence he was having to work longer hours than usual.

Kitty missed seeing him, a feeling which had crept up on her. They spoke on the telephone every day but it didn't feel the same. Since her divorce, Kitty had relished time on her own, the independence and not having to mould her ways to fit in with another person, the freedom of having no one to answer to but herself - a monumental change from having committed so much time and energy into her first marriage. But Ted was different. Their relationship had started casually, the best of both worlds; someone to enjoy spending time with, to have sex with, but without long-term commitment. She was aware that Ted found her fickleness and reluctance to commit frustrating. He wanted to take their relationship to the next level and move in together, but merely the idea of it had had Kitty running for the hills, fearful that she would be swallowed up in coupleness and lose her identity again. However, over the past few weeks she had begun to consistently feel differently about the idea of them living together. His ongoing kindness, thoughtfulness, patience, open and unwavering demonstrations and declarations of love for her, just as she was, seeped into her, offering a glimpse of what a future with him might be like. Added to that was the realisation that occasionally she now felt lonely, not because she didn't like to be alone - which she did - but because she missed him when he wasn't there. The pleasure and comfort of being together, relaxing, not having to do anything, to be able to snuggle up and exist without the necessity to talk all the time. And today, isolated in her house, she felt lonely and miserable, even the devotion and love from Daisy did little to lift her spirits, all she really wanted was a big hug from Ted.

That night Bella telephoned with the news that tractors with snow ploughs had been out along the lanes and lorries had been up and down the main roads gritting them, making them passable, though still treacherous. The gym, however, would remain closed the next day because Kim felt that it was too dangerous for her staff to attempt to negotiate the icy conditions to the isolated location.

Desperate for some human company, Kitty made plans to meet Bella the following day at the deli-cum-coffee shop in Monhurst which was located on the main road through the village. It was, they decided, likely to be the least hazardous place for Kitty to reach and Bella would be able to walk there. Despite her dislike of driving in such conditions, Kitty was determined to get there.

So on Friday morning Kitty set off having braced herself for what would normally be an easy short drive, however the lane from her house to the main road proved to be more challenging than she had expected, only a narrow gully cut through the snowdrifts allowing no room for error. After a heart stopping 30 minutes at slow speed it was with great relief that she eventually pulled up at the kerb and parked on the road just along from the deli; beads of perspiration bubbling in her armpits from the stress of it.

The deli-cum-coffee shop itself had been refurbished the previous autumn and, whilst it retained rustic features such as beams and oak floorboards, it had been spruced up to enhance further the feel of a high end deli but with local prices, excellent produce - many locally sourced - friendly service and an atmosphere conducive to browsing at leisure and of which, more often than not, resulted in customers purchasing far more than they had originally intended to.

Bella was already seated at one of the limited number of tables in the little cafe area and had managed to secure the one located by the large window which over looked the green.

Kitty wriggled out of her thick wool coat, hat and gloves, leaving her navy wool scarf wrapped loosely around her neck to keep it warm.

'How are you?' she asked, whilst simultaneously managing to order a hot chocolate with cream and marshmallows, 'after Tuesday,' she added.

'I'm,' Bella searched for an appropriate word, 'okay. I think. It kind of feels like I've let go of something, possibly some of the deep-seated fear that I had,' she shrugged.

'But?'

'I still feel a bit on edge, though I don't know why.' Bella stared into the foamy froth of her coffee.

'Bella? What is it?'

Exhaling a long sigh, Bella glanced out of the window.

'It's Dave,' she replied.

'What about him?'

'He went ballistic when I told him what I'd done, where I'd been. I've never seen him so furious and he forbade me from ever going there again. As if he has the right to forbid me from doing anything!' she said indignantly. 'I don't know what's got into him recently. He's always been so calm, slow to anger, but he's so volatile at the moment.' Bella looked miserably at Kitty.

'Perhaps he feels scared? That for some reason you visiting the house has triggered buried memories of what happened, maybe something he's not yet dealt with? Similar to you.'

Bella opened her mouth to object, but what Kitty had said may not be beyond the realms of possibility and had in fact crossed her mind.

'Possibly,' she replied.

'I think it demonstrates how much he loves you.'

They were so engrossed in their conversation that the pair had not seen Jennifer enter the shop and walk over to join them. Continuing to remain evasive about why she had been so conspicuous by her absence recently, Jennifer deftly changed the subject whenever Bella brought it up.

'I had the most peculiar letter in the post yesterday,' she said, sitting down. 'From Andrew's solicitor.'

Bella and Kitty looked questioningly at her.

'Andrew's solicitor? Why on earth would he write to you?' exclaimed Bella.

'Apparently, Andrew had recently bought and bequested a diamond tennis bracelet to me in his Will.'

'Really?' uttered Kitty a little too loudly, making other customers turn round and look at them. She lowered her voice. 'Why would he do that?'

'The letter said that the Will states that Andrew gifted it to me as an offering by way of an apology for his behaviour towards me.'

'What behaviour?' demanded Bella.

'Oh, you know, the usual thing…' Jennifer's voice trailed off.

'Ah.' said Bella, for Jennifer's friends knew that, without any encouragement on her behalf, she was irresistible to men, like catnip was to cats. She unconsciously oozed sex appeal and sensuousness, her voluptuous, shapely figure with long slim legs, rich glossy long chestnut-coloured hair which fell in luxurious curls around her shoulders, her heart-shaped face with naturally full lips, turned many a male and female head.

'Are you sure though? This sort of generosity and thoughtfulness doesn't sound like the Andrew we knew. In fact, just the opposite. What's going on?' asked Bella.

Jennifer shrugged and agreed, having gone so far as to phone the firm of solicitors in case an error had been made.

'I wonder if anyone else has received a legacy from him? And if so who?' pondered Bella thoughtfully.

'Mmm,' replied Kitty noncommittally.

Bella looked sharply at her and narrowed her eyes in suspicion.

'Kitty. You know something don't you? Spill the beans. You can't hide it from me.'

Kitty blushed deeply.

'Come on,' urged Bella.

'Okay. I do know something but I can't say. It's not my place to and no matter how much you cajole me I won't reveal anything,' replied Kitty firmly.

CHAPTER TWENTY-SIX

Feeling much chirpier once she'd spent time in the company of Bella and Jennifer, Kitty hummed happily to herself as she drove home, deciding to pop into the village shop on the way.

Betty, her grey hair looking more tightly permed than ever, appeared to be in an exceptionally good mood, Kitty smiled, then half listened as Betty chattered away to her.

'So what do you think?' asked Betty, looking expectantly at Kitty.

Kitty looked blankly back at her.

'About Dezo. It's a bit suspicious wouldn't you agree? You know, finding out that Zeno's his son, Andrew attacking Zeno and then Andrew being found dead.'

Kitty frowned. 'What exactly are you trying to imply Betty?' she said, getting a sinking feeling.

Betty looked furtively around and, despite there being no other customers in the shop, lowered her voice to a whisper.

'Do you think Dezo had something to do with Andrew's death?' she suggested in a conspiratorial manner.

Whilst this thought had fleetingly crossed Kitty's mind on more than one occasion, she knew better than to voice this to the village's most vociferous gossip.

Instead, Kitty responded with. 'That's rather a wild accusation Betty. I doubt that Dezo or Ditzi will be too impressed when they hear that you have been spreading potentially damaging and unfounded rumours.'

'Oh,' replied a crest fallen Betty.

Kitty hastily completed her shopping in order to escape the awkward silence which ensued, then politely bade Betty good bye. With her arms full, Kitty fumbled in her bag to retrieve her car keys, accidentally dropping them into a mound of dirty snow.

'Bother,' she said.

'Here, let me,' came a voice. Hetty stooped down to pick them up, brushing off the snow as she did so.

'Thanks Hetty,' said Kitty. 'How are you?' She noticed that Hetty seemed to have a glow about her, as though some of the fizz and bubble of her personality had started to return.

'I am feeling much better thank you Kitty. Obviously I am still very upset about,' she glanced around, 'you know who. But I…'

She was interrupted as the shop door burst open and Betty called out to greet her, leaving Hetty with no option but to engage in conversation with her, leaving Kitty to make a hasty exit.

Immediately she got home Kitty swiftly went straight out again for a short walk, much to Daisy's disgust who had wanted some attention. Upon her return she ate the vegetable and lentil soup she'd popped into the bottom oven of the Aga earlier and did her her best to ignore the plaintiff and persistent mewing coming from Daisy. Unable to take the pitiful noise any longer, Kitty took the kitten out for a play in the snow; ginger stripes and swirls vibrant against the whiteness of it. Satisfied that Daisy had been sufficiently worn out, Kitty quickly made a lamb and apricot casserole and popped it in the Aga to slow cook for supper. She was about to settle down with a book and a cup of tea when there was a knock at the door and was surprised to see Hetty standing on the threshold.

It transpired that Hetty had been bursting to tell Kitty her good news and had been annoyed when Betty had interrupted their conversation earlier. The news that Andrew had left Hetty one of his properties in his Will - another one he had recently purchased in Wynenden Close, not far from Venka's - along with a lump sum of cash, did not entirely come as a surprise to Kitty given the bequests she was now aware he had made, but she was still impressed by Andrew's uncharacteristic thoughtfulness and consideration.

Hetty had been so excited at the prospect of what the house and the money would enable her to do that her ideas came tumbling out in a rush; travel, set up her own business, upgrade her car, and she wanted Kitty's thoughts and advice on them.

'... I don't know if that's any help Hetty, I'm not an expert on investments or business matters but am happy to be your sounding board,' finished Kitty.

'I really appreciate it Kitty, thank you. Well, I'd better leave you in peace, I hope I haven't disrupted your afternoon too much? I was just so excited when I heard about Andrew's Will that I had to tell you.'

'I'm very glad that you did Hetty, it was lovely to see you.'

After a weekend spent in a warm comforting cocoon of time with Ted, it was with a twinge of sadness that Kitty saw him off to work early on Monday morning and subsequently left her feeling disgruntled and very moody, which in turn reminded her that she had yet to book an appointment with her G.P. Before she could forget again she telephoned the surgery and was fortunate that an appointment had just become available for the coming Friday.

With that done, Kitty felt twitchy and a need to go out and do something. She wrapped up warmly and set off slowly down the icy lane in her car, hesitating at the junction with the main road as she deliberated on which direction to take, deciding to turn left in the direction of the farm shop on the other side of Monhurst. Having driven through Monhurst, on impulse, Kitty turned left up the lane towards Florence's old house, curious to see it for herself having heard so much about it.

Half way up the lane she began to regret it as her car slipped around like a novice ice skater. The lane was so narrow that it was impossible for her to turn the car around and retreat, so she forged ahead at such a slow pace that a tortoise could have overtaken her.

Eventually she saw the track which she believed led to the property and noticed fresh tyre marks in the snow. It had not occurred to Kitty that there might be someone else visiting the house and hastily tried to think of a plausible explanation for her being there should it turn out to be someone other than Kim or Seb. It wasn't necessary and she let out a sigh of relief as she brought her car to a halt in the clearing, no other vehicle in sight.

Kitty sat for a few minutes with the engine running to keep the heat blasting out whilst she took in the surroundings. The snow made the house look picturesque enough to be on the cover of a box of chocolates or a jigsaw puzzle and less like the sort of property which should be on the At Risk Register.

She eventually switched the engine off, opened the door, stepped into the snow in her thermal boots and picked her way across to the house. The silence which engulfed her was dampened further by the blanket of snow and the birds which were mute, tucked up in their nests in the surrounding woodland. Kitty shivered, though not from the cold, and pulled her padded jacket more tightly around her before continuing on towards the house. She slipped on a patch of ice caused by water which had run off a precariously hanging section of guttering but managed to stay upright. On closer inspection, Kitty could now see the true extent of the neglect and decay and felt sad that the house had been allowed to fall into such a state of disrepair.

She reached the back door, turned the handle and gave it a firm shove. Despite the vivid description Bella had given her, Kitty was not prepared for the decrepitude which greeted her; dust, debris and decay wherever she looked. Tentatively she tiptoed through the kitchen into the hallway, then trod softly and cautiously up the stairs, avoiding the hole made in the bottom step by Bella. Bar the creak of wood from underfoot, there was an all encompassing eerie silence.

Kitty pushed the first door she came to open, which did so surprisingly noiselessly. It was the bathroom; clean and dust free with a toothbrush, toothpaste and small bar of white soap sitting neatly on the sink ledge. She frowned in consternation, retreated and turned the handle of the next one, a painful screech echoed throughout the house as the door reluctantly opened.

She stood in the room open-mouthed with astonishment.

'What do you think?' whispered a voice from behind her, making Kitty scream and heart pound furiously.

CHAPTER TWENTY-SEVEN

Kitty clutched at her chest. 'Gosh, you scared the living daylights out of me! Sorry. I didn't hear you come in and I hadn't realised that there was anyone else here,' said Kitty in her typically apologetic manner.

The petite woman who stood before Kitty looked tired but her skin was clear and unblemished. She had the most beautiful rose-bud lips encapsulated within a heart-shaped face and deep emerald-green eyes flecked with gold which shone brightly. She smiled at Kitty as she ran a hand through her short blonde elfin hairstyle.

'I should be the one apologising. Creeping up on you like that. My apologies.' She smiled again and held out her hand to Kitty. 'I'm Louise. Pleased to meet you.'

'Kitty,' she replied, her still trembling hands taking the one proffered which was cool to the touch.

'Kitty.' Louise looked thoughtful. 'So why are you here?' she asked.

'Oh. I. Well,' stuttered Kitty, feeling rather as though she'd been caught with her hand in the cookie jar. 'I've heard so much about this place that I decided to come and have a look for myself. A friend of mine is hoping to buy it and I was told that the house had been empty for quite a while. And you?' asked Kitty.

'Me?' Louise smiled. 'I own it.'

'Oh!' exclaimed Kitty, blushing the colour of a particularly ripe beetroot in embarrassment. 'Gosh. Well. I'm really sorry to have trespassed. I'd better go.' Kitty hurried towards the door and Louise stepped aside to allow her to pass.

'Please don't worry,' said Louise kindly. 'By the way, who is your friend?' she enquired casually.

Caught out, Kitty could have kicked herself for saying that she knew the person hoping to buy the property. But surely Louise already knew that?'

'Kim,' she replied.

'Kim. I see,' said Louise, wrinkling her brow in concentration.

'Yes,' added Kitty for no reason.

'Would you like a coffee?' offered Louise.

Kitty had gone off coffee and didn't relish the prospect of having one but felt that, in the circumstances, it would be churlish of her to refuse. 'Thank you. That's very kind of you. And again, I am really sorry for trespassing.'

'We don't need to say another word about it. It's forgotten.' Louise smiled again then moved passed Kitty and led the way carefully down the stairs. 'Mind that one,' she said, pointing to the bottom step. 'Not sure how it got broken,' she added, half to herself.

'Ah.' said Kitty.

'You know?'

Idiot, thought Kitty to herself. Now she'd have to drop Bella in it as well. She explained to Louise what had happened - mentioning no names - and diplomatically apologised on Bella's behalf, suggesting that she felt sure that Bella would be willing to recompense Louise for the damage.

Louise laughed. 'Really, don't worry about it. It's not like the house is in perfect condition. Was it Kim?' she asked casually.

Kitty hesitated. 'Er, no. Bella,' she said.

'Well, please reassure Bella that it's not a problem at all.'

'Thank you Louise, I will, that's very kind of you.'

Louise retrieved a flask and two mugs she had stashed inside her rucksack, along with a carton of milk. They sipped their coffee and chatted, Kitty relieved that Louise was so forgiving.

After what Kitty felt was an appropriate period of time, she bade farewell to Louise and departed, hurried to her car, waving goodbye as she drove off. When she reached the main road she turned in the direction of her original destination - the farm shop - maxing up the heat in an attempt to thaw herself out, the chill of the house having seeped into every part of her.

As always, the wares on offer in the shop were beautifully and enticingly displayed. Kitty was no exception to many other customers who could not resist temptation, by the time she had finished her jute shopping bag was filled to the brim with far more than she actually needed.

Turning to leave, she bumped in to Kim and Seb who were arriving for their weekly brief escape to have time together on their own as a couple. However they persuaded Kitty to join them in the cafe and she was soon spooning a large fluff of whipped cream and marshmallows into her mouth off the top of her hot chocolate.

'I've just met the current owner of Florence's cottage,' she said.

'Really?' said Kim in surprise. 'Where?'

Kitty looked sheepishly at them. 'At Florence's house. Sorry. I know I shouldn't have gone, but with all that Bella has told me about it I was curious, so I popped in en route.

'And she was there?' asked Kim.

'Yes. Caught me red-handed. Very embarrassing. She seems like a lovely person though and fortunately was very understanding - thank goodness,' she paused. 'What?' she said having seen Seb and Kim exchange a knowing glance between them.

'I've never met her. Nor has Seb,' said Kim. 'I've tried to arrange to meet her - through my solicitor - but she's been very elusive. I just assumed that she never visited the property.'

'Oh. I guess I was just lucky then.'

Bella felt gloomy and her mood mirrored the weather which was grey and misty. She missed her long-standing friend Mia who, along with her husband Fred, had been away on a three week skiing holiday of which they had just extended and now wouldn't be back until the end of February. Compounding her sense of misery was the fury she still felt with Dave for the way he had spoken to her and had not received any kind of communication from him since their argument.

Despite lacking the enthusiasm, she decided to take herself off to the gym in the hope that working out might improve her mood a little. Had it not been for the continued whispering and gossiping going on around her with regard to Dezo and Zeno, it would have. As it was, she came out feeling worse than when she had gone in.

Believing that many of her close friends were occupied that week, including Kitty, Ditzi, Kim, Sophie, Ariadne, Bella consequently spent the remainder of Tuesday and the whole of Wednesday wrapped up in a blanket on the sofa, alternating between watching films and staring for hours at the flames in the fire, refuelling it when needed and refuelling herself by consuming copious quantities of chocolate and ice-cream, feeling lonely and with more than a touch of self-pity.

Meanwhile, Kitty spent two enjoyable days visiting Rye, Cranbrook and Royal Tunbridge Wells, making the most of her time off. She telephoned Bella late on Wednesday afternoon and was surprised and concerned by Bella's melancholic tone. She had been under the impression that Bella was busy all week, so it didn't take much to persuade her to get out of the house and come over to Wynenden Farm the next afternoon.

Cheered by the prospect of seeing Kitty that afternoon, Bella showered, washed her hair then peered closely at her reflection in the mirror. What she saw did not please her. She looked pale and pasty and there was a crop of spots starting to form on her chin. Added to that, she felt bloated as a consequence of having over indulged in a massive sugar-fest over the previous two days.

'Come on,' she said sternly to herself as she dabbed some concealer over the spots. 'Snap out of it. It's going to be a good day.' She trotted downstairs with as much enthusiasm as she could muster and went into the kitchen where, after a little shake of the kettle to check for water, she switched it on. Opening the fridge door she was greeted by a pathetic sight; a piece of cheese with mould growing on it, a couple of out of date yoghurts, in-date butter and marmalade, which would have made a satisfactory breakfast were it not for the fact that there was no bread in the kitchen, nor in the freezer. She sniffed the small quantity of milk left in the bottle, wrinkled her nose and decided to risk it as there was just enough for a cup of tea and a small bowl of cereal. She tried to ignore the slightly sour taste, then gave up.

Determined to rectify the provisions situation as soon as possible, she finished her cup of tea, tidied up the detritus scattered throughout the sitting room from her sugar filled gloom-fest, then wrapped up warmly and set off along the drive towards the village green, crunching over the crisp snow and ice. Thursday morning meant that the weekly farmers market would be be taking place in Monhurst Village Hall. The building itself was delightful and, whilst only relatively recently constructed, it had been designed to look like a converted Kentish barn; Kent peg-tiled roof, black weatherboarding, oak windows, oak structural beams exposed internally, but which was very well insulated, making it toasty warm in the cooler weather and much cheaper to run than the building it had replaced.

Bella was surprised by how busy the hall was and it wasn't long before her shopping bag was full, replenishing her supplies with fruit, vegetables, home-made soup, milk from a local dairy farm, a couple of individual pies - one steak and ale, one curried cauliflower and chickpea - a small apple tart and two large slices of carrot cake to take over to Kitty's that afternoon. When the ubiquitous Bread Man turned up - late as always - she added a couple of small loaves of bread and half a dozen sourdough rolls to pop into the freezer as emergency supplies.

She let out a loud sigh of relief as she sat down with her mug of coffee, placing it onto a small wooden table which wobbled as she did so. She could feel the caffeine begin to buzz through her body the more of the strong black liquid she sipped, and watched the goings on around her. She saw Sharon chatting to some of the more elderly residents of the village who were seated at a rectangular table behind Bella - remarkably similar in concept to that of the Saturday morning market in Wynenden.

In need of further sustenance, Bella went back to the kitchen hatch and bought a cheese scone and another mug of coffee. She devoured the super-cheesy-in-flavour scone hungrily, particularly savouring the crunchy cheese topping. As she chewed the final morsel she saw Venka and Valentina come in, watching Valentina bewitching people with her cuteness and delightful manners. Spotting Bella, Valentina waved excitedly. Venka bent down to say something to her daughter, then let go of the two year olds hand. Valentina rushed across, flung herself at Bella then clambered up onto Bella's lap simultaneously chattering away, making her spirits rise. Venka eventually joined them, smiling lovingly at her daughter, the apple of her eye.

Sharon passed by just then and stopped to coo at Valentina. 'She is such a lovely little girl,' she said. 'She must make you very proud Venka. It's a shame she doesn't know who her father is, I'm sure he'd be very proud of her as well.'

Inwardly Bella groaned and saw Venka's jaw tighten as she clenched her teeth. Sadly, this wasn't the first time that Venka had been subjected to such judgemental and presumptuous comments regarding Valentina's parentage, not surprisingly it often ended badly, one could hardly blame Venka for snapping rudely back at whoever the inquisitor was.

'Valentina darling,' said Venka to her daughter, rummaging in her purse for some change. 'Why don't you go and choose a biscuit from the nice ladies over there,' she indicated towards the hatch.

Feeling very grown up with the task she had been given, Valentina eagerly slithered down from Bella's lap and ran across to the counter where the woman serving leant over to chat to her.

Venka turned back to Sharon and snapped. 'It is none of your business. *Never* say anything like that in front of my daughter again. Understand?' she growled.

'Well. I'm sorry if I've offended you,' bristled Sharon, unimpressed at being berated so publicly, feeling humiliated, 'but it's true. It *is* sad. I don't care what anyone says, a child needs both its mother and its father and it's selfish to prevent that from happening.' she crossed her arms definitely over her bust in defense.

Bella's jaw dropped in horror, astounded by Sharon's crassness and insensitivity. There was a perceptible frisson of disapproval towards Sharon from those who could not help but hear the exchange which was taking place.

Venka stood up and took a step closer towards Sharon, who in turn stepped nervously back.

'That,' spat Venka, jabbing Sharon in the chest with her index finger, 'is utter crap. Valentina's father is dead. So mind your own business. And,' spat Venka again, 'if you really want to know who her father was.' Sharon's face lit up with a cautious optimism. 'It was Andrew. Andrew

Battle. So do your worst with that, but do not *ever* bring the subject up again. Understood?' Venka commanded.

Bloody Hell! thought Bella. I didn't see that coming.

Sharon gaped at Venka.

'Now go. Leave us alone,' ordered Venka, swiftly switching on a beaming smile for her daughter who had come hurrying over with her half-eaten biscuit, blissfully unaware of the exchange which had just taken place.

When Valentina had finished eating her biscuit, she and Venka left, walking out with her head held high and holding tightly on to her daughter's hand. Immediately the external door had closed behind them there was a whoosh of volume, only one topic under discussion. Sensing that the teflon-skinned Sharon might pounce on her, Bella hastily gathered her bags and hurried out in Venka's wake. She knew that before the morning was out the "hot news" would have been spread far and wide.

Tucking her feet up underneath herself on one of Kitty's comfy sofas, a cheery fire burning merrily in the fireplace, Bella couldn't contain herself any longer and blurted out the mornings shock revelation.

'You don't look surprised?' she said when finished, feeling a little deflated by Kitty's lack of astonishment.

'Sorry Bells,' replied Kitty apologetically, as she licked remnants of carrot cake from her fingers whilst sprawled on the other sofa. 'Venka told me last week.'

'What?!' exclaimed a crestfallen Bella. 'Why didn't you tell me?' she added in an accusatory tone.

'I would have done but Venka made me promise not to tell anyone. She said that she was going to keep it private for as long as possible for Valentina's sake. I haven't even told Ted. So I'm rather surprised she's announced it so soon and so publicly.'

'I got the impression that she didn't mean to, that it was said in the heat of the moment, reacting to Sharon's judgemental comments. But don't change the subject. Why would she tell you? It's not as though you and she are especially close?'

Kitty shrugged, noncommittally.

'You'd have to ask Venka that,' she replied firmly in an attempt to make it clear to Bella that there was no point in pursuing the topic.

Temporarily recognising defeat, Bella decided she would have another attempt at the weekend, so instead asked Kitty what else she had been up to with her time off.

'Any progress with you and Dave?' asked Kitty once she'd finished recounting her week so far.

'Nope. It's like he's dropped off the face of the earth. No phone call. No apology. Nothing. That was over a week ago.' Bella looked miserably down.

'And he's not returning your calls or anything?'

Bella shifted guiltily in her seat.

'You have at least left a message or texted him haven't you?'

'No.' Bella replied stubbornly. '*I'm* not the one in the wrong. There's *no way* he should have spoken to me in the way he did.'

Kitty rolled her eyes. 'Bella! Honestly, you two are as bad as each other.'

Bella obstinately refused to continue the discussion and sat in mulish silence.

The silence, bar the sound of the fire crackling and popping, was eventually broken by Kitty. 'I drove up to Florence's house on Monday.'

'Really? Why? What did you think?' Bella couldn't stay cross with Kitty for very long, particularly when she knew deep down that she was right.

Kitty was about to when she was interrupted by a sharp knock at the door. She wasn't expecting anyone but got up to go and answer it, switching more lamps on as she went, the shadows of darkness having started to creep in.

Bella could hear a surprised "Oh! Hello." from Kitty in the hallway, then a few moments later heard the front door close. Looking bemused Kitty came in saying. 'Bella. I'd like you to meet Louise. I was just about to tell you about her.'

Louise entered the room and smiled at Bella. 'Bella. It's lovely to meet you… At last.'

Kitty frowned. She was sure she hadn't given any details about Bella to Louise, so why would she say "at last"?

The blood drained from Bella's face. She gasped and her mug slid from her hands, hot tea spilling over her as it fell, but she didn't seem to notice or care.

'Bella? What's wrong? You look like you've seen a ghost.' said Kitty.

Bella's mouth had gone dry, her heart was thumping and all she could do was stare at Louise in horror.

'Bella? Bella! What is it?' confused and concerned Kitty took Bella's hands in her own and patted them gently. 'Sorry Louise. Please do sit down.' She turned back to Bella. 'What's wrong Bella? I don't understand.' Kitty began to feel panicky. 'Let me get a towel to dry you and make some sweet tea.' And phone Dave she thought to herself.

'No. No!' Bella's voice rose in fear. 'Don't. Don't leave me alone. With her,' she pointed at Louise.

'What are you talking about? Bella it's okay. I'm here. Just tell me. I won't leave you. It's okay.' She could feel Bella trembling.

Bella gulped. 'That's Florence,' she whispered, pointing towards Louise.

'Florence?' Kitty paused. 'She's dead Bella. This is Louise.' she said in an attempt to reassure her friend.

'No. No. She's come back. It's Florence. Don't leave me. Make her go. Make her go!' begged Bella.

Kitty was at a loss as to what else she could say or do to comfort her friend, aware of the trauma Bella had experienced at the hands of Florence. Had visiting Florence's house triggered something? Post traumatic stress or such like? She glanced back at Louise, her mouth went dry and she felt the hairs on the tops of her arms stand on end. Louise was sitting on the other sofa with a strange smile fixed on her face. A ripple of fear ran though Kitty. What was happening?

'Listen to me Bella. It's simply not possible for Louise to be Florence. You must know that, don't you?' She felt Bella's quivering hands become clammy, and rhythmically stroked her thumb backwards and forwards in a desperate attempt to soothe her.

Bella nodded mutely, but the whites of her eyes were wide with fear.

'I can explain,' said Louise.

Kitty turned from her crouched position by Bella and looked expectantly at Louise. The fire continued to crackle, mirroring the tension within the room.

'You say that I look like Florence,' began Louise, 'but I have never met her. Nor ever even knew her. Your reaction was astonishing. It's only happened to me on one other occasion. To have that sort of response is both confusing and bewildering to me, something I feel that I will never fully be able to come to terms with because, as you correctly said Kitty, Florence is dead and I will never, ever be able to meet her.' Louise looked from Bella to Kitty who in turn were staring back at Louise in consternation.

'I don't understand. What are you saying?' asked Kitty.

'Perhaps I am not being eloquent enough. So, let me see,' Louise paused to gather her thoughts. 'My whole life I have felt as though a part of me was missing, but I didn't know why. It wasn't until I was contacted a couple of years ago by Florence's solicitor that it all began to make sense. About how I have always felt. I had no idea. None whatsoever. My parents never told me and I certainly never felt as though I wasn't their biological child, that they had adopted me. So when the solicitor finally managed to track me down, it felt as though my whole world had been blown apart. Florence hadn't made a Will. I am the closest living relative to her and therefore inherited her entire Estate. But that wasn't the end of it, I was then told that I was her identical twin sister.'

Bella gasped.

'So your reaction to my appearance is both pleasing and perplexing. In some ways it makes me feel closer to my sister, whilst still not fully being able to comprehend that there had been another living being who had been my carbon copy.'

Kitty could feel Bella relax a fraction, but could only imagine how traumatic it was for her to come face to face with a person who was the spitting image of the one who had put her through such a terrible ordeal and who had almost succeeded in killing her.

'I think I should make some sweet tea. For the shock. Or perhaps something stronger, Bella?'

Bella shook her head too dumbfounded to speak. Her brain was having trouble processing the information.

'Will you be alright if I go into the kitchen?' asked Kitty anxiously. 'Just shout if you need me. I'll come straight back.'

Bella mutely nodded.

Kitty left the room leaving Bella and Louise looking curiously at one another. She swiftly put the kettle on, picked up her mobile phone, then walked into the garden room so as not to be overheard. Dave's mobile rang and rang then went straight to voicemail.

Frustrated by him not picking up immediately, she left a garbled message. 'Dave. It's me, Kitty. Something's happened. It's Bella. She's ok. Well. No she isn't. But I think you should come here right away. To the house. Ok. Bye. Hold on it's me, Kitty. Did I say that? Oh. Anyway. Bye.'

'Here we are,' said Kitty, with a brightness she didn't feel, as she carried in a tray with cups, saucers, tea pot, milk jug, sugar bowl and spoons on it, but came to an abrupt halt. Louise had moved and was now sitting very close to Bella, too closely.

'Everything ok?' asked Kitty anxiously, a knot of fear forming in the pit of her stomach.

Bella was moving her eyes in a strange darting fashion. Kitty frowned, clearly she was trying to tell her something, but what? Slowly, Kitty placed the tray onto the coffee table and stepped back towards the door, hairs on the back of her neck now prickling like a radar picking up an emergency signal.

'Sit down,' ordered Louise with a hard edge to her voice.

Kitty hesitated.

'I *said*. Sit down.'

Kitty couldn't move, rooted to the spot with fear.

'Now!' shouted Louise.

It was then that Kitty saw a glint from something in Louise's hand.

CHAPTER TWENTY-EIGHT

'What?' Kitty stammered. 'What's going on?' She said, perching nervously on the edge of the sofa on where Louise had originally sat.

'I was just explaining to Bella,' replied Louise in an eerily calm tone, 'how I feel about never having been able to meet, or have the opportunity now to get to know, my twin sister.'

'Okay.' replied Kitty, apprehensive as to what was coming.

'And the fact that it is all her fault,' added Louise.

'Her fault? Why? It wasn't Bella's fault that Florence killed herself,' replied Kitty indignantly.

'Don't argue with me,' spat Louise. 'Of course it was Bella's fault. She was there. She's responsible. Florence would *never* have done it otherwise.'

Kitty opened her mouth to protest, then thought better of it. Why would Louise believe that Bella was responsible for Florence's death?

'Who,' started Kitty tentatively, 'told you what happened that day?'

'It didn't take much searching on the internet to find out.' shrugged Louise.

'Um. So you've not actually spoken to anyone about it? Someone who would know the truth about what happened?'

'I have. So I do.'

Despite the intense fear she was feeling, Bella couldn't stop herself from uttering. 'Really? Who?'

Louise looked at Bella contemptuously. 'You can be quiet.' she snapped.

Kitty saw Bella wince and again a glint from something metallic. Her mouth went dry as she realised that the glint was from the blade of a knife. And the knife was being pushed into Bella's side. How could this be happening? How could a seemingly innocuous meeting at Florence's old house lead to what was happening now, she wondered?

'Not that it's any of your business, but it was Andrew,' replied Louise.

Andrew? puzzled Kitty. 'Um,' said Kitty nervously, 'Andrew?'

'Yes,' replied Louise impatiently. 'You asked me who had told me. It was Andrew.'

'Andrew who?' persisted Kitty.

Louise rolled her eyes. 'Andrew Battle of course.'

'Andrew Battle!' exclaimed Kitty in disbelief. 'How do you,' she corrected herself, 'did you, know *him*?'

Louise smiled to herself, then scowled. 'We were lovers,' she replied simply.

Bella and Kitty's eyes sprung wide in astonishment. Kitty in particular couldn't believe it. Surely Hetty or Venka would have had an inkling of this? Did they know and Andrew had sworn them to secrecy? Had he used Louise to get what he wanted i.e. Florence's old house? If so, then were it not for his untimely death, he would have succeeded.

'You look shocked. Is it so far fetched that a good looking man like Andrew would find me attractive?' she glowered at them.

'No! Of course not. You're a very attractive woman. I'm sure you must have a queue of men lining up who want to date you,' offered Kitty in an attempt to appease Louise.

Appearing temporarily mollified, Louise shifted in her seat, knife remaining firmly pressed into Bella's side.

'How did you meet?' asked Kitty, playing for time, desperately trying to formulate some kind of plan in order to get the knife off Louise, hoping that by appearing calm and relaxed it would help, rather than ignite, the precarious situation they were in.

'It was last Autumn. My very first visit to the house. It had taken me a while to get over the shock of discovering that I had had a sister and then trying to find out why we had been separated. Life could have been very different,' she looked wistfully away.

Kitty and Bella dared almost not to even breathe.

'Apparently my birth parents couldn't cope.' continued Louise. 'They had my brother Charles - someone else I will never meet - all my siblings are dead. Can you imagine how that feels?' she looked at Kitty, who shook her head in response. 'And having twins was too much for them so, at three months old, they gave me up. Just like that. How could anyone do that? Separate us. Reject me. Why me?'

'That's so sad. I'm sorry. Really I am,' said Kitty, for Louise's parents to do that was tragic, yet to have made such a decision, Kitty could only imagine, must have been agonisingly difficult and one which may have haunted them their whole lives.

'It's not like I can ask them, because they are both dead too.'

Grief seemed to weigh heavily in the room. Death. Despair. Past actions and decisions rippling out over the years.

'The tea has gone cold. I'll go and make a fresh pot,' said Kitty quietly, hoping and praying that she had correctly interpreted the momentary softening within Louise. She rose slowly and reached for the tea pot. 'Would you like to stay here or come with me?' she suggested calmly.

'Be quick. We're not going anywhere. Not yet.' added Louise rather menacingly.

Attempting not to react to this chilling comment, Kitty managed to force a slight smile on her face, left the room in an unhurried manner and, once out of sight, rushed as silently as she could into the kitchen, flung the kettle onto the hotplate of the Aga, grabbed her mobile and started to text Ted.

'What are you doing?' barked Louise from behind Kitty, making her jump with fright and drop the phone which clattered onto the kitchen island. She looked guiltily at Louise who had Bella's right arm grasped firmly in her left hand, the kitchen lights reflecting off the knife which Louise was now pointing towards Kitty's phone. 'So, what were you doing?' she repeated, her emerald eyes flashing angrily.

'I was,' Kitty thought quickly, 'texting my partner, asking him to pick up some more milk on the way over this evening.' She crossed her fingers which were hidden below the island top, desperately hoping that Louise would be mollified by this explanation and watched her weighing it up.

From behind Kitty the kettle started to whistle. 'I'll just make the tea,' she said, continuing with growing desperation to think of an escape route out of the living nightmare she and Bella found themselves in.

Louise watched Kitty's every move like a hawk eyeing its prey.

'There we are.' said Kitty in a fake cheery tone. 'Let's go and sit by the fire again, shall we?' With a confidence she didn't feel, Kitty carried the teapot past Louise and Bella and led the way back into the sitting room, placed it onto the tray and left the tea to brew whilst she opened the wood-burner, poked the burning embers with a fire iron and added another log, before slowly pouring the tea, taking as much time in doing so as she could.

'Here we are,' said Kitty, passing a cup and saucer to Bella. It rattled as Bella took it, her hands continuing to tremble with trepidation. Kitty placed Louise's drink down onto a small table close to where she sat, then settled herself down on the adjacent sofa with as much of a faux relaxed air as she could muster, like a swan gliding serenely on a lake, feet moving frenetically underneath, Kitty's outer demeanour belied her inner terror.

'What do you do for a living, Louise?' asked Kitty, in an effort to steer the conversation away from the subject of Florence.

Louise frowned. 'Me? I'm a nurse. At a GP surgery.'

Bella gasped, then hastily turned it into a choking sound.

'What?' demanded Louise.

'Sorry,' gulped Bella. 'Tea went down the wrong way.'

Kitty stared at Bella, she knew she was lying but proceeded to ask. 'That must be an interesting job. Do you enjoy it Louise?'

Louise shrugged. 'I used to. But now…' she gazed off into the distance, to another place, before snapping back into the here and now, pressing the tip of the knife further and more firmly into Bella's side making her gasp as it punctured her clothes and began to press against her skin. '*She* ruined it.' Louise glared venomously at Bella. '*You* killed my sister.'

'No!' yelped Bella. 'I did *not*!'

'Liar,' spat Louise. 'Andrew told me everything. He said you were a busybody and he was right. Snooping around. Poking your nose into things which don't, and didn't, concern you.'

Kitty swiftly interrupted. 'You knew Andrew well then?' she asked. 'How did you meet?' She reiterated her earlier question.

Louise scowled. 'I've already told you,' she snapped.

'He was buying the house from you I believe?'

Louise glared at Kitty. 'That bastard conned it out of me. He made me believe we had a future together. He pursued me. Made me feel like I meant the world to him. Then, when we'd exchanged contracts on the house, he cooled off. I thought I'd done something wrong. But I hadn't. He was a complete bastard. He got what he deserved.'

A chill ran down Kitty's spine, she hoped fervently that it was simply a turn of phrase Louise was using and not an indication of something more sinister. 'He,' she started cautiously, 'could be very unpleasant but,' she paused, 'he didn't deserve to die.'

'Didn't deserve to die!' Louise laughed. 'He got what was coming to him. I went to see him. I was desperate to find out what I'd done wrong. I loved him. I thought we'd get married. Have children. Be a real family. Then I found him. Trussed up like a turkey, naked on his bed, wrists handcuffed to the bedposts. He'd been with someone else. He'd been playing the games he and I played. How could he do that to me? Betray me like that? And do you know what he said? Do you?' spittle flew out of her mouth at the vehemence of the words. 'He said "just in time. I'm ready for more." No shame. No guilt. Nothing. He'd betrayed me over the house, my *sisters* house. Now he had betrayed me over our relationship. I wasn't going to let him do that again.'

Unaware of what she was doing, Louise took the knife away from Bella's side and started tapping it against her other hand in an agitated manner.

Kitty and Bella looked at one another in horror, the implication of what Louise was implying demonstrating that it was likely she shared the same terribly sad and distressing mental instability Florence had displayed.

'What?' croaked Kitty, dry mouthed. 'Did you do?'

'I killed the bastard,' Louise stated matter of factly. 'Why wouldn't I? I wasn't going to let him get away with it.'

Perspiration trickled down between Kitty's shoulder blades; fear, dread and terror making her mind go completely blank, incapable of fathoming a way out of the current predicament. Bizarrely, all she could think about was the fact that she had not drawn the curtains and darkness was creeping in like a stealthy killer. Was her mind playing tricks? Had there been movement outside the window behind Bella and Louise?

'I'm sorry he betrayed you and treated you like that.' Bella spoke softly and in a tone which might be used to calm and placate a small child. 'He got what he deserved.'

Louise looked at her. 'You think?' she asked, eager for approval and validation at what she had done to him.

'Definitely. One hundred percent,' continued Bella. 'It was despicable what he did to you. But not every man is like that. There are some good ones out there too. Someone for you. Someone who will love and cherish you. Someone you will be able to trust, to settle down with, to marry, to have children with. Everything that you have just said you have always wanted. I've been where you have been. I *know*. I *understand*.'

Kitty watched in awe of her friend as she attempted to lure Louise into a false sense of unity, of presenting herself as a kindred spirit.

'Really? You've been betrayed? Did he get what was coming to him as well?' Louise's face was bright with anticipation.

'He did. I. I don't want to go into details...' Bella paused for effect, 'but he *definitely* got what he deserved.' She feigned wistfulness. 'And now. Now I have the love of a good man. A kind man. A thoughtful and loving man who is devoted to me,' she continued.

'You really think that that could happen to me too?' whispered Louise.

Bella nodded. 'I do Louise. I do. Don't give up hope.' She carefully reached over and took Louise's hands in her own, allowing the knife to slip to the floor where it landed silently on the rug. She looked directly into Louise's eyes and smiled whilst simultaneously squeezing her hands in a gesture of faux comfort.

Kitty could see Louise's shoulders begin to drop as she relaxed a little. She felt a draft around her feet and shivered, wanting to put another log on the fire, but not daring to move. She suddenly wondered where Daisy had disappeared to, not having seen her for a while, and began to worry. She leaned slowly backwards to see if she could glimpse the kitten through the open sitting room door and stifled a scream, immediately turning it into a coughing fit. 'Sorry,' she said, fearing that she had broken the moment between Louise and Bella.

Bella stroked Louise's hands as she held them; soothing, calming, she frowned at Kitty, puzzled. What had her friend seen?

Standing in the hallway, listening to the conversation was D.I. Allix, his index finger pressed against his lips to communicate to Kitty to remain silent about his presence.

'Bella's right,' said Kitty. 'You will find someone. Someone worthy of you.' Endeavouring not to stare at the window, convinced that police officers were responsible for the movement outside it, Kitty suddenly feeling a sense of calm. Help was here. It would be alright.

'Yes you will.' Bella took her cue from Kitty.

'I feel as though you need a hug,' said Kitty standing up slowly. 'You've been so brave. Come here.' She held out her arms, hoping that Louise would take the bait and provide Bella with the opportunity to grab the knife. Louise hesitated, conflicted. 'You're sister would be so proud,' Kitty added.

In a nano second Kitty realised too late what a huge mistake and misjudgement she had made, inwardly cursing herself as she saw Louise's brow crease, look from Bella to Kitty, then snatched her hands away from Bella. In a flurry of movement two pairs of hands dived for the knife. In that moment, sensing the change in atmosphere, D.I. Allix walked quietly in.

'Put that down Louise,' he said calmly as Louise tried to wrestle the knife from Bella.

'Never! That bitch killed my sister!' she screamed just as she managed to grasp the knife from Bella.

Kitty lunged at the pair, both she and Bella grappling to get the knife back from Louise.

Wildly stabbing, there was a piercing scream, then silence. Kitty, Bella and Louise gaped at the knife, frozen in mid air in Louise's hand, watching in slow motion as blood dripped from it.

Swiftly D.I. Allix - the room now filling with police officers - grasped Louise's wrists and removed the knife.

Kitty and Bella could only look on in horror as blood spurted profusely from Louise's abdomen through the thin fabric of her top. Louise gaped in shock and disbelief at the self-inflicted injuries she had sustained.

In a whir of activity someone pressed a small cushion down hard onto the wound. Paramedics, who had entered the house during the tussle and who had waited out of the way in the kitchen, then assessed and stabilised Louise before whisking her away to hospital accompanied by police officers.

The sitting room was sealed off from them and Kitty and Bella, in a state of daze, were taken through to the garden room and supplied with hot, sweet, tea, too shocked to say or do anything themselves. When D.I. Allix came to see them some time later, Bella asked. 'How much did you hear?'

'Enough,' he replied grimly.

CHAPTER TWENTY-NINE

Ted and Dave had turned up shortly after Louise had been taken to hospital, it transpired that Ted had been able to get his house keys to D.I. Allix which had enabled him to gain access to the property.

The evening passed in a haze of activity and Dave eventually took Bella home. His fury at her for having visited Florence's house had dissipated, but which had stemmed from the knowledge that Louise was the prime suspect in Andrew's murder. They had been close to arresting her and he feared - given her unpredictability - what Louise intended to do, particularly with regard to Bella.

Meanwhile Ted stayed close by Kitty's side, distressed that he hadn't been there to protect her. Kitty herself, once the initial shock had worn off, had been more concerned about the whereabouts of her "baby" i.e. Daisy, who was eventually found hiding underneath the antique oak cabinet in the hallway, having tucked herself under there earlier when she sensed danger.

By mid morning the following day a relative sense of order had returned to Kitty's house. Ted had flatly refused to go to work unable to bear leaving Kitty on her own. Once given the go ahead by the police, he had telephoned Audrey to ask if one of her team could come and give the whole house an extensive clean as soon as possible - there were benefits to having a friend who owned a cleaning company. Eager to help, and obviously concerned about Kitty, Audrey had turned up late in the morning with a team of three who immediately set to work, making Kitty feel like a spare part as the four beavered away, her offers of help repeatedly turned down, Ted insistent that she relax in the now spotlessly clean garden room.

She cuddled Daisy, who was behaving in a very clingy manner after the trauma and would not let Kitty out of her sight, so much so that Kitty had, on this one occasion, insisted that Daisy sleep in the bedroom with them the previous night. Ted had been rather dubious about this, feeling sure that one night would turn into another, then another, but he wanted Kitty to feel as safe and comforted as possible and if that meant having Daisy with them, it was a small price to pay

Once the house was spick and span, Audrey sat down with Kitty in the kitchen and had a cup of tea. Dressed in a conservative navy trouser suit with navy blouse; respectable but practical - Audrey was very much a hands on boss and frequently pitched in to help out when needed. Kitty could see that Audrey was debating whether to say what was on her mind, something which was clearly troubling her. But Audrey didn't want to distress Kitty further, eventually coming to the conclusion that Kitty would want to know the news sooner, rather than later.

'What's wrong Audrey?' asked Kitty. 'You look as though something is burdening you. Please don't feel you have to handle me with kid gloves because of what happened last night. I'm okay, so if there is something worrying you, do tell me.'

Audrey hesitated before filling her in; Seb had been, fortuitously, delivering the weekly vegetable box to Bastien as per usual and had found him in a distressed state having taken a substantial quantity of over-the-counter medicines in an attempt to overdose. Bastien's beloved ancient Labrador George had died of old age and was in his bed in the kitchen where Seb had found them.

Bastien had still been conscious, and whilst they waited for the ambulance had mumbled incoherently to Seb, who was able to get the gist of what Bastien was trying to communicate, that he felt there was nothing left to live for, his last connection with his parents now gone, that it was his fault that Dolly had died.

In fact that was not correct. When Seb had seen Bastien hurrying away to telephone for help, Dolly was already within moments of death having suffered a catastrophic stroke, there was nothing Bastien could have done. Bastien had panicked and gone into a state of shock - it was too soon after the demise of his parents - which explained why he had not thought to use Dolly's landline. He was still currently in hospital, having survived his attempted suicide, and Audrey told Kitty that she was going to do her utmost to ensure that he received all the support he needed to help him get better, feeling motherly and protective towards him having lost her own child too young.

It had been an eventful 24 hours reflected Kitty as she sat in the doctors surgery waiting for her appointment later that Friday afternoon. She thought about what Bastien must have been going through, about how abandoned and alone he must have felt and how awful for him to be suffering from depression, which could be a cruel and much misunderstood mental illness, and hoped fervently that he would receive the treatment and support he would need to help him on his road to recovery.

Her appointment with the doctor turned into a lengthy one and when Kitty eventually appeared from the consulting room, she looked dazed and overwhelmed.

Waiting anxiously at home for her was Ted. He took one look at her as she walked in; white as a sheet, shocked and bewildered, and feared the worst. 'Kitty. What is it? What's wrong? What did the doctor say?' his voice urgent, smile lines replaced by worry ones.

'I,' she began, shaking slightly. 'I need to sit down.'

Ted guided her into the garden room, sat her down and placed Daisy on her lap for comfort - who had been stalking round the kitchen mewing and pouncing on her toys - swiftly re-boiled the kettle and made them mugs of sweet tea. He took her hands in his and, holding them tightly, said gently. 'Tell me, what did the doctor say? Whatever is wrong, we can get through it together. I'm here for you.'

She looked deep into his blue eyes. 'I'm not menopausal,' she said. Ted nodded, holding his breath. 'I'm. I'm pregnant,' she whispered.

There was a stunned silence before Ted spoke. This was not what he'd been expecting.

'Pregnant?' he frowned.

Kitty nodded, fearing that he too would leave her, just as her ex-husband had.

'That's amazing!' A broad smile spread across his face. His eyes sparkled and he glowed with excitement. 'We're having a baby? We're having a baby! Darling, that is wonderful news!' he stopped suddenly. 'Is it what you want though?' he gulped apprehensively.

Tears were streaming down her face. 'Yes! Yes!' Relief at Ted's response flooded through her. 'And apparently I'm twelve weeks already! Past the initial danger period, although given my age there is apparently an increased risks of complications.'

'No matter what, we're in it together.' Ted said, hugging her tightly to him. He pulled back and placed his hand on her stomach, filled with wonderment that his baby was growing inside her. 'I'm so happy. What a gift! We're going to be parents!'

They spent the remainder of the afternoon and evening cocooned in a cloud of happiness, telephoning Ted's parents to tell them the good news and deciding not to tell anyone else until Kitty had had her first scan which had already been booked for the following week.

Sitting in the ultrasound department of the local hospital Kitty and Ted waited anxiously for the scan, a mixture of excitement combined with apprehension; would the scan show if the baby was developing as it should? Would there be complications?

Ted's right leg was jigging up and down from nerves. Kitty, meanwhile, shifted on the uncomfortable hard plastic seat in the waiting room, doing her best to focus on her breathing in an attempt to quell her own nerves and anxiety.

'Katherine Muier?' called the sonographer.

Kitty and Ted looked at one another, this was it. Ted took her hand and squeezed it. 'Okay?' he murmured. Kitty gulped and nodded.

Settling back onto the couch, Kitty exposed her stomach as instructed, there was a definite mound and explained why the fit of her clothes had recently been feeling snugger and snugger, she couldn't believe that she hadn't realised why.

Ted sat on the chair beside the couch, gripping her hand, both feeling the clamminess from one another's palms as they did so. They stared intently at the screen as the sonographer began to glide the probe across the gel which had been placed onto Kitty's belly.

A grainy image appeared, neither of them able to identify what they were looking at, as the sonographer clicked away on the machine as he took measurements.

'Is everything okay with the baby?' asked Kitty nervously, once the sonographer had removed the probe and placed it back into its slot.

'I'm just going to ask one of my colleagues to pop in,' he said. 'I won't be a moment, then we can go through the scan.'

Kitty could feel bile rising in her throat from dread and she clasped Ted's hand more tightly.

'There's something wrong. I know there is,' she said, beginning to cry. 'What if it's dead? There's something not right, I just know it. It could be life threatening? I don't know if I could cope, I've waited so long for this.'

'Sssh, darling, it's okay. It'll be okay. He didn't say that there was a problem, so there is no point in us jumping to conclusions,' said Ted in a reassuring manner which he himself did not feel.

The door opened, making them jump and their hearts race faster.

The sonographer introduced his colleague, who in turn smiled at them and with a softness in her voice said. 'Right. Let's have a look shall we?'

The couple of minutes she spent scanning Kitty's belly felt interminable, tears running down her face, Ted doing his best to scrutinise and understand the images in the hope that he would be able to identify what the medical professionals themselves were seeing.

The woman sat back, placed the probe down, then spoke gently to Kitty and Ted.

CHAPTER THIRTY

'May I?' asked Bella.

'Of course,' replied Kitty, smiling broadly in the May Day sunshine.

Bella reached out and placed her hands onto Kitty's belly. 'I still can't believe it. Twins!' she said in awe.

'I know! I feel so enormous and my back aches all the time. It's feeling very real now.' She stroked her expansive bump affectionately.

Kitty was now six months into her pregnancy, for the unenlightened it looked as though she were ready to give birth at any moment, yet she still had months to go, even though it was likely that she would be induced before her due date.

'And as for that ring,' added Bella, admiring Kitty's generously proportioned emerald cut diamond solitaire set in platinum. 'It's stunning. About time you made an honest woman of her,' she joked, grinning broadly at Ted.

'I am a very lucky man,' he replied, putting his arm around Kitty's shoulder and gazing adoringly at her.

He looked like the cat who'd got the cream and felt as though his life could not be more perfect; babies on the way, engaged to the love of his life, their swiftly planned intimate wedding imminent and then the birth of their offspring to look forward to.

The trio wandered around the fair which was the annual one jointly hosted by both Monhurst and Wynenden on the May Day Bank Holiday, stopping every now and then to chat to friends and neighbours as they went.

Gossip regarding Andrew, Venka and Louise was now relatively old news. Louise was in a specialist mental health unit receiving the care she desperately needed, which in itself raised the question of whether she would ever be fit to stand trial. As for Andrew, the reason behind the seemingly mysterious changes to his Will was due to a health scare. He'd delayed going to see his doctor when he had discovered a lump and eventually gone months later, only to be referred to the hospital as an urgent case and where he subsequently had a barrage of tests including a biopsy, fearing the worse, he set in place his wishes in his new Will. Sadly, he had died before he'd been given his results.

'Lovely news about Ariadne,' said Bella.

'Oh?' replied Kitty.

'That she's going to make Kent her permanent home,' she lowered her voice, 'and that she's just completed on, you know…' she glanced furtively around, 'Florence's, or rather Louise's house.'

'Indeed. Sounds like she has amazing plans for the site and thank goodness she's going to knock down that decrepit house. Whatever she comes up with, it's bound to be spectacular.'

They were interrupted by a snuffle, a lick and tickling whiskers around Kitty's ankles and she looked down to see an adorable 16 week old black Labrador puppy, his brown eyes looking eagerly up at her as she bent as best she could to stroke him. 'He's so cute Bastien,' said Kitty, tickling the puppy's soft ears.

Bastien grinned. 'He certainly is. I don't know what I'd do without him. I'm very lucky to have been given him and to continue to have so much support from within the community.'

It had been Seb's idea to buy Bastien a puppy having felt sure that it would help Bastien with his recovery, provide him with a purpose, a reason to get up every morning, a mutual need for one another. It had been love at first sight for the pair of them. Bastien had wanted to call the puppy Rupert - his fathers middle name - but out of respect to Audrey (whose late husband had been called Rupert) he shortened it and the puppy was duly named Rupe. The exuberant puppy bounced off in another direction, his puppy training currently proving to be a little problematic.

Bella wandered off in the direction of Zeno, now fully recovered and back to work, who was with Dezo and Ditzi.

'I have *got* to sit down,' groaned Kitty, leaning back in an attempt to stretch her sore back, her ankles feeling heavy from carrying the extra weight.

'Come on,' said Ted, as he guided her over to where an available table and chairs were conveniently located adjacent to the tea tent.

Kitty lowered herself down and let out a big sigh of relief, sat back and automatically started to rhythmically stroke her bump again, smiling to herself as she felt some little kicks from the babies. She watched the bustle of the fair as people mingled about it. She waved to Hetty who was serving at the temporary bar which had been set up for the event, and reflected on the future business and travel plans Hetty had told her about, along with her plans to rent out the house Andrew had left her whilst she was away.

Ted returned with a tray of refreshments, bending down to kiss Kitty gently on the lips as he placed the tray on the table.

Life, felt Kitty, was good.

Instagram @emelliotoffical

www.emelliot.com

Printed in Great Britain
by Amazon